This sports story has little to do with blood, sweat, tears, and six-pack abs. But it has a lot to do with a dental disaster, fast legs, and bad hand-to-eye coordination, plus galloping on horseback at night with a pretty girl across a Mafia-owned golf course, and learning how to make the principal of your high school so mad at you that he puts his fist through his door.

a novel

LOSERS
take all

DAVID KLASS

SQUARE
FISH

Farrar Straus Giroux
New York

SQUARE
FISH

An imprint of Macmillan Publishing Group, LLC
175 Fifth Avenue
New York, NY 10010
fiercereads.com

Our books may be purchased in bulk for promotional, educational, or business use.
Please contact your local bookseller or the Macmillan Corporate and Premium
Sales Department at (800) 221-7945 ext. 5442 or by e-mail
at MacmillanSpecialMarkets@macmillan.com.

Library of Congress Cataloging-in-Publication Data

Klass, David.
    Losers take all / David Klass.
        pages cm
    Summary: "At a sports-crazy NJ high school where all kids must play on a team,
a group of rebels start a soccer team designed to undermine the jock-culture of
the school"—Provided by publisher.
    ISBN 978-1-250-09059-1 (paperback)
    ISBN 978-0-374-30137-8 (e-book)
    [1. Sports—Fiction.   2. High schools—Fiction.   3. Schools—Fiction.
4. Individuality—Fiction.   5. Friendship—Fiction.]   I. Title.

PZ7.K67813Los 2015
[Fic]—dc23

                                                                    2015006009

Originally published in the United States by Farrar Straus Giroux
First Square Fish Edition: 2016
Book designed by Andrew Arnold
Square Fish logo designed by Filomena Tuosto

1   3   5   7   9   10   8   6   4   2

AR: 5.6 / LEXILE: 890L

For the Black Label soccer team

THE SCOREBOARD HAD BEEN DESIGNED IN Japan, and our town had bought it a year ago to record Fremont's glorious football victories and track triumphs. From the bleachers where I stood with seven hundred screaming students and four thousand equally crazed townspeople, the giant live-feed LED display and the half dozen digital timers helped us follow all the action on the track far below. Twenty runners—all eighteen-year-old toned and ripped superathletes—had turned the final corner and were racing down the home stretch. And the twenty-first runner, a much older man but in terrific shape, was coasting along in the middle of the pack when he happened to glance up at the scoreboard.

That twenty-first runner was Arthur Gentry, the principal of Fremont High for more than forty years and the man most responsible for making our school into a sports powerhouse known throughout the state of New Jersey as "Muscles High." He was the kind of principal who liked to know everything that was going on in his school, so he was always poking his head into a classroom or chatting with a new student, but it would have been much better for all of us if he hadn't glanced up at that fancy scoreboard right then.

The race was the climax of Graduation Week, which at

Fremont High meant as much sports crap as they could cram into five days. It started off with Team Appreciation Day—a pep rally for teams that had already been appreciated so much it was hard to imagine the star players hadn't gone deaf from all the applause. Then came the New Trophy Ceremony, when the sacred glass case at our school's front entrance was unlocked and gleaming gold cups for the past year's championships were carefully slipped onto shelves next to tarnishing plaques from seasons gone by. And there was Captain's Coronation, when the new team captains for next year were "crowned" by the old ones and showered with confetti while cheerleaders danced around them.

I could go on, but I think you get the picture. There's not much at Fremont High during Graduation Week to honor the valedictorian or the president of the French club, but if you happen to be an elite athlete, it's like getting a Viking funeral and entering Valhalla, or being inducted into the Hall of Fame.

WARNING—this is not a typical story about the birth of a sports team dynasty, like when Babe Ruth joined the Yankees and belted out fifty-four home runs his first year, or when Vince Lombardi took over the Green Bay Packers and promised them: "You will never lose another championship." This sports story has little to do with blood, sweat, tears, and six-pack abs. But it has a lot to do with a dental disaster, fast legs, and bad hand-to-eye coordination, plus galloping on horseback at night with a pretty girl across a Mafia-owned golf course, and learning how to make the principal of your high school so mad at you that he puts his fist through his door.

I was not an elite athlete. I'd spent years searching for the sport I was best at and never quite found it. I was a chronic hitter of foul balls, a basketball player whose jump shots slalomed around the rim before deciding to hop down rather than slip through the hoop, and a wide receiver with plenty of speed but "iron hands" that repelled footballs with an almost audible clank.

I'm tall and slender—my dad says "scrawny," and he'd been encouraging me to lift weights since I was twelve. "Bulk up and it'll pay off across the board," he assured me. "Coaches will see it, girls will notice, and you'll be able to shovel our driveway faster." I told him thanks for the advice, and I know it worked for him and my two brothers, but I'd just as soon go my own way. And that was my attitude toward our sports-crazed school, too—live and let live— till that afternoon in June when Principal Gentry glanced up at the scoreboard and everything changed.

I may sound angry, but the truth is I had nothing against pep rallies and cheerleaders dancing around next year's captains. Did I think it was nutty? Sure. But I wasn't trying to fight back or rip anything down. I did my own thing, and my first three years at Fremont I joined the computer club and kept my distance from the superjocks. Except for the fact that, by virtue of my last name, I'm one of the cornerstones of that sports culture, and you can never get far away from your own name.

Which brings me back to the grand finale of Graduation Week—Champion's Day. The culmination of Champion's Day for fifty years has been the Senior Mile Run. The twenty fastest seniors race four laps around our track while the whole school and half the town cheers them on. The Fremont record for the mile is four minutes and seventeen seconds. I know that time because the record was set by my father, Tom Logan, twenty-seven years ago. Since fewer than a dozen high school runners in all of American track history have broken four minutes, it's a hell of an achievement to have been just seventeen seconds over, especially for a big football player like my father was. It's not likely to ever be broken in our town, but every year the top twenty athletes at Muscles High take their best shot.

That day in early June, twenty-one runners were sprinting through the sunshine for the finish line. Battling it out were four team captains, two hyperathletic girls in orange Lycra, five members of our track team, and a baseball star who had been drafted by the Yankees. But the runner drawing the most attention was old Principal Gentry, a schoolboy champion in his day, then a track letterman at Princeton, and now, at seventy, still a rail-thin specimen and a competitive runner.

"Look at the old geezer go," my friend Frank grunted. "If he's not careful, he's going to keel over."

"Have some respect," I told him. "Let's see you do that when you're seventy."

"I can't even do that at seventeen," Frank admitted. "And you know what? I'm fine with that. When I'm seventy I plan to be on my back in a hammock, eating SunChips." It's not hard to picture Frank with white hair, swinging in a hammock, staring up at the clouds and popping SunChips. He's a gentle giant who loves to pig out on junk food and take long naps, and he avoids all physical exercise with a laziness that a sloth would envy.

Principal Gentry was made of tougher stuff. He was clearly not going to win this race—Al Flynn, the center-fielder headed to the Yankees, was neck and neck with Ramon Hernandez, the captain of the track team, for that honor. They had opened up a twenty-yard lead over the rest of the field, and the crowd was roaring and stomping so that it felt like an earthquake was shaking the bleachers. Ramon put on a final spurt and crossed the finish line in four minutes and thirty-one seconds, with Al just an eyelash behind. The two gods of sport slapped five and everyone gave them a cheer, and then all eyes swung back to our principal.

These days serious older runners compete in their own track meets, and there are records for every age group. Principal Gentry's best time was twelve seconds off the state record for seventy-year-olds, and I don't think he intended to try to break the record that day.

But forty yards from the finish he glanced up at a digital display and saw that he was seven seconds from the record. This was a man who had climbed Mount Kilimanjaro at sixty, and scuba dived with hammerhead sharks when he turned seventy, and whose motto was "Just go for it!"

The crowd began roaring again as Principal Gentry dug into his last reserves and sped up. His stride was fierce and determined as he churned down the home stretch, passing runners fifty years younger. I can still see his bony elbows pumping like pistons and the sunlight flashing off his sweaty forehead that was half-lowered toward the finish line as if ready to break an invisible tape with the point of his nose.

7

"GENTRY, GENTRY, GENTRY," the crowd chanted.

He passed the captain of the basketball team, who broke stride to wave him on.

I spotted my father lower down on the bleachers, near the green turf, chanting, "GENTRY, GENTRY." Dad is six feet three inches tall and his thick head of black hair tossed in the spring breeze as he stood with his best friends—most of them old teammates from his high school days—and cheered and shook both fists. Dad watches lots of sports events, live and on TV, and he often gets so personally involved with them that my mom and I have to tell him to calm down.

Fifteen yards to go. Gentry was only two seconds off the record. He threw himself forward with guts and willpower, as if to set a shining example and say to each of us: "This is what you can achieve, if you just lower your head and go for it."

"GENTRY, GENTRY!" The bleachers felt like they were going to collapse at any second. I didn't shake a fist, but I did put my arms out to steady myself. On my left, my friend Dylan Sanders, who is usually far more critical of the jock culture at Fremont than I am, got caught up in the moment and started leaping up and down. It was impossible not to get excited. I found myself clapping and shouting.

Five yards to go. Principal Gentry hurled himself at the finish line with everything he had. He zipped across, nose first, right arm following as if throwing a punch at time itself, and then his trim torso, with his left arm trailing. He raised his arms and turned to the scoreboard, and saw that he had missed the record by half a second.

There was a loud, deflating sigh from the crowd, like the air hissing out of a hot air balloon. Principal Gentry put his hand dramatically on his heart, as if to say, "I gave it my all." The applause swelled. And then he went down on one knee, as if saying a brief prayer to the Olympic gods, and the cheering got even louder because he looked so noble kneeling there, and he had come so close and fought so well.

And then old Gentry toppled over onto the blue synthetic track that he had helped raise the money for, and the crowd went totally silent. "Oh my God," I whispered.

The ambulance crew was tending to him in moments.

"I didn't mean for it to really happen," Frank whispered to me, sounding scared. "I swear I didn't."

We were all scared, and I saw several people start to pray.

"He'll get back up in a second," I whispered back to Frank. "He's probably just winded."

But he didn't get back up. The sad fact is that he died right there in front of nearly five thousand people, and a week later they named the whole turf field and track after him—Gentry Field. There was even a proposal to bury him beneath it, but apparently that had to be abandoned for zoning reasons.

Now, you'd think that Gentry's dramatic death might have given Fremont pause to say, "Maybe we've pushed this sports thing a little too far. Maybe as a school, a town, a community, we owe it to our kids to take our foot off the gas and hit the brakes and emphasize reading and writing and algebra a little more and biceps curls a little less." But it didn't go down that way at all.

THE SURPRISE ANNOUNCEMENT WAS MADE
at a school board meeting just three weeks after Gentry's
death. It was very unexpected because there had been talk
of a search for "an educator" from outside our community—
a new principal with impressive scholarly credentials who
would give our school a fresh look and feel.

I wasn't at the meeting—I was spending most of my
summer vacation hanging out with Dylan and Frank, playing video games or swimming in Hidden Lake, and most
of my evenings at my miserable summer job busing tables
at Burger Central.

But I heard the news right away because Dylan's mother
is on the board and forces him to come to meetings, and he
had dragged Frank along. So my two friends were in the third
row when the board president, Mr. Bryce, announced that
they had not needed to search far. In fact, it seemed like
they had just rolled over the nearest rock and scooped
up the biggest and meanest critter that scampered out.

When the meeting ended Dylan and Frank texted me
that they had a news flash, and they headed right over to
Burger Central to try to score some free fries.

"Muhldinger?" I said, staring back at Dylan. "You're
kidding me."

"There was applause when they announced his name," Dylan reported. "In fact there was a spontaneous standing ovation. Everyone seems to think he's a brilliant choice."

"Brilliant how? What qualifications does he have?" I asked.

"He's a proven leader," Frank pointed out with his usual sarcasm. "What about some fries, Jack? When I'm stressed out I need to eat."

Frank must be stressed out a lot, because his eating habits resemble those of a great white shark. He seeks out food twenty-four hours a day, or at least every minute when he's awake, and it wouldn't surprise me if he occasionally took bites out of his pillow in his sleep. He would be fat if his growth spurt hadn't matched his appetite—when you're six foot five you can carry fifty extra pounds like an overnight bag.

"Proven at what?" I demanded. "Just because he can win state championships in football doesn't mean he can run our school. And if you want fries, go order fries from Becca. I'm not in charge of handouts—I just wipe the tables, and I'm still trying to get over Muhldinger. What the hell were they thinking?"

"The word 'legacy' came up several times," Dylan informed me. "As in 'We have to stay true to Gentry's legacy.' And also the word 'tradition,' as in 'We have a long and glorious tradition to uphold here.' And the news only gets worse, Jack, so a little snack might brighten things up."

"If we had the money for fries, we wouldn't need a friend," Frank pointed out. "Just wander through the kitchen and slide some into a napkin when no one's looking. We're all doomed, so we might as well have a last meal."

I studied Dylan's face. "How could any news be worse than Muhldinger taking over our school?"

Becca was returning from a bathroom break and overheard my question as she walked past. She jolted to a stop and stared at us. "Muhldinger?" she asked in shock and outrage. "No freaking way. How is that possible? He's not even a teacher. He's just a big muscle-head. He doesn't even have a neck. They can't do that to us. He's the worst kind of sports Nazi."

It was true. Brian Muhldinger, coach of the Fremont football team, chief of the audiovisual department, which made him a nonteaching member of the faculty, and now apparently the new czar of our high school, had a broad chest that seemed to be welded directly to his fat, bald head. It was as if the millions of pounds of weights he had pumped had reconfigured his body to eliminate all thin and weak areas.

Becca's real last name was Knight, but everyone called her "Becca the Brain" because she was focused on school all the time and had never gotten less than an A on any test since third grade. I'd always admired her long legs and sharp sense of humor more than her GPA, but Becca didn't date or do anything that might waste precious time that she could spend studying. During the summer she worked the computerized register at Burger Central, punching orders at hyperspeed and using slow periods to study impossible vocabulary words that might appear on the SAT.

"Neck or not, it's Principal Muhldinger now," Frank

explained. "And you guys don't want to hear the *really* bad news."

Becca looked back at him. "The football team is taking over the library as their new weight room?"

"I think that's actually quite possible," Frank told her, "but no, that's not the bold new policy Muhldinger announced in his speech at the board meeting—the one that got him the standing ovation."

Andy Shimsky, who waited tables, had heard enough to join our little group of social outcasts. He was a string bean of a kid, with long, greasy black hair and wrists like toothpicks, and had been mercilessly bullied by jocks since middle school. "What bold new policy?" Shimsky demanded warily.

There was a moment of ominous silence when Dylan and Frank exchanged looks and Becca, Shimsky, and I waited for the bombshell to explode.

"In honor of Arthur Gentry's legacy . . ." Dylan began. "And to continue his unique vision of the Fremont High School scholar-athlete . . ."

Frank finished in a mocking tone: "Starting in September all seniors will be required to join at least one school sports team and stay with it through an entire season. This will develop strong bodies along with keen minds, and create a unifying school spirit that will keep alive the legacy of Arthur Gentry."

"But that's three hours of practice a day," Becca pointed out.

"Not to mention weekends and traveling to away games," I added. "What if we're not good enough to make any of the teams?"

"They're adding B-team and even some C-team options, and expanding the rosters," Dylan said. "I believe Arthur Gentry would tell you to just go for it."

"Part of the new policy is no cuts just 'cause you happen to suck," Frank informed us. "They'll keep you on the roster of one team or another and make you practice your ass off and sit on the bench. You can scrape mud off the cleats of the football stars, or sponge sweat from the basketball court during halftime, or re-lime the baseball diamond after the starters have kicked up dust and left. I guess the good news is that we all have important roles to play."

"They can't do this to us," Becca declared. "They can't make me play a sport I hate. I already have my sport. Show jumping. It's part of my story."

"Your story?" I asked, trying not to stare too intensely at her extremely pretty hazel eyes.

"The one I'm going to tell about myself in my college application essay," she informed me like I was clueless. "Perfect grades aren't enough these days. Twenty thousand applicants to the top schools have nearly perfect grades and test scores. You need a story to set you apart. And mine is about horses, and how I helped raise one named Shadow that had a damaged hind leg, and nursed him back to health, and won ribbons riding him. I've already written the essay. It's called 'Knight and Shadow.' I don't need another sport and I can't afford to waste three hours a day on a stupid team I'll never play for."

"It's not as if Muhldinger's offering you a choice," Dylan told her.

"There's always a choice," Shimsky announced, sounding

like he was preparing to lead a revolution. He had suffered a lot—getting beat up all the time. In sixth grade his nose had been broken by a creep who'd rammed his face into a garbage can. Our town has its tough side—the jocks rule, and if you don't show them respect you pay. It had made Shimsky tough and crafty in his loner way. "Whenever there's a rule there's a way around it."

"Not this one," Dylan said. "This is about legacy and tradition. The school board confirmed the new policy. My mom was the only 'no' vote. Ladies and gentlemen, start your engines and get ready to suffer. The lunatics have taken over the asylum and we're at their mercy."

"We're all dead meat," Frank agreed. "Sports road-kill. If I go out for shot-putter, do you think they'll make me run laps with the track team? I could run one lap, or maybe two, very slowly on a nice fall day." Frank was being optimistic—he runs about as fast and gracefully as a fully loaded garbage truck grinding up a steep hill in low gear.

"I heard the track team ran ten miles a day last year," Becca told him.

There was a moment of unhappy silence as we looked at each other and pondered what senior year would be like with Muhldinger in charge of our school.

And that was when Mr. Psilakis, the night manager, hurried up behind us and started screaming: *"Get to work, all of you!* I don't pay you to gab. Jack, a table of ten just left a royal mess. Shimsky, there are two orders of nachos getting cold. Nobody likes cold nachos. Becca, we're short-handed at the registers. *Let's go, move your butts!"*

I hurried over to the royal mess and started clearing up half-munched french fries and greasy bits of uneaten cheeseburger. Frank ambled up next to me, picked up a discarded onion ring, studied it as if debating whether he should pop it in his mouth, and then tossed it reluctantly into my tray of garbage and dirty dishes. "Sorry to be the bearer of bad news," he said.

"I just don't get why they're doing this," I told him. "Why don't they just do their legacy thing and leave the rest of us alone? What happened to live and let live?"

"Ours is not to reason why," Frank answered. "Ours is just to join a team and die." He hesitated and then said softly, "Jack, your father was one of the first at the board meeting to jump to his feet and start clapping."

"No big surprise there," I muttered, picking up a broken ketchup bottle and turning it upside down in my tray to avoid the jagged glass edges.

Frank lowered his voice even more. "After the meeting broke up I saw him talking to Muhldinger, and I heard him say something about you trying out for the football team. Muhldinger was nodding his head. Sorry, but I thought you'd want to know."

3

"THIS IS NOT REALLY TACKLE," ROB POWERS
told us. The park was empty because of the summer heat,
and as the sun dipped lower the shadows of old oak trees
reached out inch by inch across the grassy field, as if getting
ready to trip us up.

Twelve of us had shown up for this "friendly game," and
now that I was here I could tell that it would be neither
friendly nor a game. "So it's two-hand touch?" I asked
nervously.

"Not exactly," Rob said. "We call it half-hit. Which
means you're trying to bring each other down, but not do
any serious damage. You don't need helmets or pads for
half-hit—just have fun out there."

Rob had been my closest friend once upon a time, before
the school pecking order took shape. His father had played
quarterback on the state championship team that my dad
had captained. When they drank beers together, Rob's
father still sometimes called my dad "Captain." Rob and
I had hung out into middle school, and then we had gone
in very different directions. I was scrawny, to use my
father's phrase, but Rob had sprouted muscles, not to
mention chiseled features, cat-quick reflexes, and a rifle
arm. Now he was contending for the starting quarterback

job, earning cash from modeling gigs, and dating a swarm of cheerleaders.

He had called me up the day before and invited me to this friendly game, and he hadn't hidden his real agenda. "One of our starting receivers just tore his ACL. Coach Muhldinger is looking for someone with good wheels to replace him, and your name has come up."

"Thanks, Rob, but I really don't think I'm varsity material," I had said.

"It wouldn't hurt you to try," he'd pointed out. "We're not allowed to have team practices during the summer, but we're going to have a friendly pickup game in the park—just an informal toss and catch kind of thing. No coaches, just some of the guys. Why don't you come and give it a run, and see where it leads?"

My dad had been in on the plan. "Just try," he encouraged at the breakfast table the next day.

"Dad, I've got iron hands."

"Cover them with receiver's gloves."

"Do I look like a football player to you?"

He lowered the sports section and glanced across at me, as if evaluating me with his gray eyes. At forty-five he still had the muscular body of an All-State running back whose toughness was legendary in our town. His nickname had been the "Logan Express" and people who'd seen him play said that it had taken three or even four tacklers to bring him down. If a knee injury in his senior year of college hadn't ended his playing career, Dad would have turned pro. It was hard to know what he was thinking as he looked back at me, but he said: "Sure."

"I thought I was scrawny."

"The point is there's one thing nobody can teach and that's speed."

My mother had been listening to the conversation, and she gently said: "Tom, if he doesn't want to do it, don't push him."

"I just want him to try," Dad told her. "Is that such a horrible thing?"

So here I was, giving it a try.

Rob wasn't the only varsity player who had shown up. Sprinkled in with seven of us newbies were five starting members of the football team who had come, presumably, to check us out. Coach Muhldinger—or perhaps I should say Principal Muhldinger—wasn't there, nor were any of the other dozen or so assistant football coaches. So Rob and a guy named Barlow were running the thing.

They staked out a grassy rectangle with orange cones and divided us into two teams, and I was put with Rob and four other guys I didn't know well. We huddled up around him before we kicked off. "Stay loose," he told us, "no pressure at all, guys. But it's still a chance to show what you've got. So if you go in for a tackle, make sure you wrap him up and bring him down. You never know who might be watching."

I looked past him, to the parking lot, and saw a big man get out of an SUV and sit down on a bench near a duck pond that offered a good view of the field. He was too far away for me to see his face clearly, but he had the bulk of a weight lifter, and even from this distance I could see that he had no neck. Another tall man strolled up and sat next to him. He was wearing a cap that shadowed his face, but I could tell it was my father.

We lined up facing the other team, with Rob in the center, holding the ball. I tried to stay calm. There was nothing to lose. I didn't even want to make the stupid football team. If I did well it would be fine, and if I screwed up it might be even better. The June day had been sweltering— nearly a hundred degrees—and even though the sun had started to sink, it was still steamy hot. I felt a sweat break out on my legs and arms and across my chest, and took a few quick breaths.

Rob gave me a wink, as if to remind me of Gentry's motto: "Just go for it." And then he took two steps and kicked off into the setting sun—a twisting kick so high that the ball seemed to disappear for a second in the purple clouds, soaring over the receiving team's heads. As they scrambled back to pick the football up, we raced toward them, and I found myself in the lead.

I've always been fast. It's my saving grace as a mediocre athlete—the thing that partially makes up for my scrawny build and lack of coordination. I'm not the fastest in our school—there are probably two or three sprinters on the track team who can edge me out over fifty yards. But that evening in the park, when six of us sprinted across the grass toward the other team, I quickly took the lead.

As I raced ahead of my teammates, I wondered why I was doing this. It was almost as if a little voice was shouting: "Stop. You don't have to do this. You hate football. None of these guys are your friends. Not even Rob—don't kid yourself. You don't have to prove anything to Muhldinger—he's a sports Nazi, just like Becca said. Your dad should just accept who you are, or it's his problem and not yours. Slow down and let somebody else get there first." That's what the little voice said, and I heard it as I ran, but my arms were pumping and I was flying over the grass. Instead of slowing down I sped up, and quickly pulled away from my teammates.

The football rolled deep into what would have been their end zone if the field had been lined, and stopped in tall grass. Barlow got to it first and could have just downed it. But he chose to pick it up and run it out, and I slanted toward him.

One of their players tried to block me, and I dodged around him. Barlow saw me coming and shouted to his teammates: "C'mon, you losers, block for me." One of the losers threw a nasty block at me and the bony point of his right elbow dug into my ribs, but then I was past them all and facing Barlow one-on-one. He was about my height but not scrawny at all—a star running back, one of the co-captains of the varsity team, and a furious competitor in every sport known to man.

I darted toward him, and he held his ground, watching me come on. The truth is I wasn't even thinking about tackling him—I figured my job was just to contain him till my teammates arrived to help.

Barlow faked right and went left, and I bought the fake for a half second and then reversed direction. My feet got tangled with each other, and as I took off after him I tripped myself. I knew that any second I would do a face-plant into the grass and look like the biggest clown since the Three Stooges stopped making movies.

I fought gravity and my own clumsiness, and somehow I kept running for three more steps, if you can call that running. It was halfway between a sprint and a dive—I was already nearly horizontal and my arms were windmilling for balance.

And then I couldn't fight it anymore and went down hard, chest first, but at the very last second my arms grabbed on to something and I held on.

In my battle to stay upright I had forgotten all about Barlow, but my three-step dive to the grass had made up the distance to him, and my thrashing arms had wrapped around his knees. Instead of the clumsiest dry-land belly flop in the history of Founders' Park, I had by sheer luck executed a nearly flawless open-field tackle of the football team's starting running back.

We both went down hard and rolled over on the grass. I let go of his knees and lay there for a second, stunned. Then Rob's excited voice crowed above me: "Way to hit, Jack. That was awesome, man. A safety on the first play of the game!"

He pulled me up, and my teammates surrounded me and thumped me on the back. "Great stuff!" "Massive hit, Logan." "You're the man."

Barlow walked over, wiping mud off his forehead. He muttered, "Good hit," and tapped me on the shoulder, but there was a sharpness to his voice and his dark eyes didn't look particularly friendly.

"Thanks," I said.

"That was a safety," Rob reminded Barlow. "We get two points and you guys kick off to us. Nice way to start a game, huh?"

Barlow made a growling sound deep in his throat as he turned away.

We lined up for their kick, and a kid named Garrett caught it and ran it back. Rob moved us up the field with two short and accurate passes. He pointed to me in our third huddle. "Three complete and we get a first down," he said. "It's your turn, Logan. Slant right. I'm going to count your steps. On your fifth step stop short, turn back to me, and the ball will already be in your chest. Got it?"

"Five steps," I agreed. "Got it."

"It's a timing play," he said. "Can't miss."

Our huddle broke and we walked toward the line together. "Don't drill it," I cautioned him softly. "I don't have the best hands."

"You're playing like a beast," he whispered back. "If you get daylight after you catch it, turn on your jets. The way you're going, you'll get a shot at a starting job."

I slid the receiver's gloves my father had bought me out of my pocket and pulled them on over my sweaty hands as I walked back to the line. Those two words kept tap-dancing around in my head. *Starting job.* Who was I kidding? I wasn't a star receiver on the Fremont football team. Not me. Not close. Not ever. Tap, tap. But still . . . *starting job.* Playing before crowds. Cheerleaders at parties. *Tap, tap.* I glanced at the duck pond. The two men on the bench hadn't budged. My father pulled out a bottle of water, tilted himself a drink, and stared right at me.

Garrett stood over the ball. "Forty-seven," Rob called out to him. "Sixty-five. Twenty-two. *Hut.*"

Garrett hiked him the ball, and I slanted right. As I ran, I heard one of their players shout out, "One Mississippi, two Mississippi, *watch Logan!*"

I was already on my second step, with a kid named Dumont trying to cover me. He was fast, but he knew he couldn't run with me, so he gave me three yards of cushion off the line. I counted my steps—three, four, five—and slammed on the brakes. I turned back toward Rob and *BAM*, the football arrived by express mail.

I hadn't expected it that hard and fast, and I couldn't quite hold it. It popped up out of my iron hands, and as I tried to grab it, other hands reached for it. Dumont had closed the distance, and he tried to grab the loose ball and run it in. I managed to get both my hands on it as Dumont's momentum carried him on past.

I realized that I was now alone, undefended, safely cradling the football. It was time to turn on the burners and run it in for a touchdown. Once I got going, no one on this field could catch me. I started to spin back around, toward their end zone, and as I was in mid-pivot, a freight train ran me over.

The next thing I knew I was lying on my back on the grass, tasting salt and pebbles, and looking up at the purple clouds that seemed to twist and billow mysteriously, like a magician's cloak during a good trick. I tried to stand up, but Rob told me to "Stay down, buddy. Jesus, look at his mouth."

I put my hand to my lips, and it came away crimson. I

realized to my horror that I wasn't tasting salt and pebbles but rather blood and my own busted teeth.

"Sorry, Logan," Barlow's voice said. "Didn't mean to hit you that hard."

As the shock of the impact wore off, the pain came on in waves. I lay flat on my back and closed my eyes and made my hands into fists.

Then I heard my father say, "Stay down, Jack. There's an ambulance on the way." And then more softly, in the closest he had ever come to a loving voice: "You did good, son. I'm proud of you."

MY TWO BEST FRIENDS STOOD BY MY BEDSIDE,
but they couldn't bring themselves to look at my mouth.
Dylan was staring past me out the window where a gardener
was mowing the hospital's large lawn, while Frank had
focused his eyes on a lunch tray on my bedside table that
hadn't been cleared yet. Given my condition, there wasn't
any solid food that he could snag, but there was an uneaten watermelon Jell-O that he was eyeing hungrily. "I
didn't even know hospitals had dentists," Frank said. "But
he did a pretty slick job. Wrapped you up like a Christmas
present."

"Oral surgeon," I tried to say, but it sounded like a frog
croaking over a windy swamp. My dislocated jaw had been
popped back into place by an oral surgeon, which I think
is like a dentist on steroids. I had seen enough dentists,
nurses, and oral surgeons in the past two days to last a
lifetime. I'd lost track of the number of people who had
come into my room, studied my X-rays, and poked around
inside my mouth like it was an interesting renovation
project.

A bandage now wound around my head and under my
chin to prevent me from opening my mouth too wide. Two

of my front teeth had been knocked out, but one of them had been saved and brought to the hospital with me and replanted. Several more had been chipped and cracked and jarred loose, but they had been splinted to healthy teeth and were all somehow still rooted in my gums. I had also been diagnosed with a grade one concussion—the mildest kind, they told me, as if I should be grateful—and I was floating on pain pills.

"Don't try to talk," Dylan advised me. "Stick with thumbs-up, thumbs-down. Are there any cute nurses here?" Dylan thought about girls a lot and talked about them as if he were highly experienced, but the truth was that he was almost painfully shy and didn't have any success with dating in the real world.

I gave him a thumbs-down.

"How's the food?" Frank asked, following up his own main interest.

Another thumbs-down.

"He can't chew food anyway," Dylan reminded Frank. And then as if on cue they both glanced right at me at the same moment—at my swollen face, bandaged jaw, and splinted teeth.

Dylan shook his head and said, "Jesus, Jack, didn't your mom teach you not to play in traffic? What the hell were you doing out there banging bodies with the football meatheads?"

"He was doing something he should be very proud of," a deep voice answered from the doorway. I recognized the distinctive rumble of our new principal. Heavy footsteps approached and then he was standing at the foot of my bed, his bald head shiny as a cue ball under the fluorescent lights. "Giving his all for his school."

"Looks like he gave most of his teeth for his school," Frank observed. "Anyway, I thought it was just a pickup game."

Muhldinger folded his massive arms across his barn door of a chest. "Sometimes when you play hard you get your bell rung. A few months later, you don't even remember it."

"That could be because concussions cause memory loss," Dylan suggested.

Muhldinger glared at them, and then he said, "I'm not surprised you two don't understand. I've never seen either one of you put on the school colors. But that will change soon enough. Now, I'd like a word alone with Jack."

Dylan rolled his eyes and headed out. Frank hesitated, as if reluctant to leave me with this maniac, but then he, too, left, and Muhldinger pulled the door shut. "I was going to stop by yesterday, but your dad said you were pretty much out of it," he told me. "You seem much better this morning."

I didn't say anything back. For one thing my mouth was all wired together, and while I was curious why Muhldinger had come, he was just about the last person I wanted to see in my hospital room. So I just lay there on my back looking up at his flat nose that had been broken and reset badly, and his hard black eyes that seemed to flash down and challenge me, as if saying: "Get up, Logan. Get out of that hospital bed and answer the bell for the next round."

But I wasn't getting up for any next round. I had thrown in the towel and I was staying down for the count. Screw him and everything that he stood for.

Muhldinger saw my face twitch, and misread my anger for pain. "I can see you're hurting," he said. "You know, I broke this schnoz three times." He pressed his index finger against the tip of his flat nose and grinned. "No worries, Jack. They'll cap your teeth and your jaw will heal up and in a few days you'll walk out of here on your own steam. A month from now you'll be eating steak and running again. And I have to say—you can run pretty fast. Sometimes you even remind me of the Logan Express." He broke off for a second and continued in a low voice: "I played with your father, and watching you in the park brought it back for a second."

And I think that was the moment when I started to truly hate him. Or maybe it wasn't him at all, and I really just hated the part of myself that had needed to impress him and my dad and had landed me here. I vowed to myself that I would never make that mistake again, whatever it cost me.

He stepped closer, and began to walk around my bed. "But that's not what I came here to tell you. Or maybe in a way it is." Again the grin, as if we were buddies now and about to share a secret. "Jack, I have some very good news." I tried to imagine what his good news might be. Maybe he had taken a job as the assistant line coach of the Giants and was resigning as principal before the school year even started.

Muhldinger walked to the head of my bed, till he was standing right above me. "You are exactly what I'm trying to bring to our school," he told me. "The guys on the football team already know what they can do. But you challenged yourself and stepped up big-time, and pickup game or not, you really showed me something out there."

Suddenly I was positive his very good news could only turn out to be really bad news. I didn't like the way he was smiling down at me. If I had become his poster boy for sports recruitment, I was in serious trouble. I wanted to say: "Whatever it is, you've got the wrong hospital patient. Put me on the poster that says: 'Stay off the field and save your teeth for your old age.'"

But of course I couldn't say any of that because the oral surgeon had wrapped me up tightly, so I just looked back up at him and wondered how much it hurt to have your nose broken three times.

Muhldinger lowered a big paw onto my shoulder. "Forget about tryouts, Logan," he said. "You're on the team. I'm the coach, after all. We'll have a uniform and a number waiting for you." His eyes were shining, as if he had just given me the greatest gift in the world. "You're a Fremont Lion. Come see me when you're healed up and we'll talk some more about what it means to be a varsity football player. You're one of my pride now."

He pulled his hand off my shoulder and walked out of my hospital room.

I HAD INTENDED TO TELL MY DAD AT THE
dinner table, when my mom could be an ally. I knew that
was a little cowardly, but cowardice had taken a big step
forward in my playbook since my teeth has been pulver-
ized and I'd started my involuntary liquid diet. But my
brother Carl showed up for dinner with his wife, Anne,
and I didn't want to turn this into a big family discussion.
Carl had been an All-League middle linebacker whose life
in high school had revolved around football and the weight
room, and I knew he would think I was chickening out.

So I waited till they left, and then I played a computer
game and cleaned my room, and after half an hour I ran
out of ways to waste time and headed downstairs.

Mom was in the kitchen, reading a thick novel. She's a
part-time librarian in our town library and she's always
bringing home new books to read herself before recom-
mending them. "Want some ice cream?" she asked. "Might
feel good on your mouth."

"Not hungry."

She glanced up from what looked like page five hundred.
"Since when do you turn down ice cream?"

"Mom, I'm not going to play football."

She understood immediately and nodded. My mom

raised a family of intense athletes, but she never played any sport beyond a little friendly tennis, and she's never pushed me to do anything. Maybe the truth was that she'd had enough of standing in the snow, rain, and wind, cheering on her first two sons and shivering. "When are you going to tell him?"

"I figure it's better to face the firing squad sooner rather than later. Want to give me a blindfold?"

"No blindfold necessary. Just be honest," she advised. "He'll understand."

"Sure he will." I couldn't keep the skepticism out of my voice, and maybe there was just a little bitterness, too. I remembered my dad's hand on my shoulder and his whisper that I had made him proud, while I tasted my own blood and teeth.

"Give him a chance, Jack," she urged.

"I hope he gives *me* a chance," I said, and headed into the family room.

My father was sitting in the leather armchair, sipping a beer and watching the Yankees get clobbered by Boston. "Swing the bat, damn you," he growled at the batter on the screen.

"Dad, he can't hear you," I said. "That's a digital image of a man who's in the Bronx."

"He's lucky he can't hear me," my father muttered. "If there's one thing I hate it's guys who take a called strike three with men on base."

I glanced around the room. Sports memorabilia was everywhere, from a black-and-white photo of the Mick belting a home run, to a framed Giants jersey signed by Eli

Manning, to our family trophy case. The glass case took up a whole wall, and while it was smaller than the case at Fremont High, for one family it was pretty damn impressive. My father and brothers had been studs at every possible sport, and mixed in with the forest of football trophies were gold men shooting basketballs, and silver wrestlers with their arms spread wide, and bronze batters with bats cocked.

"Got a minute?"

"Sure." He clicked the game off and pointed to the couch. "Have a seat. How's the old mouth?"

"Better," I told him, remaining standing.

"Try not to take the pain pills unless you have to."

"Okay, no pills tonight. Dad, I made a decision."

"Good," he said. "About what?"

I opened my mouth but I couldn't get the words out. I finally settled for just one: "Football."

I think he sensed the truth, but he didn't help me. He just waited as the seconds dragged by.

"Sorry," I finally told him. "Not going to happen."

Muhldinger had called up to tell my dad that I had a place on the varsity team, and I think it was the proudest he had ever been of me. Now he studied my face as if trying to read an answer there. "You're afraid you'll get hit again," he finally said. "That's normal. I used to feel that way sometimes after I got popped. I know you don't believe me, but it's true. Everyone has those moments, Jack. You took a real hard shot. But you weren't wearing a helmet, and you'll see that playing with pads feels a lot safer, and they've taken new precautions so—"

I cut him off and my words came out loud and angry. "It's not 'cause I'm afraid. I just don't want to play on the stupid football team."

"Because?" he asked softly.

"That's not who I am."

"Okay," he said, "then don't." His gray eyes looked sad, and when he spoke again his voice held no anger, but only sympathy, as if he could see me making a big mistake and wanted to help. "But, Jack, are you sure you know who you are? Because sometimes we only find that out by trying something new. Brian was offering you an opportunity. One of the most exciting chances you've ever had to step up and challenge yourself. Are you sure you just want to chuck it in the garbage can and go on with business as usual?"

I stood facing him, and the case of glittering family trophies on the wall behind him, and I wished I could have answered: "This is who I am, this is what I'm good at, and here's what I plan to do with my life, or at least my senior year. I want to explore this subject at school, date that girl, and get into such and such a college so that I can spend the rest of my life doing something that I love." But this was a moment for truth, and the truth was that I had no such answers. I'd never had a girlfriend, there was no subject I was particularly good at or drawn to, I was only applying to a few mediocre colleges, and the map for the rest of my life hadn't arrived in the mail yet, so all I could tell him was: "Maybe I don't know who I am, but I do know for sure that I don't want to be on the football team. I know how much it means to you. And it's not a stupid team—I'm sorry I said that. A lot of people get great things out of it. But not me. I don't want it and I'm not gonna do it."

Dad shrugged his big shoulders and clicked on the game again.

He settled back in his chair and focused all his attention on the TV, as if I had already left the room. "Throw your fastball," he growled at the Yankees pitcher on the screen. "Challenge him with a heater."

HIDDEN LAKE ISN'T ACTUALLY HIDDEN. SIGNS on nearby roads have arrows that point to it like a target, and a street called Hidden Lake Lane leads right to our busy town beach with a lifeguard on duty all summer long.

But a few hundred yards from the town beach is a rocky little cove that's hard to get to. The only way in is a twisting, unmarked trail that leads down from the paved road and winds through briar bushes. Suddenly you pop out at the water's edge and find yourself on a narrow beach that's more pebbles than sand.

It was a Wednesday afternoon in July and the sun was sinking toward the trees on the far side of the lake. I sat on a beach towel, trying not to stare at Becca, who was twenty feet away in a red bikini. She was studying a book with great concentration and occasionally making notes with a pencil—probably memorizing vocab words for the SAT or something.

I had been out of the hospital for a little over a week, and had already had two follow-up visits with my dentist. I was off the pain pills and feeling better, except that I knew one more hellish conversation about the football team was going to kick off in my direction very soon. I was still two days away from my first shift back at work.

"You need to tell Brian," Dad informed me the morning after our talk in the family room. He works long hours on a construction crew and most days he leaves home before I wake up, but on weekends he sleeps late and we all eat breakfast together.

"Why don't you tell him?" I suggested.

"Because he's holding a spot for you, so don't you think you should be the one to let him know that you won't be taking it?" My dad probably thought I wouldn't have the guts to tell Muhldinger, and I admit I wasn't looking forward to it. I couldn't predict exactly how our new principal would react when I told him I didn't want to be part of his mighty Lions, but I knew he wasn't going to slap me on the back and wish me good luck in my future endeavors.

Near me, Dylan and Frank were discussing one of their recurring subjects of the summer—which team they were going to go out for in September, or avoid.

"Ping-Pong," Dylan said. "I have a wicked backhand slice. I can literally bend the ball around a pillar in my basement."

"The only problem is that there's no Ping-Pong team at our school," Frank pointed out.

"I can start one," Dylan said hopefully. "Millions more people play Ping-Pong than football or basketball. It's an Olympic sport."

"Muhldinger's not a Ping-Pong kind of a guy," Frank told him. "He likes sports where people bleed."

Dylan nodded miserably. "Not many injuries in Ping-Pong, unless you get a splinter from the racket. What about you?"

"I'm using the process of elimination," Frank announced. "Figuring out the ones I definitely don't want to go near." He yawned. "Basketball is off my list for reasons having to do with mass and gravity. My vertical leap is . . ."

"Nonexistent."

"I can get airborne," Frank insisted, "but not for long. Football is also out. Collisions on frozen fields are not my idea of a good time. Forget cross-country. I just don't see the point since the invention of the gasoline engine. I once went out for a long jog after lunch and fell asleep while I was running."

It was probably true—Frank could sleep almost anywhere, especially after a big meal. I'd seen him fall asleep in theaters during earsplitting action movies and in math class in the middle of an algebra test, and I once found him snoring away on a leaf pile in his backyard while the blower that he'd been using roared beside him and his worried dog licked his face. I had no trouble believing that he could start to nap while in the middle of a run.

I knew Frank and Dylan were joking around, but it was also clear they were worried. They had been dismissing sport after sport, trying to figure out what would be the easiest and least dangerous teams. Now that August was just around the corner, their conversations were taking on real urgency. It was kind of pathetic that on this perfect summer afternoon the specter of Principal Muhldinger was looming over Hidden Lake, haunting us all.

I stood, walked down the beach to the water, and waded out three steps. Then I dove in from where it was knee deep and the cold lake swallowed me. I stayed under for as long as I could, and when I finally surfaced I was more than forty feet from shore. I turned over onto my back and floated. The sun felt warm on my face, and I tried to soak it in and clear my mind of worries about sports, my father, and an inevitable conversation with our new principal.

Someone broke the surface near me. I expected to see Frank or Dylan, but instead I glimpsed long black hair and the flash of a red bikini. "Hey, Becca," I said, a little surprised. I figured she must have seen me dive in and followed me out here, but I didn't have a clue why. We weren't exactly friends. I had tried to chat with her a few times at work but she'd never seemed that interested.

Becca treaded water near me, and for a few moments she didn't give any hint that she even knew I was there. I began to wonder if we had just randomly ended up in the same part of Hidden Lake.

Then she asked: "How're your teeth?"

"Rerooting themselves. It's nice to be able to eat again."

"I heard about what happened from Meg. Her dad works for the volunteer ambulance corps. It sounded like a real bad accident."

"It wasn't an accident."

She gave me a curious look. "Somebody did that to you intentionally?"

"After I intentionally put myself in the stupid position of trying out for the football team."

Becca slowly stretched out on her back and floated a few feet away from me. "At least it paid off. I heard you made varsity. That's a big deal."

At Muscles High it certainly was, but I was pretty sure

she was being sarcastic. "I've decided to turn that great honor down."

She studied my face. Her hazel eyes sparked in the bright sunlight. "Wow. Muhldinger's not going to like that at all."

"I haven't told him yet. Not looking forward to it. But whatever. A lot of people have more serious problems than whether to play on a stupid football team."

"That's probably true," Becca admitted and fell silent. We floated near each other for a while. We had worked together at Burger Central all summer and had never had more than a thirty-second conversation. Now at least we were sharing a deep silence.

Wind rippled the water, and I could hear the lifeguard's whistle all the way from the town beach. A dragonfly looked us over as possible landing pads and whizzed past. "It's nice out here," she said, and I couldn't figure out why she suddenly sounded uncharacteristically nervous. "That stupid book gave me a headache."

"What were you studying?"

"Would you like to go to a movie sometime?" she asked.

"What?"

"Multivariable equations," Becca said quickly. "They're the most common algebra problems on the SAT. The whole trick to them is isolating the variable—"

"Wait a minute," I said, cutting her off. "Did you just ask me out?"

"No big deal. I've been studying a lot lately. I thought it would be fun to see a movie, but if you don't want to, no problem."

"How's this Friday night?" I asked, maybe a little too quickly.

Becca gave me a shy smile, and it was one of the prettiest things I'd ever seen. Who knew that such a serious girl had a smile like that hidden away? "Friday's great. We can go right after work. You pick the movie—I'll see anything."

She turned and glanced toward the beach, and I thought she was going to swim off, but then she looked back at me and said: "I'm glad you're not going to play football, Jack. What's happening at our school is disgusting, and making us all join sports teams is . . . fascistic."

"Right," I said, trying to remember exactly what "fascistic" meant.

"Somebody needs to tell them to shove it."

"If there's one thing I never wanted to be, it's a rebel."

But she was busy giving me advice. "When you tell Muhldinger, don't try to reason with him. These people are total wackos, and he's off the scale. Just say your piece and get out of there fast, before he eats you alive."

She wasn't exactly making me feel better. "Believe me, I'm not planning to get into a debate with him on the value of football." To change the subject, I asked her the question that had been bothering Dylan and Frank: "So what team are you thinking about going out for in September?"

Becca didn't hesitate. "The one that's going to cost me the least time and effort. I saw on the school Web site they may start a C-team for soccer."

"What's the criteria?" I asked.

"At the C-level they'll take anyone with a heartbeat," she

said. "But it'll probably never happen because they need to find a coach and dig up enough other teams for us to play. If they get it together, it will be a Dumpster team for non-athletes, which suits me just fine. See you on Friday." Then Becca dove under, and she must have had lungs to match her long legs because she didn't surface again till she was all the way back to our cove.

I floated on alone in the middle of Hidden Lake, smiling for the first time since I had gotten my face mashed. Friday night was not far away. I was kind of in shock at the idea of taking Becca to a movie, but I also found myself thinking about soccer—a sport I had fooled around with. We'd played in gym class, and with my speed I'd always been more than decent at it. I had a surprisingly strong shot with my right foot, but I'd never thought about joining a team. I'd watched some MLS games on TV with my dad—he'll watch any sport known to man. But he had a football player's dislike of soccer, and after a while he'd mutter, "One hour and the score's still zero to zero. I'd rather watch ice melt," and switch the channel.

At Fremont, with its crazed cult of football, soccer was barely tolerated. The varsity boys and girls rarely won any trophies to contribute to the Fremont case on New Trophy Day, and the JV teams were invisible. Becca was right—a C-team would be a joke, if anyone noticed it at all.

But that probably meant we could control things a little bit—I was pretty sure Frank and Dylan would join up if I did, and Becca could get her best friend, Meg. If we found the right coach, I could spend the fall hanging out with friends and not worrying about setting records or crushing opponents or getting crushed myself.

I licked my tongue over my messed-up teeth. Becca might also be right that, like it or not, my new role was to tell Muhldinger to shove it. There was probably no better way of doing that than turning down the mighty Fremont football team in order to play on a remedial soccer squad with a bunch of slackers.

A TALL SECRETARY WITH WHAT LOOKED LIKE

orange hair told me to wait in a sitting area. There was a table with some magazines, but I was too nervous to read any of them. After about ten minutes she came back and told me to follow her. We walked through the administrative offices and reached a closed door, on which she rapped three times. The door was brand new, and so was the gleaming bronze nameplate on it that proclaimed in large letters: BRIAN MUHLDINGER—PRINCIPAL/HEAD FOOTBALL COACH. Muhldinger had wasted no time putting his name on the door, and I guess he was working through the summer getting ready for the school year, now that he was running the show.

"Come on in," a deep voice ordered. The secretary opened the door and I stepped in, and then she pulled it shut behind me.

I had been in this large, sunny office a few times when it had belonged to Arthur Gentry, and I noticed the changes. Gentry had loved sports, and on the walls of his office he'd hung photos of great athletes who'd used courage, speed, and skill to upset brute force or beat the odds. Growing up in my family had given me a pretty good knowledge of sports history, and I'd recognized many of the classic pictures: Billy Mills coming from behind to win the gold medal in Tokyo, Muhammad Ali towering over a downed Sonny Liston, Joe Namath with his arm cocked on the day the Jets upset Baltimore, and Michelle Kwan spinning lightly on the ice.

But Gentry had been a Princeton graduate who loved to read, and his office had also been crammed to the bursting point with books. They had overflowed his shelves and been stacked up on his desk and even on the window ledges—educational journals, literary and historical classics, and a few trendy teen novels he'd read to stay connected with his students.

Muhldinger had taken down Gentry's pictures and hung photos of his own. His new pictures were all football related and captured moments of jolting impact: linemen slamming into linemen, free safeties demolishing receivers, and pass rushers crushing quarterbacks. High above his desk I saw a large framed color photograph of Arthur Gentry crouched at a starting line, eager to begin a race. A caption gave his name and the dates of his birth and death, with a quote from Thomas Jefferson: "If the body be feeble, the mind will not be strong." In the photo Gentry looked very alive and eager to go for it. For a moment I remembered his brave final sprint down the stretch, and the way he had sunk to his knees and then collapsed onto his back.

Gentry's books were all gone. It was like they had been sucked out with a giant vacuum, the bookcases along with them. I did a quick scan and only saw three books in the whole office—a dictionary, a James Patterson murder mystery, and a biography of Lawrence Taylor. On the right side of the desk was a whiteboard with an intricate pattern of X's and O's, no doubt charting a complex new top secret play designed to win our first game of the season.

Muhldinger was seated at his desk, which looked out a large picture window at emerald lawns and playing fields. He was wearing a short-sleeve shirt that showed off his biceps, and was flipping through some papers with a scowl. When he glanced up and saw me, he put down the papers gratefully. "Meetings," he growled. "Meetings about meetings." He stood up and walked over to me and held out his enormous right hand. My own hand disappeared into it, and Muhldinger gave me a handshake firm enough to squeeze oil from a walnut. "Good to see you, Jacko," he said. "How're you feeling?"

"Better."

"All done with the dentist?"

"I hope so."

"Smile," he commanded.

I drew back my lips.

"You're not going to win any beauty contests, but then you probably weren't going to before you got hit," he said with a laugh.

"Probably not," I agreed, trying to find a way to start the real conversation that had to take place. "But I've had some time to recover, and—"

"Injuries suck when they happen, but a young body heals and you move on," he said. "I bet you don't even remember the worst of it—am I right or am I right?"

I glanced up at the photo of poor old Arthur Gentry. "Actually, I remember all of it."

He seemed a little surprised. "Well, that's good," he said. "You can use that for motivation. Sit down, Jack. I've got something to show you." He waved me to a chair, and then he walked over to the whiteboard and rummaged around behind it. He soon found what he was looking for and came back holding a box. I didn't know what was in it, but suddenly I felt an urge to get this over with as quickly as possible.

"I have something to tell you—" I started to say.

"And I have something to show you," he said, opening the box. "A special order. Check this out!" He pulled out a red-and-gold Fremont football jersey. It had a lion on the front, its mouth open as if preparing to devour someone. He turned it around, and with a sinking heart I saw the number—32—and the name. LOGAN.

"I gotta tell you," he said, "when I saw it I choked up. I couldn't help remembering your dad. I was a freshman when he was a senior and had his state championship year. Undefeated, untied—the Lions dominated at every position. That was the best team we've ever had at Fremont."

I didn't know what to say, but I had to say something. "Principal Muhldinger, I'm afraid I—"

He cut me off with a smile. "No one could fill his shoes, Jack. And I don't expect you to. The important thing is what's here," and he tapped his heart. "And you've got it there—you showed it to me that day when you bled for Fremont. And you don't know how much that meant to me.

Because if you can do it, anyone else at this school can do it, and I don't mean that in a bad way. It was inspirational." He handed me the shirt, and I didn't know what else to do so for a moment I took it and held it in front of me. It felt light in my hands, and hung down well below my hips. Number 32.

"The same number your dad wore," Muhldinger said reverently.

My hands shook and the shirt rippled. "I can't take this," I told him.

"I thought of retiring his number as one of my first official acts," he told me. "But I don't believe in sacred ground. Wear it with pride."

"No, you don't understand. I can't—"

"I understand perfectly," he said. "But there's nothing to worry about. He loves it that you're going to be wearing his number. I checked in with him this morning, and he told me he thought it was a great idea."

"He said that this morning?"

"His exact words were 'Love it!' I left him a message, just to make sure it was okay with him," Muhldinger said. "He texted me right back."

So my dad hadn't told Muhldinger that there was no point in giving me his old number because I wasn't going to join the team. He had left it up to me to break the bad news, and had made it harder by approving this new wrinkle. If I rejected the team, I would now also be rejecting his number and legacy. Anger came to my rescue. "My dad should have called you back and told you—" I started to say.

"A text was fine." Muhldinger cut me off with a smile. "Your dad and I go way back. Lord knows we've had our differences over the years, but when it comes to football I've never respected anyone more. I was suited up and on the sideline the day he scored the winning touchdown against East River. It looked like half the East River team was trying to drag him down, and there was your father somehow taking step after step as time ran out. I don't mind telling you that I cried that day."

His eyes were shining, like he was remembering the moment as a young man when he had seen the face of God. Becca was right—he was a total wacko. Watching him, I felt something welling up deep inside me. At first I thought I was going to break down in his office and have a little cry myself. Then I realized that something much worse than tears was coming, and I had to find a way to get out of there fast.

"I've only cried three times in my life," Muhldinger went on softly. "When my father died. When I had to put my dog to sleep. And when the Logan Express scored that winning touchdown against East River."

I put my hand over my mouth but I couldn't stop it. A laugh burst out.

Muhldinger looked confused and a little offended. Then he relaxed and his face softened as he broke into an unexpected smile. "Yeah, I know. It's a little corny, but, Jack, I've never seen anything like what your father did that day. He refused to lose. What it meant to me was that if he could do it, any of us could, if we just dug deep enough."

I laughed harder—I just couldn't stop.

Muhldinger began to chuckle himself. It was some kind of weird bonding thing, except that he thought he was laughing with me and I knew I was laughing at him. "So maybe I get a little emotional sometimes," he said, and he waved his hand in a "what the hell" gesture. "I'm proud of those tears, Jack. They were manly tears. Say what you want about your father, but he went to war that day."

I was laughing so hard I started crying manly tears of my own. My gasps turned into deep sobs, and I thought I might choke to death. Muhldinger stopped smiling and stared at me as if trying to gauge something. "What's so funny?"

Suddenly I was almost shouting at him, and it's a strange thing to shout at your principal in his office. "Look at him!" I said, pointing to the color photo of Gentry. "He died flat on his back in front of five thousand people because he also went to war and was trying to break some kind of meaningless state record at the age of seventy."

"Maybe that's how he wanted to leave us," Muhldinger said. "Why is that funny?"

My voice got even louder. "*It isn't funny at all!* Heart attacks are agonizing. If he hadn't died that day he'd be in this office right now, reading a book, and then he'd go home and kiss his wife and play with his grandkids."

Our new principal couldn't argue with those observations, but his jaw moved under the skin, as if he was chewing on something that had an unpleasant taste. "Lower your voice," he commanded, and stood up. "Take your shirt and go, and ask your dad to teach you some respect."

I stood up to face him. "Keep the shirt."

Muhldinger towered over me. "I must've told fifty people you're coming on the team."

I took a breath, and the truth came tumbling out: "Sorry, but I don't want the shirt, and I don't want to play for your football team. That's what I've been trying to tell you."

Muhldinger's forehead turned red, and then his cheeks, and in a few seconds the point of his nose and the stub where his neck should have been were also scarlet. His voice grated out from between clenched teeth: "I feel sorry for your father."

"This has nothing to do with my father."

He took a step closer. "It has everything to do with your father," he insisted. I had a feeling he wanted to lower his shoulder and drive me through a wall, but of course he couldn't. "Do you think I would have offered you a spot on my varsity team if you weren't a Logan? Now, goddamn it, I'm running this school and you're going to be suited up and on my sideline on opening day, and that's the end of it."

The Logan side of me must have taken over, because suddenly I wasn't afraid of him anymore. I looked right back into his hard black eyes and said: "No I'm not. I'm going out for the C soccer team."

"Get the hell out of my office. You're an embarrassment."

I saw him start to lose it, and he turned away very quickly. I thought he was going to open the door and shove me out, but then I saw his right hand clench into a fist and start to swing. His body pivoted, and *BAM* his fist went right through half an inch of solid wood. A karate black belt couldn't have done better.

The next thing I knew there was a big hole in his new door. Muhldinger was holding his right fist in his left hand and cursing, and the secretary with orange hair was telling me: "I really think you should go now."

IT'S A LOT EASIER TO GET THROUGH FOUR hours of busing tables when you know you're going to be taking a girl like Becca to a movie afterward. Half-chewed cheeseburgers didn't seem as gross as usual, and I didn't even mind the french fries that had been stomped on and ground into the red carpet like thin wads of chewing gum.

We finished up at nine, left our bikes chained up behind Burger Central, and headed over to the mall on foot. It was a four-block walk on a warm summer evening. Becca was wearing tan shorts and a red V-necked top, and her long hair blew in the evening breeze. She smoothed it back as we talked, and everything would have been great except that she seemed obsessed with finding out what had gone on between Muhldinger and me. "I hear he broke his pinky. Meg saw him yesterday, and she said he's got his fingers taped together in some kind of splint. What did you say to him?"

"Nothing."

She studied my face. "That must have been some pretty good nothing. Was he aiming at you or the door?"

"If he'd been aiming at me, I wouldn't be alive now to take you to this movie," I told her. "Could we talk about something else?"

Becca finally let it go. "Sorry. What else would you like to talk about?"

I ran through a couple of possible stupid questions in my head at rapid speed and chose one that I actually was curious about. "Why do you study so much?"

She frowned. "At other schools kids study much harder than I do and no one thinks they're freaks."

"I wasn't calling you a freak," I told her. "I was just trying to get to know you a bit."

"Ask me a better question, Jack, and I'll give you a better answer."

She seemed to be challenging me to take a risk. I blurted out what I was really curious about: "Why did you ask me on a date? We've worked together for two months, and I didn't think you were at all interested."

I got another one of those smiles. "It was a slow day at Hidden Lake," she teased.

"That's what I figured," I told her. "Either that or you felt sorry for me because I got my teeth bashed in."

The lights of the mall shone two blocks away, and cars streamed into the parking garage, but the sidewalk was deserted. We walked side by side in silence.

"I did feel sorry about what happened to you," Becca admitted. "I was going to visit you in the hospital, but you got out fast."

"Not fast enough," I told her. "Doctors and dentists were all over me for two days. I hate dentists, and I'm not fond of nurses or oral surgeons, either. I couldn't eat any solid food for a while. Just stuff Mom ran through a machine till it was goopy."

"Why do you hate dentists?" She seemed intrigued.

"They're creepy."

"My father's a dentist," she told me.

"You're kidding, right? I've never heard of a Dr. Knight in this town."

"His practice is in Mapleville."

"No offense," I said quickly. "I had no idea what your dad did. I'm sure he's a nice guy and a very good dentist."

She smiled at my awkward apology. "Actually I sort of agree with you that it's a little creepy. He wants me to follow in his footsteps, but it'll never happen. I might end up as a doctor, but there's no way I'm going to spend my life looking into people's mouths. He doesn't take no for an answer, and sometimes he can get really stubborn." She broke off as we reached the mall and headed up the escalator.

The comedy I had picked was horrible. The jokes were so lame that no one in the theater was laughing. After half an hour people started filing out, and Becca touched my arm and whispered: "Enough?"

"Let's go," I agreed.

We joined the stream of people fleeing out the exit. "You really know how to choose them," she said.

"Dylan told me it was good. But then again he has no taste."

"Clearly," she agreed.

I glanced up at a clock. It was just a little before ten. I didn't want our first date to fizzle out so quickly. "Do you want to do something else? It's still early."

"What did you have in mind?"

There wasn't much to do in our town, even on a Friday night. "Bowling?" I suggested.

"I hate bowling more than you hate dentists," she told me.

"Then you choose."

Becca thought for a minute. "Let's go see Shadow."

"Look out the window," I said. "It's night. No sun, no shadows."

She laughed. "Shadow is my horse."

"Does he see visitors this late?"

"They have evening lessons at the stable on Fridays. We can just make it. Come."

We hurried to get our bikes and headed over to Brook-farm Stables. I had driven by it many times, but I had never been inside. I followed Becca through the front gate. She waved to the guard, who waved back, and we biked up a long driveway.

We rode past a lighted riding arena with a lesson going on. Beyond it were dark barns.

Becca led me to a side entrance and hopped off her bike. "We don't have to lock them up," she said. "I've been coming here for years and it's totally safe. We just need to make sure we're out by ten-thirty when they lock the front gate." She slipped in the door and I followed her.

The barn was dark and had a musty stench of everything having to do with horses. Becca switched on a row of bare bulbs hanging from the ceiling and led me down a narrow corridor past dozens of gloomy stalls. The horses were on their feet. Some of them were eating oats, but most were standing silent and motionless. Occasionally I saw tails twitch and heads swing in my direction.

"Do they sleep standing up?" I asked.

"It's not really sleep," she told me. "They're napping."

"How come they don't doze off and fall over?"

"They were originally prey animals," she explained. "They had to be able to run from predators so they developed the ability to lock their legs and rest standing up. That way if a predator came, they could wake in an instant and break into a run. They nap for fifteen- or twenty-minute stretches all day long, standing up. Every so often they need to lie down for an hour and really crash."

She stopped by a stall, and I saw the outline of a horse, facing away from us. "Shadow," she whispered just a bit louder. "Hey."

The horse recognized her voice and swung around to face us. He was one of the bigger horses in the barn, and had a reasonably kind expression on his brown-and-white face given that we had just woken him up. He stepped over near the bars of the stall, and Becca reached in and fondly patted his nose. "Hey, boy." Shadow nuzzled her hand and then looked at me. "Talk to him," she said.

I wasn't sure what to say to a horse. "Hello, Shadow."

"Go ahead and pet him," she urged.

Shadow looked me over, and I think he was wondering who the hell I was and what I was doing with his girl. "He's jealous," I told her.

She patted Shadow's nose. "Jack's okay," she told the big horse. "Please don't bite him."

I reached out and tentatively patted Shadow's nose, and he let me. My hand brushed her hand. "Did you once tell me that Shadow hurt his leg?"

She nodded. "Five years ago. They wanted to put him down. I wouldn't let them. My father kept telling me I had to do it, that it would be for the best in the long run. That's one of his favorite sayings—'It may be painful now, but it will be better later on.' But there are a lot of ways of excusing cruelty . . ." Becca's hand trembled. I noticed she was breathing a little fast.

"You okay?" I asked.

"No," she said. And then she started to cry.

I didn't know what to do. I was in a dark barn on a first date with a girl who was shivering, and tears were streaming down her face. This wasn't in the first-date manual. She pulled her hand back from Shadow and wrapped her arms around herself, as if the temperature had suddenly dropped fifty degrees.

"Should I go get someone?" I asked.

She shook her head. "No. I'll be okay. Sorry," she said, gasping as if she were having trouble breathing. "I have these sometimes. They pass. Sorry, Jack."

"Stop saying you're sorry," I told her. "Was the movie that bad? Or is it me? Did I say too many stupid things?"

Becca smiled through her tears. "No, you're fine. I'm the one who's a mess."

"Can I help?" I asked.

I watched her take a series of short breaths, inhaling and exhaling at regular intervals. When her breathing got more regular, she said in a low voice: "I haven't told this to anyone else, but my parents aren't getting along."

"That sucks."

She nodded and took a couple more breaths. "It's been bad for a long time. But lately it's gotten much worse. And . . . I just can't handle it sometimes."

She trembled again and I put my arm on her shoulder to steady her. "Okay?"

"Yeah, I'll be okay," she said. "I just need a little time." We were silent for a moment, and then slowly we leaned into each other until I was holding her and she was holding me. And we stood together like that in the dark barn for a few minutes, and gradually her breathing became normal again. "Sorry I unloaded on you," she said. "Thanks for not thinking I'm a complete wacko and running away."

"As long as you don't put your fist through a door, I'm not going anywhere," I told her.

I pulled back and looked at her face. Her hazel eyes fixed on me, still wet with tears. For a crazy moment I thought she was going to kiss me, but she just pressed close again, and then there was a loud snort that broke the moment.

I glanced over and Shadow was staring right at us, and he wrinkled his nose at me. "Definitely jealous," I said.

Becca looked over at her horse and laughed. "Maybe he should be," she said. "Come on, Jack. They're going to lock the gate. Let's go home."

9

OUR LIONS HAD JUST BEEN NAMED BY A
major newspaper as the high school football team to beat
in the whole state of New Jersey, and the town was throwing itself a big party before the season even started.

The gym seats a thousand people, and it was packed
to the rafters. A banner read in giant letters: FREMONT
LIONS—TRADITION, PRIDE, POWER! The varsity players had
been called out onto the darkened gym floor one by one, with
a drumroll before their names and a spotlight strobing
their path. They were now standing together on a raised
platform in their red-and-gold jerseys, in three imposing
rows. In front of them the cheerleaders had formed a pyramid that looked just a little smaller than the Great Pyramid of Cheops. Muhldinger sat in the middle of the raised
platform with the president of the board of education and
the mayor, watching the goings-on with a proud smile.

I was not out on the floor with the football team. I
had turned that honor down, and I sat with Dylan, Frank,
and Becca on a middle bleacher, dreading what was about
to happen. My friends couldn't understand why I had
dragged them to this late-summer pep rally. "There's a reason I need to go, that I can't talk about," I had told them.
"But you guys have to come and support me."

"If you need us so badly, why don't you share your secret with us?" Dylan had demanded. "Why do we have to pretend to cheer for Muhldinger's meatheads?"

"Yeah, if we're gonna miss one of the last afternoons at the lake, don't we deserve to know what the hell's going on?" Frank agreed.

"You'll understand soon enough," I promised them.

Becca had also been reluctant to come. She hated Muhldinger and everything he stood for, but I pointed out I'd risked everything to pat her dangerously jealous horse, so she had to come to support me. We had gone out on a few more dates, and Frank and Dylan were starting to accept her as part of our little group. Becca probably found them strange, but she seemed to enjoy occasionally hanging out with my two nutty friends.

The four of us were sitting in a row, clapping noticeably less enthusiastically than our neighbors, as Muhldinger stood and walked purposefully toward the mic.

"Hey," Frank said to me, "your whole family has the school spirit bug. Even your bros showed up." He pointed to where my dad, mom, and two brothers sat at the very front. "Why are they all dressed up?"

I saw Becca following the direction of his finger with interest. She had never met my parents, or my two brothers. Carl was sitting next to Anne, and my oldest brother, Billy, was there with his wife, Charlotte, and their two young kids.

It felt very strange to see them sitting together in a group and for me to be so far away. It had been my choice, but now that it was happening I didn't like the feeling at all.

Before they could ask me any more questions, Muhldinger grabbed the mic, ripping it from its stand like a hungry bear harvesting a cob of corn from its stalk. He looked around at the big crowd for a moment and then brought the mic to his lips. *"Let's hear it for Fremont!"*

The answering applause swelled to a deafening roar. At least a solid minute must have gone by with people clapping, hooting, and whistling while the cheerleaders shook pom-poms and turned cartwheels and the gym's sound system blared the music to the school fight song. The last line of the song is: "Fremont High will rise to the sky, to be number one!"

"LIONS NUMBER ONE," Muhldinger shouted above the din, picking up the final refrain. A chant began: "NUMBER ONE, NUMBER ONE." He pumped his ham hock of a fist in time to the chant, and people started stomping on the bleachers.

"Can we leave now?" Dylan asked. "Before I go deaf or this building collapses?"

But the roar was ebbing, because Muhldinger was holding up his hand for silence. "My friends," he said. "Thanks to all of you for giving up a summer afternoon to show your support for our Lions. The reason we're number one now is because of all of you, but we also owe a huge debt to those who've gone before us. And of course I'm talking about Arthur Gentry, who is watching over us today and always. As I'm sure he would say: when this new football season starts up, let's 'Just go for it'!"

There was another explosion of cheering. I had to admit that Muhldinger looked completely at ease in his role of school leader, at least when it came to football. "But we also have other Fremont heroes to remember," he reminded us. "And I've decided that my first official act as your principal should be to do something that's only been done once before in the history of Fremont High."

I tensed up. My arms were locked straight, my palms on my knees, while the balls of my feet pressed into the wooden bleacher floor.

Muhldinger walked toward the front of the platform, which brought him closer to the crowd. "Today," he said, "we're going to honor one of the best players to ever walk through the halls of our school, not to mention tear up the football field. I'm talking about the all-time rushing leader at Fremont High—the Logan Express—Tom Logan!"

A spotlight picked out my father, and everyone in the gym seemed to look at him except for Becca, who glanced at me.

"They wanted me to be part of the ceremony," I whispered to her. "I said I'd come and watch with my friends."

Muhldinger walked over to where my parents and brothers were sitting. He was still talking to everyone in the gym through the microphone, but he was now looking at my father: "Six thousand two hundred and twenty-three yards. A hundred years of Fremont football and nobody else has even come close to that. And I gotta tell you, I saw him play, and I carry that memory around with me. It reminds me of what we can be if we try hard enough, and *refuse to lose*. So let's not talk about it anymore—let's see it!"

A big screen lowered behind him, and a football game

from years past conjured to life on it. I sat forward—I had seen lots of film of my dad playing college football, and even a few grainy clips from his high school days, including a ten-second dark and poorly filmed version of this famous play that had put a last exclamation point on his brilliant high school career. But these images on the big screen were so bright and lifelike that I almost felt like I was on that snowy field when Fremont broke their huddle and lined up for their final play of the season.

Fremont had the ball at the East River twenty-two-yard line. The clock showed seven seconds left, and we were losing by five points. There was time for one more play, with the state championship on the line. The Fremont quarterback hiked the ball, rolled to his right, and handed it off to number 32. My dad tucked the ball away and charged forward, but he was hit behind the line of scrimmage. The tackler bounced off him like he had tried to bring down a tank, and Dad roared toward the East River goal line, twenty-two yards away.

An East River lineman dove at him and got a straight-arm for his trouble. It was like a punch to the face mask, and the lineman's head snapped back as he fell to the snow. The footage we were watching was soundless, but I could almost hear the impact of my father's straight-arm reverberating across the years, and the one thousand people in the Fremont gym seemed to all hear it also. They let out a collective gasp.

Fifteen yards to the goal line. Dad was motoring in heavy traffic. He was following a lone blocker, but when that blocker stumbled, Dad darted away toward the left sideline, completely exposed. A big East River tackler grabbed him from behind, wrapping both arms around my father's waist. He should have been able to pull Dad down, but somehow number 32 dragged the guy with him.

At the ten-yard line, a missile struck. A high-flying East River player flashed in at shoulder height and exploded into my father's right side. The impact spun Dad around but somehow he stayed on his feet. The airborne tackler latched on to my father's right arm. So there were two of them clinging to him now, but the Logan Express chugged forward to the eight, and then the seven.

This was where it got a little hard to believe. Two more East River players hit him high and low from opposite sides. It was hard to see exactly where they grabbed on, because Dad was wearing the opposing team like an outer layer. His red-and-gold shirt was almost completely hidden beneath East River blue. Our gym had gone quiet, and watching, I felt a cold tingle down my back, as if a bit of the snow from that long-ago afternoon were sifting across two decades onto my spine.

Five yards to go. Four. The East River players were getting desperate. You could see them not just holding on but trying to trip him up and drag him down. But the engine that carried them forward refused to quit.

Dad neared the goal line, and a wall of East River brawn was waiting for him there. Three gargantuan players reared up in his path, and their body language said clearly: "Thou shalt not pass."

Dad hit that blue wall at the one-yard line, and for the first time he lost his momentum and was pushed back. We were watching the play in regular time, but the action seemed to slow to second by second. My father was knocked backward and looked like he would sink down beneath all that weight and fall a few inches short. Then he found some secret reserve of strength, and he surged forward again with a tremendous second effort. And this time, incredibly, the wall in front of him sagged and buckled.

Ever since my teeth had been mashed I hadn't been able to think about football without feeling furious. I'd turned down the team and rejected my father's shirt and his legacy, but when the silent gym came alive with cheering I found myself cheering, too. I couldn't deny the pride I felt at what was happening on the screen.

The four players clinging to my father and the three more in the wall all had hands and arms and legs wrapped around him, but somehow number 32 reached the plane of the goal line. He seemed to freeze there for a heartbeat, neither in nor out, teetering on the brink, as if the football gods wanted this moment time-stamped and immortalized.

Then he burst forward into the end zone and fell to the ground with what looked like half the East River team on top of him. The referee raised both arms signaling the winning touchdown, and the crowd behind the end zone went berserk. The camera panned to a few shots of celebrating spectators and then returned to my father, who had climbed back up to his feet.

His helmet had been ripped off, and his long black hair glistened with snow as his mouth opened wide and he gave a shout of triumph and raised both fists high over his head. He stood like that for a long second, alone in his moment of glory, and then his teammates mobbed him and the tape cut off.

Twenty-seven years later the Fremont gym was rocking with applause. Muhldinger walked into the audience and grabbed my father's arm and made a little joke out of hauling him to his feet. Dad is a shy man who usually shuns the spotlight, but this was his moment and he seemed willing to just go for it.

A drumroll sounded, and then a spotlight led him out onto the gym floor to where Barlow—the varsity co-captain who had slammed me to the ground in Founders' Park— stood holding a red-and-gold shirt with the number 32. I was pretty sure it was the very shirt that Muhldinger had ordered for me—the one I had refused to wear.

Barlow handed the shirt to my dad and shook his hand. Dad held the jersey over his head as the crowd cheered, and then I heard Muhldinger say something to him that sounded like "Go ahead, Tom, hook it up." My dad slid something through the shirt, and while he was working on it I saw that two cheerleaders were escorting Carl and Billy out onto the gym floor. "Ladies and gentlemen," Muhldinger boomed, "we thought Tom might need a little help, so here are two other brave Lions from years past—Carl Logan, twice All-League, and Billy Logan, former team captain and All-State!"

Becca's hand tightened on my arm.

"I knew this was coming," I whispered to her. "It's fine."

But it wasn't fine. Now that it was actually happening, I was sorry I had come to this stupid pep rally. I should have gone to the lake with my buddies, or allowed Becca to take me horseback riding. I could have been on a horse lost in the trees, far away from this gym where my father and two brothers now stood in a golden pool of light. They were each holding on to something. "Go ahead and raise it up," Muhldinger told them.

They started to pull, and the football jersey spread out magically on whatever wire was supporting it and began to fly through the air like a red-and-gold bird. But before it rose more than ten feet above the floor I heard my father say, "Wait a minute."

The shirt stopped rising.

Muhldinger and my dad were standing close together and the mic picked up their voices. "What is it?" our new principal asked.

I heard my father say my name. My stomach knotted up and I felt a little dizzy.

The overhead lights came on. Dad was holding the mic and scanning the crowd. "Jack? Will you come down?"

I told myself that I didn't have to do this—we had discussed it and come to an agreement—but a second later I felt myself standing up and the people near me were clapping and patting me on the back as I walked past them.

I guess there are some things in life that you do without thinking about them too much. I walked to the end of that row, and then hurried down from aisle to aisle and bleacher to bleacher, and I don't think I had a single clear, conscious thought till I hit the gym floor and walked out to join my father and brothers. Dad stepped forward with a happy smile and grabbed my right arm, and then

Carl and Billy were passing me a rope and Carl ruffled my hair and said, "'Bout time you got your butt down here, bro."

The lights went out and a spotlight came on the shirt, and we hoisted it up together. My brothers were on one side of me, and my father was on the other, and our arms and hands pulled and churned together. The jersey rose above the gym floor, above the rows of wooden bleachers, until it reached the iron girders that interlaced just below the gym's ceiling and the banners from our nine State Championship seasons that hung there. One shirt already had a place of honor near those banners and the giant American flag. This was the jersey from Gene Hamilton, who had been the first Fremont football coach back at the turn of the twentieth century and had led the team for four decades. Dad's shirt found its spot right next to his, and the clapping built to a crescendo.

The lights were still off, and two strong hands fell over my shoulders in the darkness. I heard my father's voice tell me softly: "Sorry, Jack, but I needed you with us."

Instead of being angry at him, I heard myself answer, "I wouldn't have missed it for the world."

Then the gym lights came back on, and Dad's ceremony was over. The cheerleaders launched into another routine, and I didn't want to walk through it so I moved off to the side and stood in semidarkness at the edge of the gym floor, watching.

"Nice moment," a familiar voice said, sharp with sarcasm. Muhldinger had walked up next to me.

"Sure was," I agreed, watching a baton circle skyward and then spin back down until it was snatched out of the air by a blond girl in a short skirt.

"That shirt's better off up there than on your back," he said.

"Could be," I agreed, turning to face him. "How's your hand?"

His black eyes sharpened. "All healed up," he answered softly. "By the way, we're pulling the plug on that C soccer team."

"Why?" I asked.

"No coach," he told me. "A team needs a faculty coach, and none of the teachers seem interested in cesspool soccer. To tell you the truth I can't blame them. But there are lots of other choices for you. Come talk to me in my office and we'll go over some options. Good stuff today, Jack. I'm sure it meant a lot to your dad and mom to have you out there."

He gave me an extra-hard thump on the back with the same hand that had punched through the door, and then he was walking out to the center of the floor where the cheerleaders had finished their routine and was saying into his mic: "How about that, Fremont? Let's give it up for our lovely cheer girls!"

"THIS IS A BAD IDEA," I WARNED BECCA, AS
we locked our bikes up outside a sprawling, ugly brick
five-story apartment building in the city of Hackensack. It
was called Woodview Towers, but it was not towering, it
had no view of woods, and the man we had just biked ten
miles to see seemed to me to have less potential as a soccer coach than our seventy-seven-year-old school nurse.

"I ran it by him and he didn't say no," Becca told me as
we headed for the front entrance.

"That doesn't sound like an enthusiastic yes," I pointed
out. "And he's not exactly a sports coach kind of a guy."

"Sometimes you remind me of the people who bashed
your teeth," she said. "Try not to pass judgments."

"Live and let live is my motto," I assured her. "But in
school I once saw him reading a book and making notes
while he walked down some stairs. He tripped on his
own feet, tumbled down a whole flight, and nearly killed
himself."

"That could happen to anyone," Becca said.

"Not to anyone else I've ever seen. He got up with a
bloody nose and his busted glasses hanging off his face, but
he was still holding on to the book."

"I think that's sweet."

"He'd nose-dived right in front of my gym class and everyone was laughing—except the few of us who were worried he'd broken his neck. But he dusted himself off like it was just another day in the life of a Latin teacher and walked off reading."

"Well, maybe a guy who trips and falls and doesn't care if people laugh at him is exactly the kind of coach we need."

We reached the main entrance to Woodview Towers, and Becca walked in through a stone archway ahead of me. She was wearing snug blue Lycra biking shorts and a yellow T-shirt from some horse show, and just watching her leaning forward on her bike with her legs pumping and her hair flying behind her had taken my breath away for a good part of the ten miles from Fremont to Hackensack. She seemed so free-spirited and happy that it was hard to imagine this was the same girl who'd had the panic attack in the barn.

She found a list of tenant names on the side wall near the locked front door. "Haskell," she muttered, running her eyes down the list. "Here it is, Percy Haskell."

"Percy?" I repeated dubiously.

"He told me he was named for Shelley," she explained.

"For who?"

Becca gave me an exasperated look and rang the buzzer. "Don't play dumb. Percy won't understand it and I don't like it either."

"I'm not playing dumb. Listen, he's a part-time teacher, he has no connection to our school or town besides teaching one course there twice a week, and he may be the most unathletic man I've ever seen in my life. I'm not being judgmental—I'm just saying that I don't see how this is going to help us with Muhldinger."

"Hallo there, friend or foe?" a voice called down in a British accent.

"Friend," Becca said into the mic. "It's Becca and Jack."

A loud buzz sounded, and we pushed in and headed to the elevator.

"Friend or foe?" I repeated.

"I like the way he talks," she told me. "He uses the language beautifully—he even writes his own poetry in verse. And part-time or not, he's technically on the faculty. If he wants to be our coach, then we have a faculty coach."

"And why would he want to be our coach?" I asked her. "What's in it for him?"

"Good question," she admitted. "But it won't hurt to try."

We took the elevator to the fifth floor, and Percy Haskell was waiting for us in gray flannel pants and a purple polo shirt. He was several inches shorter than me and so thin I wondered if he had been ill. "Welcome," he said, greeting Becca with a smile and then shaking my hand. "I don't think we've met."

"Jack Logan," I told him. "I take Spanish. But I hear you're a great teacher."

"I wouldn't rely on my favorite student for an accurate opinion on that score," he said with a laugh. He led us into his small apartment, and the door swung closed. It looked very solitary, like a jail cell or a hermit's cave. Besides an old bicycle and many well-thumbed books, there weren't much in the way of personal touches to indicate he had friends or a girlfriend or any kind of outside interest. I didn't see a computer or a TV or any electronics. I wondered how such a smart guy from England had ended up alone in a dingy one-bedroom apartment in Hackensack, with a job as thankless as part-time Latin teacher at our jock school.

"Tea?" he asked us.

"I'm fine with a glass of water," I said.

"Me too," Becca told him.

"Cold tap water it is then," he said, "coming right up."

He waved us into the living room. There was a couch and a table near the one window, which looked down at an auto parts store. Several old books with leather bindings sat on the table, some of them propped open. Wedged inside were file cards with notes written in tiny handwriting in different-colored ink.

He came in with two glasses of water and handed them out. "Sorry I don't have much in the way of snacks." He began gathering up the file cards and books. "I was just doing a comparison of the differences between Livy's account of the Battle of Cannae and the way Polybius describes it," he told us, as if we would know what he was talking about. Actually, Becca probably did. "I've always been keen on strategy and tactics in the Second Punic War. That's Hannibal, right there, by the way." He pointed to a wall near the window where a poster from the British Museum was taped up. It was a photo of a warrior's face on an ancient coin. He looked out defiantly from beneath his helmet, glowering across a few thousand years at us. "Of course, nobody knows what he really looked like, but there are a few commonly accepted images . . ."

Percy dropped one of his books, and as he tried to grab it he knocked over a stack of file cards, then swatted one of the water glasses, which sailed through the air and shattered on the floor near the window. He hurried into the kitchen to get paper towels, and Becca and I got down on our hands and knees to gather up the fallen file cards.

"Quick," I asked her. "When was the Second Punic War?"

She shrugged. "After the First Punic War?" And then she asked me: "Any idea where it was fought?"

"Punica?" I tried.

She grinned. "Punica?" I smiled back. She looked so cute beneath that table that I was trying to come up with the right strategy and tactics to go in for a first kiss, but Percy had returned from the kitchen with paper towels and was saying, "Frightfully sorry. Please don't go anywhere near the broken glass. I don't want the Second Punic War to cause any new casualties," and he laughed at his own joke, a high-pitched warble that sounded like the call of some weird tropical bird.

In a few minutes the mess was all cleaned up, and the three of us were seated at the table. "So," Percy said, "Becca explained that you two are thinking of starting a team. That's very enterprising of you."

"We kind of have no choice," I told him. "Our school—"

"With Muhldinger now in charge," Becca cut in.

"Yes, he has certainly let the faculty know that he is sweeping in with lots of enthusiasm and a very new broom," Percy added, and I wondered what kinds of e-mails Muhldinger had been sending to the teachers over the summer.

"Our school," I continued, "has a new policy that all seniors have to join a sports team. Most of the teams are super serious and obsessed with winning, and we're trying to start a soccer team that isn't."

"Which means," Becca added quickly, "that it will be low-key and dedicated to everyone just having a good time."

"Splendid," Percy said. "I was never much of an athlete myself, and I took some ribbing from the other lads who were a bit more serious about their rugby. And they gave me a couple of hard knocks, too, along the way." His voice held a note of bitterness, as if a few old schoolboy bruises were still healing.

I tried to imagine Percy playing rugby. I knew very little about the game except that it was like football without pads. This toothpick of a guy must have been smashed seven different ways.

"Yeah, that goes on at our school, also," I told him. "I got some of my teeth cracked earlier this summer."

"Sorry to hear it," he said. "A friendly soccer team seems like an eminently sensible solution." He smiled at us. "But I'm not sure how I fit in."

"We need a coach," Becca told him, wasting no words.

Percy looked back at her in surprise. "You want me to be a football coach?"

"Soccer coach," she corrected him.

"Your soccer is my football. And I'm touched that you

would peregrinate all the way to Hackensack to ask me. But I'm afraid I wouldn't make a very good coach."

"No problem," I told him, standing up. "Thanks for hearing us out."

"We're not looking for a good coach," Becca said, remaining in her chair. "I won't say we're looking for a bad coach, but what we're definitely looking for is a nice person who won't make us run wind sprints or do push-ups."

"He already said no," I pointed out.

But Becca didn't give up easily. "Look, Percy . . . I mean, Mr. Haskell . . ."

"Percy is fine outside of school," he told her.

"Look, Percy, we wouldn't be asking you if there was anyone else willing to do it," she said. "I don't want to put pressure on you, but you're our last hope. And there is a little money as a coaching salary. I think it's a thousand dollars for the season. I know you hate jocks as much as I do, it's a big time commitment, and the weather's gonna get cold . . ."

"You're not doing a good job of selling me on this, Becca," he told her.

"But we want to have a very different team than the others. We're getting together a really nice group, and we won't care if we win or we lose. So there won't be any pressure—just fun. Sometimes it's good to try something new."

He looked thoughtful. "Yes, sometimes it is," he agreed. He glanced at me. "Anything to add?"

"No," I said. "Except that maybe you could use some

strategy and tactics from the Second Punic War. We're going to need all the help we can get."

I had meant this as a joke, but he seemed to take it seriously. "I'm not sure a double envelopment will work on a football pitch . . . sorry, a soccer field. Let me think this over for a moment."

He folded his hands behind his neck and began to pace back and forth the full length of his apartment, as if forgetting that we were even there. I glanced at Becca, who was also watching him pace. He was more than a little nutty, but I already sort of liked him and also felt sorry for him. He reminded me of a trapped animal in this small apartment, and I had the uncomfortable feeling that we were trying to trap him another way.

I was absolutely positive he would never in a million years leave his Latin classics to commit to coaching a Fremont soccer team, and I couldn't blame him. It had been a crazy idea from the start.

Suddenly he stopped pacing, unknitted his hands, and looked at us. "A bit of fun wouldn't hurt. Count me in," he said decisively, jabbing the air with his index finger and knocking over a lamp, which fell on the carpet but somehow didn't break. "Let's hitch up our shorts and give it a run." Which I think was his peculiar way of saying: "Let's just go for it."

GIVEN THAT I HAD NEVER HAD A GIRLFRIEND
before, I had also never brought a girlfriend home before,
and I was pretty nervous. But almost from the moment
Becca walked in the door, she hit it off with my mom. She
recognized Becca from the library, they got into a discussion about their favorite writers, and it turned out they
had half a dozen in common.

I took her on a quick tour of the house, and Dad was in
the family room watching a mixed martial arts fight. He
clicked it off as soon as she walked in and stood to shake
her hand. I wasn't sure if she'd seen the fight, but I did
notice her glance at our trophy case and I knew she was
probably thinking that we were a bunch of total sports
wackos. She did her best to pretend to look impressed by
the trophies, and she asked Dad about the biggest one. He
explained he had gotten it for being the best offensive player
in his senior year.

"The best in the league?" she guessed. "In the county?"

"In the whole state of New Jersey," I bragged from the
doorway.

"Wow," she said, looking at the three-foot silver cup.
"That's really something."

"It was a weak year," Dad said modestly. "I'd better go fire up the grill."

We ate outside on the back patio. August was giving way to September and there was a chill in the air with a 100 percent chance of school in a few days. At first our conversation seemed awkward. My father kept asking Becca about her parents, which was perfectly reasonable except that she didn't seem inclined to talk about them. I had a pretty good idea why she kept trying to change the subject, and I felt a little uncomfortable. But then a strange thing happened—my dad and Becca hit it off over fishing.

My father had grilled up bluefish using his favorite recipe, and she asked for seconds. "I love the sweetness," she told him. "What's that flavor?"

"Mayo and citrus," he explained. "It couldn't be fresher. The blues are running and I pulled it out of the water this morning."

Becca surprised me by saying, "My father used to have a boat down at the shore and caught everything from mackerel to makos, but he always said if he could only catch one kind of fish it would be blues."

"When you hit a school of them it's like nothing else," Dad said enthusiastically. "What kind of boat did he have?"

Up to now Becca had been guarded about discussing her parents, but when it came to fishing trips of years past she seemed to relax. "A seventeen-foot Grady-White. He kept it in Tom's River, and took it out as often as he could from March to October. I used to go with him a lot when I was ten and eleven. He had favorite spots in Barnegat Light, and farther out all the way to the lumps."

"What happened to the boat?" Dad asked.

"Hurricane Sandy smashed it up. It was insured and he could have replaced it, but he loved that boat and I don't think he's fished since then."

"Sometimes you just have to let something you love go," Dad told her.

After that, the two of them got along well, and I could tell he liked her and was proud that his son had a smart, cute girlfriend. We finished off several pounds of bluefish and put away most of an apple pie, and it was just about time for Becca to leave when she brought up the team we were trying to start.

"Soccer?" Dad asked me, as if I had just told him I was taking a rocket to Jupiter.

"It's the most popular sport in the world," I answered, trying to keep things light. "Played with a round ball by more than two hundred million people."

"I'm familiar with it," he said, "but I didn't know you played."

"Well, I'm not ready for the World Cup," I admitted.

Becca cut me off. "We're gonna play it together," she told him. "Our team is gonna be co-ed. But we need your help."

He looked from her to me. "So this is a setup?"

"No," I said.

"Absolutely," she contradicted me, and grinned at my father. "We're ganging up on you, Mr. Logan."

"Maybe you'd better just do what they want, Tom," my mother said with a smile.

But Dad didn't think it was funny. I knew he would be

polite because we had a guest, but he wasn't on board with this at all.

"The thing is," Becca told him, "we've done everything we can. We've got a faculty coach and we've signed up fourteen players. But Principal Muhldinger says our coach isn't on the full-time faculty and that fourteen aren't enough. Which is ridiculous because we've got a full team and three subs."

"I guess the rules are the rules," Dad said, and that was his way of saying we were done talking about it.

Becca didn't follow his game plan. "But none of those are *real* rules," she pointed out. "He invented them to mess us up."

"Why would he want to do that?" Dad asked.

"Because of me," I said.

Dad looked at me, a little surprised. "Go on."

"Muhldinger has it in for me because I'm a Logan and I didn't join his football team. So he's torpedoing our soccer team to get back at me."

"That sounds like his style," Dad agreed, glancing quickly at my mother. "Brian has a long memory and he always had a mean side. And I think I heard something about a door being demolished." I hadn't told them the details of my visit to the principal's office, and Dad had never mentioned the door till now. He said it with a faint smile.

"I was thinking maybe you could give him a call," I told him. "Ask him to let us have our team. If you ask him, he'll say yes."

"Probably," Dad admitted, and he looked just a little

angry. "But you shouldn't ask me that in front of your friend, because it puts me in a position I don't care for."

"We've had such a nice dinner," Mom jumped in quickly. "Why don't we take a break from this and finish off the apple pie?"

None of us could have possibly eaten more pie, and Becca confessed: "It was my idea to ask you, Mr. Logan. Jack didn't want to. But we've done so much to get this team going, and you're our only hope now."

"Tom, maybe it wouldn't hurt to give Brian a call," Mom suggested hesitantly.

Dad thought it over for two seconds, drumming his fingers on the tabletop. Then he told us, "Sorry. I'd like to help you guys out, but I won't make that call. Now it's getting late. Jack, are you going to walk Becca home?"

"Yes," I said. "Come on, let's get going."

But she was just as stubborn as he was. "If you don't mind my asking, Mr. Logan, why won't you call him?"

Dad managed a tight-lipped smile, but he clearly did mind her asking. "I can see that you're a very determined young woman, and I'm sorry I can't help you guys out. I don't have Brian's mean side, but he and I do agree on a lot of things about life and sports—particularly when it comes to sports at Fremont. Soccer's not my game and I don't know anything about that team you're trying to start, so it's not my place to throw my weight around. Please come back and have dinner with us again soon, and tell your father that if he ever wants to go fishing for blues I've got a friend in Waretown who has a boat we can take out anytime."

My mom walked us to the door and shook Becca's hand.

"Come back soon," she invited. "And stop by the library this week so I can show you that new novel."

"I will," Becca promised, and then we were out the door and walking through the darkness.

We walked in silence for a few blocks, and then Becca took my hand. "Sorry I made you do that."

I closed my fingers over hers. "My dad can be a real hard-ass."

She surprised me by saying, "I've read about lots of heroic tragic figures, but he's the first one I've actually met in person."

"Tragic because he's too stubborn to make one stupid phone call to help his son out?" I asked.

"No," she said. "He's the guy everyone in this sports-crazy town wants to be—the one who gained the most yards, ran the fastest mile, and could have played in the NFL. But he never got to do it because of an injury. What happened to him?"

My voice dropped, even though there was no one else listening. "In his senior year of college he led his team to a bowl game. One of the minor ones, but still. He was one of the best Division One running backs in the nation, projected to go in the first few rounds of the draft. But in the last practice before that bowl game he got into a freak collision and busted up his knee."

"Couldn't they fix it?"

"They did," I told her. "He can run on it. But he could never play in the pros."

"Wow," she said. "What does he say about that?"

"Nothing. What I just told you I've picked up from my

mother and my brothers, but I've never talked about it with my dad or heard anyone bring it up with him."

"Probably because you all sense that he's got to be an incredibly strong man not to go crazy with bitterness," Becca guessed. "God, living in this town where he was such a star, his number is retired, and he's surrounded by his old trophies . . ."

"All that gives him pride," I told her. "He's either coached or come to every game that my brothers and I have ever played, in any sport. He stands on the sideline shouting and shaking his fist, and he relives his glory days through us— or at least he did through Carl and Billy. I haven't given him much to cheer about."

We reached her house. It was set back from the street behind a row of bushes, and I could see that there were lights on. "Thanks for walking me home, Jack."

"Should I come in and say hello to your parents?"

She hesitated, tempted, and then she seemed to think better of it and said: "Let's leave that for another night. C'mere." And she drew me into her driveway, in the shadow of her old garage. "You're lucky," she said softly. "Your parents are so sweet together."

"They get along okay most of the time."

She stepped closer and I could feel her breath on my face. "Don't you see the way he looks at her?"

"Maybe it was because she'd just baked him an apple pie."

"He adores her," Becca said, and suddenly she was very close. "And he should. Your mom's great. And her son's not so bad. Good night, Jack." She reached up and kissed me lightly on the lips and pulled back.

"What's the matter?" I asked.

"Nothing," she whispered. She pressed forward for a much longer kiss, and I nearly passed out in her arms. "Good night," she finally said, and headed up the walk.

Oh man. I don't think my toes touched the ground all the way home—I just floated. But when I reached my house, my father was waiting up. "Let's talk," he said.

I followed him into the family room, and he pulled the door closed. "Your girlfriend's great," he told me with a little smile. "I can't imagine what she sees in you, but there must be something."

"She's a big fan of you, or at least your bluefish," I told him. "Listen, I'm sorry we pressured you. I knew it was a bad idea. I should go to bed now."

"I called Brian," Dad told me. "Your soccer team is a go."

I wasn't expecting that. "Wow. Thanks. I really appreciate it, Dad."

His face turned unexpectedly serious. "Don't make me regret it. It was a harder favor to ask than you know. Make sure you don't embarrass me."

I didn't exactly know what I was committing to, but I nodded and stood up. "I won't. I promise. Good night," I said. "And thanks again."

He held his hand up to stop me. "Jack, there's something you should know. It's about your mother."

I had no idea where this was going.

"Many years ago he used to date her," Dad told me.

"Muhldinger?" The world rocked for a minute. I couldn't believe what I was hearing.

"They were in the same class in high school. I was

three years older. When I came back from college I took her away from him and married her. That's always been between us."

"But he looks up to you so much," I said. "The first thing he did as principal was retire your number."

"That's football," Dad told me. "There's always been lots of mutual respect when it comes to sports. And he's a new principal so he probably wanted to do something that would be popular in the town. But on the personal side we've had our rough moments. It wasn't easy for me to ask this favor from him, and he wasn't too enthusiastic about giving you guys the green light. Okay?"

"Okay," I told him. "Wow. I thought Mom had better taste."

He grinned. "She must've had a soft spot for big dumb football players." And then he looked serious again. "But let me give you one piece of advice. I got you your team but I can't help you anymore, and this isn't over yet. Brian doesn't like you, and I wouldn't underestimate him."

12

IN THE MUD PITS TO THE SIDE OF GENTRY
Field, the football team was hitting the tackling sleds. We
were several hundred yards away, but the sounds of jarring
collisions reached us on the afternoon breeze, along with
shouted commands from the assistant football coaches:
"Slam that dummy. Keep your legs moving. Drive it into
the mud." Occasionally I even heard Muhldinger's growls:
"You wanna play for the Lions? Show me what you've got."

The cross-country team streaked by us like a herd of an-
telope, with Delaney, their tall, redheaded coach, running
right with them, checking his watch. "Everybody under
seven for the next mile. Come on, guys. Nice and relaxed.
Lift those knees. Let's go!"

Our team had gathered for the first time, and we weren't
running, or even walking. We were sitting on a grassy hill,
beneath the branches of an oak tree, listening to our coach.

"Some preparatory matters," Percy said. "The athletic
department tells me we need a team captain. Does anyone
have any suggestions?"

There was a moment of silence and Dylan raised his
hand. "I nominate Jack."

"What are you doing?" I whispered. "I don't want to be
captain."

"You're the one who got me into this," he whispered back. And then he said out loud to everyone: "Jack's a great guy and the Logans are famous athletes in this town, so the sports Nazis should like the sound of him as our captain."

"I second the nomination," Becca said.

I looked from my best friend to my girlfriend—they were ganging up on me. Before I could think of a way to turn this down, Percy said: "By a show of hands, how many of you think Jack would be a good team captain?"

Every hand went up.

"So voted," Percy said.

"Congratulations, captain," Dylan whispered.

"I'll make sure you regret this," I promised him.

Meanwhile, Percy had moved on from voting to a lecture. "I thought it might be useful to begin with a historical overview," he told us. "The earliest derivations of soccer seem to be from the Greek sport of *episkyros*, which the Romans renamed *harpastum* . . ."

Right then, I decided that Percy was going to be the perfect coach for us. I half listened to his history lesson, which was actually pretty interesting, and looked around at our team. There were fourteen of us sprawled on the grass. On my right, Frank had finished emptying a bag of pretzels into his mouth and lapsed into an afternoon nap. Becca and her friend Meg, a girl with freckles who had a great singing voice, were on my left, covertly checking their cell phones. Dylan was picking blades of grass and tossing them into the breeze. Shimsky had earbuds under his long hair and was listening to some classic punk rock and ignoring everything that Percy was saying.

I knew only a few of the other kids who had signed up, and they weren't exactly imposing physical specimens. There was a flabby guy named Pierre, who had moved to our town a year ago from France and was a talented tuba player in the band. His father ran a bakery and Pierre looked like he enjoyed a few too many croissants for breakfast every day. Surprisingly there was Chloe Shin, our school's ace record keeper, who updated the stats on the sports Web site for all the Fremont teams. She was barely four feet tall, wore thick glasses, and didn't seem likely to set any records herself. And there was a nutcase with curly black hair named Xander Zirco whom everyone called Quirko because he talked to himself.

I looked around at them and wondered where we were going with this bunch of misfits and oddballs.

Pretty much everyone was wearing their normal clothes. I had changed into shorts and a ratty tee and had put on some old cleats I'd found in a closet at home. Percy had on lime-green sweatpants and a brown-and-red-checked sweater that looked like it had been through World War II, and his lecture on soccer was still going strong. "In 1848 the Cambridge Rules ushered in the era of modern soccer," he droned on, "by prohibiting tripping, kicking, and carrying the ball. At that point soccer branched off from rugby, and became a popular school and college sport in England, and quickly began to spread throughout the world."

I was pretty sure Muhldinger wouldn't consider this history lesson a proper practice. He had approved us on a provisional basis—he could cancel our right to exist at any time if we didn't prove ourselves. Were we going to try to win at least a few games and get better the way most sports teams try to improve? Or was this a bunch dedicated to the fine art of losing?

If we made a joke out of what our school cared about, Muhldinger would shut us down fast. And when Percy was done with the history lesson, what were we going to spend our time doing in practices? I have to admit that while I had gotten my teeth busted and wanted to rebel, I was still a Logan, and there was a part of me that thought if we were going to have a Dumpster soccer team it should at least be a half-decent Dumpster soccer team.

Percy wrapped up his lecture on soccer history and moved on to our coming season. He set a whiteboard up on a stand and passed out copies of a schedule. "We're looking at a six-game season," he said. "Marion Day Junior High School in Aurora has agreed to a game next week—"

Frank cut in. "We're going to be playing a junior high school?"

"Yes, that will be our opening match." Percy nodded. "Their coach is from Birmingham—that's England, not Alabama. We had a nice chat. And after that there are five high schools that have freshman teams that have agreed to play us. Does anyone have any questions?"

"Blue house," Xander Zirco said.

Percy looked at him. "Excuse me?"

Zirco was gazing off into the distance, as if he could see something in the treetops and the low-hanging clouds that no one else could. "I want to live in a blue house," he said, and snapped his fingers so loudly that it sounded like a firecracker going off.

It was pretty clear that he was off in his own fruitcake world. "Blue houses are indeed nice," Percy said. "I grew up in one myself. Anyone else?"

Meg raised her hand. "My cousin goes to Marion Day. It's a girls' school."

"Yes, but I wouldn't take them lightly. They were undefeated last year," Percy said. "It should be a good first test for us. Now, I believe it's time to actually kick the ball, so here it is." He unzipped a duffel bag and gingerly took out a soccer ball as if it might explode if he touched it the wrong way. "Let's go over the basic rules," he said, turning back to the whiteboard, "and then let's hitch up our shorts and give this ball a few kicks. The most important thing to know about soccer is—"

He'd made it all the way to his favorite saying about hitching up shorts, but he never got any further. That was when the Lions pounced. Charging football players seemed to come from all directions at once at high speed, trampling the grass and the bushes, upsetting the whiteboard and its stand and knocking over several of our players. They were shouting, their red-and-gold helmets gleamed in the afternoon sunlight, and one of them kicked Percy's soccer ball into a cluster of trees fifty feet away.

There were screams of surprise and fear from my soccer teammates, and my first instinct was to step toward tiny Chloe, who was right behind me, to shield her. As I did, one of the charging Lions almost knocked me down and we grabbed each other by the shoulders. I recognized him—it was my childhood friend, Rob Powers. When he saw me, Rob looked a little guilty and veered off. Then someone else blindsided me from behind and knocked me flat onto my chest.

I put my arms out to break my fall, but for a moment I was back in Founders' Park, lying in the mud, tasting my own blood. By the time I shook the blow off and Becca helped me back up to my feet, the attack was over.

"What was that?" Percy demanded, as team members dusted themselves off and Shimsky climbed down from the tree branch where he had taken refuge. "I will lodge an official complaint with the highest authorities."

"Don't bother," I told him. "The highest authorities already know about it. That was our official welcome to Fremont sports."

"DO YOU THINK MEG LIKES ME?" DYLAN
surprised me by blurting out a few minutes before the
soccer party was supposed to start.

We were setting out sodas and cups, and plates of chips
and pretzels. His basement was large and carpeted and had
a Ping-Pong table, a foosball table, and a flat screen TV.
Dylan thought about girls all the time, and hinted that he'd
gotten to know ones in other towns through his church
group, but I doubted it. I had never seen him say two words
to a girl, and this was the first time he'd admitted liking
one at our school. I thought it was a step forward, and called
for a little gentle teasing as encouragement. "Are you kidding? She's not that desperate."

"Don't bust my chops," he pleaded. "Maybe she'll be
impressed when she sees my backhand slice."

I feared that he was serious. "Dylan, in the whole history of the world I don't think a girl has ever liked a guy
because of his Ping-Pong backhand. If you really like her,
try saying something to her."

"You could be right about that," he admitted, and chewed
nervously on his lower lip. "Like what?"

"Meg always gets the lead in the school play. Ask her
what role she's going out for this fall."

"I don't know anything about theater."

"Then ask her what she had for breakfast. It doesn't really matter what you ask. The important thing is to show some interest."

The doorbell rang, and it was Chloe, with Pierre a few steps behind her, holding a box of cookies from his dad's bakery. I didn't know how many people would show up for our soccer party, but I guess our team members didn't have busy social schedules, because the basement was soon noisy and full.

Frank and Pierre parked themselves on the couch in front of the flat screen. They kept most of the cookies, a giant bag of corn chips, and a bowl of salsa. It wasn't surprising that neither of them could run more than fifty feet without a time-out—their afternoon snack sounded like a swarm of locusts descending on a cornfield.

Zirco danced weirdly by himself in a corner.

At the Ping-Pong table, Dylan was hitting one killer backhand slice after another. He threw occasional glances at Meg, who was standing alone by the fish tank, looking bored. She kept dialing someone on her cell phone, and I figured it was Becca. I didn't want Meg to leave until Dylan tried to talk to her, so I went over and asked if she'd try a foosball game. "I've never played before," she told me.

"Not an obstacle," I said, pointing to Chloe and Shimsky, who were waiting for us on the other side of the table. "Those two don't exactly strike me as foosball pros."

But there are some things in life you can't predict. Shimsky, dressed in his usual black, gave the impression that all he cared about in life was surviving high school, listening to his iPod, and eventually leading a revolution that would change the world order so that the thin, weak, and victimized would take over. But somewhere along the way he must've spent a lot of hours on a foosball table, because the moment the ball dropped through the hole his thin wrists started snapping, sending the foosball rocketing toward our goal.

Chloe had good coordination and a competitive side I didn't expect from a nerdy statistician. She defended against me furiously, and every time Shimsky scored a goal she slapped five with him and urged him to "Keep the pressure on." Shimsky had finally found something he could be aggressive at, and each time he scored he repeated, "No mercy."

Meg and I were soon toast. "Sorry," I told her, leading her over to the drinks table. "I didn't know what we were up against."

She had her cell phone in her hand and had already forgotten all about foosball. "Becca always texts back in five seconds. She's still not answering."

"I talked to her an hour ago and she said she was heading over," I told Meg. "Something must have come up."

"Well if she doesn't get here soon, I'm leaving."

The party was in full swing, and everyone else seemed to be having fun. I glanced at the Ping-Pong table, where Dylan was undefeated. I walked over to him and said, "Let other people play. It's time to have a drink and mingle with your guests."

He glanced in the direction that I was trying to lead him, and saw that Meg was standing alone near the drinks table. "But I haven't been beaten yet," he said. "I gotta keep playing till someone beats me. Rules of the house."

I yanked the racket out of his hand and gave it to Zirco, who looked at it like he might try taking a bite out of it. "Come have a root beer," I said to Dylan, grabbing his wrist.

I half dragged him over to where Meg was studying her cell phone and scowling. "It's like she dropped her phone in a lake."

"I'm sure she's okay," I told her. "Dylan was asking me about the school play. He's thinking about trying stage crew. What're you guys putting on?"

"Stage crew?" Dylan repeated, as if he wasn't even sure what that was.

"*Hairspray,*" Meg told us. "Auditions are next week. It's gonna be great. I saw it on Broadway." She gave Dylan an encouraging nod. "We need help with crew."

He poured himself some root beer and looked down into the cup as if counting the ice cubes.

"What kind of help do you need most?" I asked. "Is it mostly set building?"

"Everything," she said. "Carpentry, lighting, grips. Everyone wants to be in the spotlight and nobody wants to work behind the scenes."

"I don't think Dylan minds being out of the spotlight," I observed. My shy friend was so nervous that he couldn't even look up at her. "And Dylan's great at carpentry."

"Not really," he mumbled.

"He built that foosball table," I said.

Meg glanced at the table where we had just been humiliated. "You built that?"

Dylan shrugged. "I just followed the instructions and put it together."

"That's more than I could have done," I said, and gave up. It was up to him now.

Shimsky walked by and touched my arm. "I'm out of here."

"What about my chance for foosball revenge?" I asked.

"Forget about it, you'll never beat me." And then in a lower voice, he said, "We should talk." And he headed for the door.

I looked at Dylan and Meg. "Be right back, guys."

The fact that I was about to leave prodded Dylan into action. He cleared his throat, and I could see him racking his brain for something to say to Meg. He must've come up empty, because when he finally spoke he asked her the question I had suggested, jokingly, earlier: "So, what did you have for breakfast this morning?"

She stared back at him. "What?"

There was no way out, so he repeated: "I was just curious what you ate for breakfast this morning."

"Why do you possibly care?" Meg demanded.

He looked at me wildly for help.

I didn't have a clue what to say, so I took my best shot. "Dylan's parents make him eat giant breakfasts," I told her, "so he's always asking other people if it's normal to eat three eggs and bacon and toast, and whatever else."

"I usually just have a yogurt," Meg said. "God, do they stuff you like that every morning?"

I walked away quickly. Dylan was really on his own now.

Even if he failed miserably, at least he'd actually said something to her.

Shimsky was waiting on the front lawn. "So," he said, "what are you going to do?"

"About what?" I asked.

"We were attacked yesterday," he said.

"You mean at soccer practice? They were just sending us a message."

"The message was that that was the first punch, before the second punch," he said, as if he knew everything there was to know about being punched. "So what are you going to do about it?"

"Why do I have to do anything?"

"You're the captain."

I looked back at him. "So what? If you think we need to do something, let's take a team vote."

Shimsky flashed me a little smile of disdain. "Those who vote decide nothing. Those who count the votes decide everything."

"Who said that?" I asked him.

"Joseph Stalin. If you don't do something fast, it will just happen again, even worse." Then he stomped off quickly in his black boots.

I watched him leave, and thought that in his loner way Shimsky might be a little bit dangerous. Then I turned back toward the house. My cell rang, and I saw that it was Becca. "Where are you?" I asked. "The party's almost over and Meg's been driving me crazy asking about you."

"In the Corolla," she said, and I knew right away that

something was wrong. A silver Toyota Corolla was parked down the block, beneath a tree. I could just make out a figure behind the wheel.

"Since when do you drive?"

"Come with me," she requested.

"Should I get Meg?"

"Just you."

So I jogged toward the Toyota. Like me, Becca had just gotten a learner's permit recently, and she wasn't allowed to drive unless there was an adult driver in the car with her.

She was alone in the front seat, gripping the wheel with both hands as if she didn't care about steering but just needed something to hold on to. "You missed a weird party," I told her. "Dylan's crushing on Meg. I can't tell if she's got any interest. And Zirco was dancing with himself." I got in and sat down next to her and closed the door. "Bec, what's up? Are you okay?"

"Put on your seat belt," she said softly, and it almost came out like a threat that she knew she might wreck the car. I saw that her eyes were red and puffy.

"Maybe we should just sit here and talk for a minute."

She shook her head.

"Then let me drive. You might have a panic attack."

"If I feel one coming I'll pull over," she said, and she switched the car on.

I fastened my seat belt. "Where are we going?"

"Away," she told me, and steered us from the curb with a screech.

BECCA DROVE FAST AND DIDN'T SAY A WORD.

I asked her several times what was wrong, but she just kept looking straight ahead, as if concentrating on the road was all she could manage.

We left Fremont and were soon on the Garden State Parkway, heading south at more than seventy miles per hour. I phoned my mom and told her that the soccer party had ended, and that I was with Becca and would come home late. I neglected to mention that we were on the Parkway, heading south at more than seventy miles per hour.

I clicked off my cell and asked Becca: "Where are we going? Do you want me to call your parents and tell them something? They'll be worried."

She shook her head.

"Okay," I said. "Just don't go too fast," and she slowed a little bit. I took that as a good sign. Her hands on the steering wheel looked steadier, as if putting distance between herself and Fremont was good for her. "What's going on?" I asked her again. "Did something happen at home?"

Becca finally answered, "Two people who hate each other shouldn't get married. And if they do they really shouldn't have kids."

"I'm sure your parents don't hate each other."

She glanced at me and then back at the Parkway. It was late afternoon, and cars were just starting to turn on their lights. "Did they have a fight?" I asked.

She shrugged. "It's over."

"The fight?"

"My family," she said. "Could we please not talk for a while?"

"Okay," I agreed. "Just tell me this. Do they know you took the car?"

"My father drove off in his Lexus and he's not coming back tonight. He sleeps on the couch at his office, or at least that's what he says he does. And my mom is locked in her room. She took a pill and she's either asleep or lying there staring up at the ceiling."

Becca turned on the radio, and hip-hop pounded for the next thirty miles.

She drove us to Seaside Heights, a beach town with a boardwalk that had been badly damaged by Hurricane Sandy and then rebuilt. The summer was over and the giant crowds were gone, but it was a warm Saturday evening and the boardwalk was still busy. There were food stalls and game booths, and steps that led down to the sand.

We walked the boardwalk for a while, and I bought us slices of pizza. I tried my hand at knocking down milk bottles, and on my third attempt I actually won a small orange teddy bear. I gave it to Becca. "It's gotta be the ugliest color in the world, but it will bring you good luck."

"Thanks," she said. "I think I am going to need some."

Sunset was coming on, and she led me down the stairs

to the beach. We walked along the dark gray sand above the waves. She asked me, "Do you remember on our first date when you asked me why I study so much?"

"Sure," I said. "It was a stupid question. It made you mad."

"Studying in my room, with the door shut, always felt safe."

"I get that," I told her.

"Today I went to my room and shut the door and put on headphones, but I could still hear every single word."

"What were they fighting about?"

Becca stood very still, looking out at the dark water. A tanker was a big dot at the edge of the horizon. She fixed on it, as if she wanted to climb on board and sail far away.

"There was a crash," she said. "He must've thrown something. My mom said she was going to call the cops, but I doubt he threw it at her. My dad can be a real jerk but he doesn't try to hurt people—at least directly. But suddenly they had pushed each other over the edge. It all just came tumbling out."

Becca shivered and I put my arm around her shoulder.

"He told her the marriage was a mistake," she went on in a low voice, as if she had hit Rewind and was now playing it back word for word. "The biggest of his life. That it had ruined his whole life. He said that he'd never loved her. That he felt trapped. That's the word he kept using. Trapped. He had been trapped. He felt so damned trapped. And of course what he was really saying was that I'm a big part of that trap."

"Your father knows how lucky he is to have you for a daughter."

She turned away from the ocean to look at me, and those hazel eyes had no room for excuses or politeness or anything but the sharp truth. "He wishes I had never been born," she said. "If I hadn't been born he would have left her years ago."

"He didn't say that."

"He didn't have to. Then my mom told him if he wanted to leave he should leave. She said she knew he had a girlfriend, and why didn't he just go to her and stop pretending. So he left, and this time when the door slammed I knew it was slamming for good."

"I'm sorry," I told her, not knowing what else to say.

Becca shrugged. "So I was sitting there with my college applications all spread out on my desk. I was rewriting my stupid application essay, 'Knight and Shadow,' about how I saved my horse."

"It's not stupid," I told her. "You did save him."

"It's pathetic that I've rewritten it two dozen times," she said bitterly, her voice getting a little out of control. "You know why I've done that? To escape. And the truth is I'll still never get into Stanford or Yale or Harvard. Because I'm just not quite smart enough or original enough, and it's a vapid, meaningless essay about a stupid horse. And you know what, Jack? It doesn't matter. None of it. I looked around at my textbooks, arranged in order on my shelf, and my homework done perfectly. Year after year I sat in that same stupid white chair and did it all just the way the teachers asked, and the truth is that none of it matters, not my grades, not our joke of a soccer team, not Latin or calculus, it's all crap. I had to get away. So I took the car and . . . *Screw them*," she snapped out, biting off each word. "I wish I had never been born." And then she stopped talking.

I didn't know what to say so I didn't say anything. Eventually, she took my hand and we just stood like that, watching the lights of the tanker melt away into black. Finally I whispered: "It's getting late. We should probably go back."

"Okay," she said. And then, "You'd better drive. It's kind of amazing I got us here in one piece."

"You drove fine," I told her. "And you're gonna be okay."

"You really think so?"

"I know it. Just give it a little time."

I drove us back, and for someone with a learner's permit who'd never been on a highway before, I did okay. We didn't talk much, but I noticed how Becca tightened up when we got near Fremont, and when we pulled into her driveway she looked terribly tense. "Let me come in with you," I asked.

I thought she would say no, but she just whispered, "Okay."

Her front door was open, and we stepped into her house. It was super neat and eerily quiet. She headed up the stairs, and I followed her. When she reached the second floor, Becca walked down a short hall to what I guessed was the master bedroom and rapped loudly on the double doors.

There was no response, and all kinds of crazy thoughts ran through my head.

"Mom," Becca called. And then she pounded on the door: *"Mom?"*

Seconds passed. Then the door opened and a petite woman with disheveled hair was standing there in a yellow bathrobe, squinting out into the light. She looked a little lost, as if she had just stumbled out of a fog. "Becca?" she asked.

"This is my friend Jack."

"Nice to meet you, Mrs. Knight," I said.

But her mom didn't even glance at me. She was staring at her daughter, and then she stepped forward and took Becca in her arms. "Becca, oh, Becca," she said, halfway between an apology and a sob.

Becca started hugging her and sobbing, and I quickly backed up and headed quietly down the stairs.

IT WAS A TOP PREDATOR CONTEST—SHARKS
versus lions—and Gentry Field was rocking. More than
five thousand students and fans had filed through the main
gate, past a new bronze statue of Arthur Gentry in full
stride, and were now seated on the red metal bleachers.
Smithfield is west of Fremont, and there's always been a
crosstown rivalry. They can't compete with Muscles High
when it comes to the major sports, but they're just dumb
enough to try. A loud contingent of Smithfield fans decked
out in navy blue were hooting and hollering for their be-
loved Sharks to gobble up our Lions. They were waving
plastic dorsal fins and screaming that the Lions weren't
going to be state champs but rather stupid chumps, and
that our team was too scared to even show up.

"Where the hell are they?" Frank demanded. The game
was scheduled for a noon kickoff and it was already 11:40.

"Maybe Muhldinger's punching a few extra holes in the
locker room wall during his pep talk," I suggested.

"They're probably waiting to make a big last-minute entrance," Becca said. The Lions liked to enter their den in
style. They always sprinted in through the gate closest to
our school while the band played "Fremont Forever"—the
starting quarterback in the lead with both arms raised, his

seniors running along with him, while the underclassmen and coaches trailed behind. I kept glancing at the gate, waiting for it to swing open and the band to strike up the first notes of the fight song, but seconds just kept ticking away.

I'd been surprised that Becca even wanted to come to this game. She'd had a tough week—her parents had separated, and her dad was now living in a hotel near his dental practice. She couldn't sleep and didn't eat much, but somehow she came to school every day, kept getting A's on tests, and even came to all our weird soccer practices.

We'd had five so far, each one stranger than the next. I guess any kind of physical activity can make you a little better at soccer, but I doubted that these nutty practices would teach us anything about scoring goals or playing tough defense.

Muhldinger had shown up unexpectedly at our Thursday practice. He'd sauntered up just as Coach Percy was finishing a lecture on tactics, and he'd watched, baffled, as our coach drew wavy lines around a big circle on his whiteboard. "What the hell is that?" Muhldinger demanded.

"Lake Trasimene," Percy explained enthusiastically. "I was telling them about the ambush there in 217 B.C.—the best tactical use of terrain in all of military history."

Muhldinger studied the whiteboard. "What does Lake Tra-whatever-the-hell have to do with soccer?"

"Lake Trasimene is south of the Po River in Umbria," Percy told him. "Hannibal ambushed the Romans there in 217 B.C. and killed fifteen or twenty thousand of them, depending on which historian you trust. Livy is more dramatic, but I personally lean toward Polybius because he was Greek and therefore had less reason to exaggerate and embroider, wouldn't you agree?"

Muhldinger stared back at him as if even trying to answer such a question made you insane. Instead, he growled: "And that is important because . . . ?"

"The Romans never even had a chance to fight back!" Percy said reverently. "Stay hidden and let the terrain do the fighting for you—that's today's message. Now we're moving on to our stretching."

"Good," Muhldinger said. "Let me see some calisthenics. Don't go easy on them, Haskell. Pain in September, trophy in November."

"Actually, we're trying to alleviate stress so we use free form yoga," Percy told him.

Muhldinger glanced at Frank, who'd assumed a position that I was pretty sure had nothing to do with yoga but a lot to do with deep sleep. "When do they actually kick a goddamn soccer ball?"

"We'll get to that very soon," Percy assured him. "Do you want to wait?"

Muhldinger had glanced around at the fourteen inferior physical specimens folding themselves into yoga positions and meditating or napping. "No," he'd growled. "I've seen more than enough. But I'll be at your first game against that girls' junior high school. And you'd better show me something."

Now we had come to watch his first game, and even though our soccer team was full of kids who hated football, a surprising number of us had shown up.

Frank, Becca, Meg, and I were standing together on a high bleacher. Dylan was supposed to join us, but his stagehands' meeting for the fall production of *Hairspray* must have been running late. Pierre was first tuba in the marching band. Chloe was working her wonders on the pre-game stats that flashed on the high-tech scoreboard.

Game time came and passed. There was a nervous energy crackling through the stadium now—it was clear that something odd was happening. Rumors flew around Gentry Field. According to league rules, it was a team's responsibility to show up, no matter what. If either team was more than an hour late, they would forfeit. I couldn't imagine Fremont forfeiting its home opener and ruining its shot at a state championship season. But as the digital clock ticked past 12:30 that began to seem increasingly likely.

Sirens sounded, and they weren't ambulances but rather fire engines and police cars. They raced into the parking lot, and from the bleachers we could see Fremont police and firemen sprinting into our school building. People around us speculated that someone had gotten sick or violent inside, but I couldn't dream up a scenario that would keep all members of the football team inside the building.

Then Dylan found us and told us what he'd heard. "Someone locked them in."

"In where?" Meg asked.

"The Keep," he explained. Our locker room is in the oldest part of the school, the basement. It was built more than a century ago, and there's a small room in the very back of the locker room nicknamed the "Keep" because it's like a castle keep—the oldest and strongest part of a fortress. Fremont teams traditionally gather in the Keep for pep talks and good luck. It has no windows and just one heavy old door. "But the Keep door is always open," I said.

"You might not have noticed, but it's got a thick iron hasp and a loop built into it that look like they belong in the Tower of London. Somebody brought in a humongous padlock and locked the team inside."

"Can't they cut the lock?"

"They tried. It's thick anodized steel."

"Why don't they just take the hinges off the door?" Frank asked.

"They tried that, too, but nothing's worked so far," Dylan said. "I heard they're trying to melt it now with an acetylene torch."

Seconds ticked on. The bands played. The cheerleaders did routines. But all eyes were on the digital scoreboard that now read 12:47.

I spotted my father down on his usual bleacher, standing with his friends. He looked tense and frustrated, as if he were witnessing a car crash but couldn't help save anyone.

12:50 came and the bands had stopped playing. The stadium was eerily still. I imagined the football team crowded into the Keep, standing around the locked door, watching their season tick away.

"I can't believe this is actually happening," Dylan said.

"Yeah," Frank agreed. "It's freaky and kind of sad."

"But interesting," Becca said softly, so that only we could hear her. "I'd like to see Muhldinger's face."

"I'm sure it's not pretty," I told her. "But if they do

forfeit the game, I'm sure he'll appeal it. It's not his fault someone locked them in."

"Lots of luck with that," Dylan said. "I remember when the Green River bus broke down and they arrived here seven minutes late. Muhldinger held them to the letter of the law, and said it was their responsibility. They appealed and lost. He's been a real hard-ass to the other coaches in the league for years. I'd like to see him try to explain to them why he deserves a second chance because he got trapped in his own locker room."

12:55 came and passed.

Then at 12:57 the far gate swung open and the Lions sprinted through it. They weren't in their usual carefully choreographed formation. Instead, they ran in a panic, like they were late for the last bus home. Muhldinger was near the front of the pack, his face scarlet with fury. He sprinted over to the officiating crew and they had a quick conference with the Smithfield coach. Then the teams lined up for the opening kickoff and the game was on.

Fremont had clearly been knocked off stride. Smithfield jumped out to a two-touchdown lead, and when the Lions tried to claw their way back the game got rougher. My old friend Rob Powers had lost out in the battle to be starting quarterback, and because he was fast and a superb athlete he was on the kick coverage team. Halfway through the second quarter he was hit from the side and knocked to the turf so hard that he was carried off the field on a stretcher. I was glad to see him moving his arms and legs, but he was clearly in pain.

At the half, Smithfield led thirty to fourteen, and it

seemed like Fremont's predicted state championship season was going to end before it began.

I don't know what Muhldinger told the Lions during halftime, but they came out so fired up it almost looked like they would burst into flame. Man for man, they were a much better team than Smithfield, and they fought their way back through old-fashioned smash-mouth football. They took over the line and made crunching tackles that knocked three Smithfield players out of the game.

Muhldinger urged them on, screaming like he was possessed. Watching him pacing up and down the sideline, I realized how much this football team meant to him—it was literally his life. The Lions finally tied the game in the fourth quarter and won it on a thirty-yard field goal as the last seconds ticked off the giant digital clock above Gentry Field.

Our home crowd gave a cheer, but it came out more like a collective sigh of relief. The band played our victory fanfare, but somehow it sounded a little sad, almost like a dirge. Fremont was supposed to be the best team in the state of New Jersey, but the Lions had used one of their nine lives to get away with a squeaker, and everyone knew it.

What was worse, someone had tried to sabotage our season, and it was clearly someone who knew Fremont High School well.

MUHLDINGER PULLED THE DOOR CLOSED,
locking the two of us into his office, and his tiny black eyes
fixed on me. "Talk to me, captain."

I glanced at his office door. It had been replaced since
he put his fist through it. This version was a darker wood,
and it looked expensive. I kept silent.

"You know why you're here?" he asked.

"No, sir."

"You turned down my team for a bunch of losers. And
then you came to our opening game."

"It's the biggest show in town," I said. "Everyone came.
But if you think I had anything to do with what happened
on Saturday, I didn't, so . . ."

A sharp command: "Sit."

I sat and he sat down across from me and folded his massive arms. "Of course I know that. If I thought you were at
all involved, we wouldn't be sitting here like this, having a
friendly chat. I have my sources."

"I'm sure you do," I replied. "But I'm not one of them."

Muhldinger smiled. "Sometimes you seem nothing at all
like your father and your brothers, and other times you
remind me of them. It's that cocky attitude you Logans get
when someone pushes you. I can see it in your eyes."

"I didn't mean to give you attitude. Can I go now?"

"It made your father a kick-ass football player," Muhl-dinger went on, ignoring my request. "He had the speed and size to be very good, but certainly not first round draft pick material. But that Logan quality, 'If you push me, I'll knock you flat,' made him a college star, and I think he would have done fine in the NFL if not for that knee injury." I couldn't tell from the way he said it whether he was sad my dad's career had been cut short, or whether he was actually pleased. He leaned forward: "But, Jack, that cocky attitude cuts two ways. Twenty years later he digs holes on a construction crew. And you'd better watch yourself."

"My dad's done just fine—" I started to say.

Muhldinger cut me off. "We're not here to talk about him. My point is that sometimes to get ahead in life you have to know your place. That goes for all of us." He sat back in his chair and ran his eyes around his large corner office as if to say, "Look at my place. I'm the king of the world."

"I didn't want to play on your football team, but I would never have locked you guys in on Saturday," I said.

He nodded. "No Logan would do something like that. But I don't see your place as captaining a bunch of losers, one of whom just took a shot at this school and everything it stands for. I appreciate that you're loyal to your team-mates, but you don't have to protect a dirtbag."

"I never wanted to be captain," I told him, "and I'm not protecting anybody."

"Good," he said, leaning forward. "Because a monumental tragedy was barely averted on Saturday. Someone almost destroyed our whole season. And that person will have to pay."

"It could have just been meant as a bad joke," I pointed out. "Nobody got hurt."

"There are lots of ways people can get hurt," Muhldinger snapped back. For just a moment his mask of self-control slipped, and I saw how furious he was. With an effort, he calmed himself down. "But the key question is who would do such a sneaky, cowardly thing?" he asked softly. "It was kind of like fighting without fighting, letting the terrain do the fighting for you. The way Hannibal did around that stupid lake in Italy, right?"

"It didn't have to be someone from my soccer team. I'm sure you have the police looking into it."

"They may not have to look far," he informed me. "There are security cameras all over this school. I already know who was in the basement on Saturday morning before the game. All of my sources point to your joke of a soccer team."

"Great," I told him. "Arrest whoever did it and leave me out of it."

"Your girlfriend was there," he said, studying my face carefully.

"Becca was with me in the stands, waiting for your team."

"She was inside the school before the game was supposed to start," Muhldinger said. "And I know what she thinks of me and my team. She's got as much attitude as you do, plus she thinks she's smarter than everyone else."

"She is smarter," I told him. "Becca's gonna be the vale-dictorian and she's never broken a school rule in her life."

"I know her type and I don't trust her. Then there's your pal Sanders."

"Dylan was at a stage crew meeting with a dozen other people," I said. "His mother's on the school board."

"His mother's a pain in the ass," Muhldinger growled, "and he's a little snot."

I kept silent.

"And that Chinese girl, Shin."

"Chloe was doing stats for the pregame," I pointed out. "And she's Korean."

"The scoreboard controls are in the basement. She was fewer than fifty feet from the locker room. And I think she's got a thing going with that shifty son of a bitch who wears black. He was there, too. Slinky."

"Shimsky," I said. "I never saw him."

"He was skulking around."

I remembered Shimsky taking me aside after the soccer party, telling me we'd been punched and asking me what I was going to do about it. Had he decided to do something about it himself? And I recalled Becca on the bleachers telling us she wished she could see Muhldinger's face. She certainly hated him, but she would never risk her whole school career on a stupid prank. I also couldn't believe that Dylan or Chloe was involved, either. "It sounds like you have a really short list of suspects," I said a little sarcastically.

"Short enough," he told me. "Why don't you save me some time? Be smart and talk to me, captain. Your parents and I go way back. It's time to be a Logan."

"Sorry, but I don't have a clue who did it," I told him, standing up. "And even if I did, I wouldn't rat them out to you. But if you want me to tell you something, I will. There are dozens of kids at Fremont who hate being forced to play for a team and who are pissed off at the direction you're taking our school. Any of them might have done it, just to take a shot at you."

Muhldinger stood to face me. "Since we're being frank, I'll tell you something back. You're dead wrong about your father. I've known him a lot longer than you have and he's not exactly thrilled with the way things have turned out, spending his life digging holes for people's bathrooms. Shoulda, coulda, woulda can eat you up inside, no matter who you're married to or how brave a face you try to put on it. You get too cocky, Jack, and you pay for it." A dangerous look came into Muhldinger's eyes that I recognized from the moment when he had put his fist through the door, but this time he controlled himself. "And just so we understand each other, if someone takes a shot at me I come back at them a lot harder. Someone gave me a kick on Saturday, and that person—and everyone who protects them—are gonna feel my size thirteens on their backside."

THE MARION GIRLS WERE ALREADY OUT ON
their gleaming emerald field when we drove up in our
clanking yellow school bus. There must have been twenty
of them in home white "Wombat" uniforms, running a
shooting drill with machinelike precision. They weren't
very big—after all, they were only in junior high school—
but as we watched out the window, shot after shot whistled
off their feet into the yellow netting at the back of the goal.
Dylan was sitting next to me, and he muttered: "We're in
a lot of trouble."

A girl with a ponytail let loose a ferocious kick. The
ball soared over the goal, zoomed above a chain-link fence
like a guided missile, and slammed into the side of our
school bus.

"No, we're not in a lot of trouble, we're dead meat,"
Frank corrected him. "We're about to be obliterated by a
bunch of feral wombats."

"What exactly is a wombat?" Pierre asked.

"An Australian rat," Becca said. It was probably on one
of her vocabulary lists.

"Actually, I believe wombats are marsupials," Coach
Percy corrected her. He was decked out for our opener in
brown trousers and an Argyle sweater, which looked like

it might be the right outfit to wear to a foxhunt. "The interesting thing about wombats is that their pouches are backward to protect their young from getting covered with dirt when they dig burrows, which they do very splendidly."

"There's nothing that's gonna protect us from getting crushed," Dylan noted.

"Why does it matter?" Becca asked. "It's a gorgeous day. Let's just have a good time."

It was a beautiful fall day, and a large crowd had come out to see the curiosity of a girls' junior high team taking on a co-ed high school squad. Thirty Marion girls stood on the sideline, ready to cheer on their friends. There were also several dozen Marion parents camped out on folding chairs, with cell phones and cameras ready to record the coming game.

As far as I could tell, no one from Fremont had come to see us, which was probably a good thing. I knew Becca was right and we should just enjoy the beautiful day, but the Logan in me was dreading getting annihilated by a bunch of junior high school girls.

We even looked awful—they had given us ratty old red-and-gold uniform shirts that the boys' JV soccer team had discarded, and we all had bought our own different-colored shorts. Except Zirco, who was in blue jeans.

Our warm-up was ice cold. We lined up and one by one kicked balls at the goal. Shot after shot went wildly off target. My teammates hit weak dribblers, and a few of them missed the ball completely and laughed. One dork named Alan Jenks, whom everyone called Jinx, managed to miss the ball as his leg kicked forward, and then as he stumbled back he somehow back-heeled it behind him. That was the most awkward shot, but there was an even stranger one—Pierre's shoe flew off his foot into an upper corner of the net while Frank dodged and hooted with laughter.

Frank had volunteered to play goalie—I think so he wouldn't have to do any running. His six-foot-five-inch frame filled up a lot of the goal's mouth, but he wasn't exactly as quick as a cat in covering the sides and the corners. Low shots were a particular problem. He apparently didn't like to lower his center of gravity so he just waved at low rollers, as if ushering them into the goal with a cheerful "Go ahead, be my guest." Midway through the shooting drill Frank got both of his thick arms caught in the netting, and three of us had to untangle him.

I glanced at our sideline and saw that we now had two fans. Principal Muhldinger was giving up an afternoon football practice to see our first game. And my father surprised me by showing up. I hadn't told him about this game, but he must have seen it on the school sports Web site. My dad had a perfect record of coming to all family sports events. The two football icons of Muscles High stood together on the unfamiliar territory of a soccer sideline, towering over the Marion parents nearby. It reminded me of the evening in Founders' Park when they had sat side by side on a bench and watched me get oral surgery the hard way.

Percy gathered us in for one of the strangest pregame talks I've ever heard. "You may be overmatched," he said, "but the important thing is your own positive mental attitude. Remember what Hannibal said when his army first saw the Alps and realized what a daunting journey lay ahead. His fierce warriors had conquered Spain and were setting out to try to destroy Rome. But when they saw the snow-capped Alps rising to the clouds, they despaired and were ready to mutiny. Hannibal gathered them together and asked them: 'What are the Alps but just high mountains? Is there any height insuperable to men?'"

Percy gazed out at us as if he had just said something inspirational, but my teammates didn't look impressed. They weren't exactly fierce warriors setting out to conquer Rome. They looked like the least athletic and most out of shape bunch who had ever put on Fremont jerseys, and it was clear from their faces that they couldn't care less about conquering anything. I tried to tell myself not to care either, but then I glanced at my father and he gave me a thumbs-up.

The ref called over: "Hey, Fremont, you guys ready? I need your captain."

I trotted out to midfield to face the girl with the ponytail whose shot had nearly knocked over our bus. Her face was tight with determination.

"Fremont, call it in the air," the ref said, and flipped a coin.

"Heads," I shouted, hoping I could at least win the coin toss.

It was tails. "We'll take the ball," the girl said.

"Which goal do you want, Fremont?" the ref asked me.

"The smaller one," I replied, trying for a little humor. Nobody even smiled. The ref raised his eyebrows, and the line judge blew a stream of warm air across his knuckles. The girl with the ponytail stared back at me like she was a Viking raider preparing to burn down my home and sack my town.

"We'll take that one," I said, pointing to the goal behind me.

"Good luck," the ref said. "Let's have a good clean game."

I trotted back to our team and found my teammates finishing their yoga stretches. "How did it go?" Becca asked.

"We're going to get clobbered," I told her.

"Fine," she said. "It's a good day for it." She saw something in my face and added: "Jack, remember why we did this. You could have played on the football team. You didn't want to buy into that."

"True," I agreed. "Did you see that my dad's here?"

She nodded. "Don't look so worried. I'm sure he's seen family members lose before."

"Not often," I told her. "And not like what's about to happen to us."

Then it was game time and we walked out onto the field and took our positions. I lined up at center mid, looking across at the girl with the ponytail who was playing center forward for Marion. She stared back at me for just a moment, and then down at the soccer ball at her feet.

The ref blew his whistle to start the game, and for about two minutes we looked like a reasonably competent soccer team. We actually managed to kick it into their half, and Pierre took a shot, which their goalie easily saved. She rolled the ball out to the left fullback who one-touched it up to their center midfielder.

I stepped forward to challenge her, but she passed the

ball up to the girl with the ponytail, who took off with it right at our goal at a hundred miles per hour. Chloe and Zirco were playing center defense and ran to take her on, but all they managed to do was collide with each other. Chloe's glasses broke, and Zirco caught an elbow to the groin.

The girl with the ponytail sped by them and let loose a rocket of a shot that caught Frank full in the face and richocheted off him into our goal.

Frank sank to his knees, both hands cupped over his nose.

Zirco rolled around on the ground holding his groin and making a high-pitched bleating sound like a lamb just before it's slaughtered.

Meanwhile, Chloe was on her knees, feeling around in the grass for a missing part of her glasses frame.

Coach Percy ran onto the field, but he didn't seem to know which wounded player to help first. Our season was less than two minutes old, the score was one to nothing, and we were already bruised, bleeding, and whipped.

I'm sure it felt worse to be ambushed by Hannibal at Lake Trasimene, and that in the long history of world soccer there have been teams that looked worse than we did and were more thoroughly thrashed, but I doubt it's happened very often. When Marion went up ten goals to zero—shortly after the half—their coach told his girls to stop scoring and just pass the ball around.

The only thing more humiliating than having a bunch of junior high school Wombats score goal after goal on you is having them invoke a mercy rule and kick it back and forth for thirty minutes as you chase the ball hopelessly and their parents shout *"Olé, olé!"*

Some things happened that afternoon that I doubt have ever been seen on a soccer field before. When Marion stopped shooting at Frank he lost interest and leaned against a goal post. A few minutes later the ref blew his whistle and pointed to where Frank was lying. I sprinted over to him, afraid the shot to his nose had caused some kind of concussion, but he was snoring peacefully. Coach Percy shook him, and Frank opened his eyes. "Are you okay?" Percy asked.

"Oh, sure," Frank said blearily, blinking and looking around. "I guess I just dozed off. How's the game going?"

"Not so well, big guy," I told him. "Try to stay vertical."

A few minutes later Pierre ran a little faster and farther than he had trained for, and then he stopped, bent over, and threw up right near the sideline, where the Marion girls watching the game screamed disgustedly.

Meg might have been a great actress, but she spent the whole game standing in one place, as if waiting for a cue that never came.

Becca was fast and athletic, but she didn't seem to care at all that we were getting massacred. When a ball was stolen from her near our sideline I heard my dad shout: "Fight for it. Win it back!" but Becca just turned to Meg and shrugged, and Meg grinned and shrugged back.

Near the end of the game Zirco did a spinning three-sixty and kicked the ball as hard as he could out of bounds, as if he were aiming at a goal three soccer fields away.

Several of us gave chase as the ball bounced across a baseball infield and rolled into a cluster of trees. On the other side of the trees was a lake, and by the time we reached the bank Zirco was wading into the water after the ball. The bank was steep and he slipped and floundered around in the water, yelling wildly. It took four of us to haul him out, and when we finally dragged him onto the reedy bank he shook himself dry like a dog.

With five minutes to go in this nightmare, I stole the ball from the Marion game of keep-away. I dodged around their center midfielder, and when their sweeper came up to tackle me I kicked it by her and tried to run onto it. Suddenly it was a race between the two of us, and I usually win races. There was something unexpectedly thrilling about sprinting toward the opponent's goal and pulling away step by step from the last defender. I took one final dribble, and as their goalie came out to cut down the angle I kicked it low and hard past her, for our first and only score.

I turned to see my father's reaction, but he had left. Muhldinger was still there, however, standing with his hands on his hips and his jaw locked tight. He didn't say a single word till the game was over and we congratulated the Marion girls and got onto our bus. He got on last, and told us to move to the back.

Muhldinger stood in the aisle, looking down at us. "That was," he said, "the single most embarrassing thing I have ever seen in my entire life. The word 'losers' doesn't do it justice. Nor does 'disgusting.' Or 'pathetic.' The word 'vomit' comes a little closer." He glanced at Pierre.

No one said anything. We just looked up at him and

waited for the storm to pass. He was clearly angry at how badly we had stunk up the soccer field, but I knew there was something else lurking behind his fury. I remembered how certain he'd been that the person who'd locked his football players in the Keep was on our team. He looked around the bus at us like we were all guilty. When he started venting, his anger came spewing out like lava from a volcano.

"You wanted a team and I gave you one, but I thought in return you'd have some respect for our school and our traditions. Clearly I was wrong. You have no respect. The opposite—you want to tear down all the things we're most proud of at Fremont. Falling asleep on the field, puking on the sideline, running into a freaking lake—you're wastes of your parents' genes! Spastics. Morons. Garbage. You have no pride in our school, and you have no pride in yourselves, and I sure don't blame you for that because if I were one of you I'd dig a hole and bury myself."

"To be fair," Percy spoke up hesitantly, "it was our very first game. Of course there is plenty of room for improvement, but—"

"Shut up, you idiot!" Muhldinger bellowed at him. I had never heard anyone talk to a teacher that way. "There's no room for improvement because I'm pulling the plug on this pathetic experiment in losing. When I want to see a clown show I'll go to the circus. Your team is finished and good riddance to it."

"But we've made commitments to play five other teams," Percy pointed out bravely, ignoring the insult. "I realize you're disappointed with our effort, but isn't it in the spirit of Fremont High to honor those commitments?"

Muhldinger looked momentarily flustered. *"I run this school, not you!"* he shouted at Coach Percy. "To hell with those commitments. Those teams will be better off without playing us. You call this the C-team. *C* is for cesspool and I'm flushing you turds." And he slammed his open hand into the metal ceiling, then turned and stalked off the bus.

There was complete silence.

"For a Neanderthal, he does have a way with the potty talk," Becca admitted softly.

"It was a fun season, but a little short," Dylan added sadly.

"Spaghetti," Xander Zirco chimed in mysteriously. "No meatballs."

MY MOTHER WAS WASHING DISHES AND
throwing mystified glances at the door that led to the
basement steps. The thuds from below were muffled but
ferocious, like someone trying to chop down a tree with a
blunt ax. Dad didn't usually work out in the evenings, but
when his anxiety spiked—for example, when he had a problem at his job or a son who disappointed him—he headed
down to the basement that he and my brothers had turned
into a mini-gym, and he worked out his stress by running
on a treadmill at maximum speed or walloping a heavy bag.

"Do you know what's gotten into him?" Mom asked me.
"He barely said a word at dinner. Did something go wrong
at work?"

"It's not his job."

"Well, then what? My lasagna wasn't that bad."

BAM, BAM. The house seemed to shake.

"It was great lasagna," I said. "But it came after the
worst sports performance any Logan has given in fifty
years."

Mom put a dish in the drainboard and looked at me.
"This is about a soccer game?" she asked incredulously.
"But it was your very first one."

"And the last," I told her. "Muhldinger's pulling the plug on us. We stank it up today."

"You'd never played before," she pointed out.

"That must be why we were destroyed by a bunch of junior high school girls."

"Your team will get better," she promised. "Just stick with it."

"The team is finished," I told her. "Muhldinger was at the game, standing with Dad. They were both disgusted, and Muhldinger canceled our whole season. He told us we were turds and he was flushing us."

"That's a side of Brian I never liked," she said. "He can be a real bully. Will you have to join another team?"

It was strange to hear her use his first name. "I don't know," I said. "This has never happened before at Fremont." I paused, and couldn't stop myself from asking, "Mom, how could you ever date that jerk?"

She lowered her sponge. "Who told you about that?"

"Dad."

She looked surprised, and not particularly pleased. "It was a very long time ago."

"Yeah," I said, "but he's horrible."

"In some ways he was always a jerk," she agreed, "but he was a sports star and super confident, and when I was eighteen I found that attractive."

"Was it just a few bad dates?" I asked hopefully.

Mom hesitated. "No. It was serious. We even talked about getting engaged. But then your father came home and that was the end of that."

I stared at her. "You almost married Muhldinger?"

"I'm not sure I was thinking so clearly when I was in high school," she said, a little defensively. "Would you say you're always thinking clearly?"

"No," I admitted. "Sorry. I shouldn't have brought it up."

"That's okay," she said. "I married the right guy in the end." A punch thudded from below like a cannon going off. "Even if he gets a little hotheaded sometimes."

I glanced toward the basement stairs. "He's on full boil. What should I say to him?"

"You don't have to say anything. It's not your fault that you're on a lousy soccer team," she told me. "He'll get over it."

"No, I owe him an apology. I let him down today." I headed for the basement stairs. They were steep and narrow. *BAM*, *BAM*, a one-two rattled the walls. The lightbulb blinked. It felt like I was descending into the lair of an angry monster.

Then I saw him in his black shorts and sweaty T-shirt, the muscles of his arms and back standing out as he circled the bag, feinting and pretending to search for an opening. He was concentrating hard, his eyes sharp with fury. I wondered who he was pretending to hit. I reached the basement floor and walked toward him.

Dad darted forward, his weight balanced, and his right fist flashed out—*thud*. The iron supports groaned and a dusting of plaster came down from the ceiling. He saw me and lowered his fists.

"You're going to wreck the house," I said with a cautious smile.

He hadn't said one word all during dinner and clearly

wasn't in a talkative mood now. Without acknowledging my presence he walked to a stool, sat down, and started taking off his gloves.

"Need help getting those off?" I asked.

Dad shook his head and used his teeth to bite the gloves off, then set them carefully on a shelf. He still hadn't looked at me. He grabbed a towel and wiped some sweat off his face. "You and your girlfriend asked me to do you a favor," he said. "Against my better judgment, I made the call. But I asked you something in return—not to embarrass me."

The heavy bag was still swinging from his last punch. I watched its shadow move slowly back and forth across the cellar floor. "That's true," I admitted.

"I can't tell you exactly what I felt today," he went on, "because I've never felt that way before. But it didn't feel good, Jack."

"I scored," I told him. "Near the end of the game. I kept us from getting shut out. I looked for you but you'd left. I guess you were too disgusted to stay."

"It wasn't disgust," he said. "I was afraid." He finally looked right at me, and his words came out fast and angry. "Afraid I might run onto the field and grab someone and shake them and say, 'Stop joking around and fight!' I went for a drive and tried to calm down. I stopped up near Highland Lake and walked through the woods down to the water, and I kept thinking about my own father. He came to every game I played in. He was a damn good athlete and he gave me lots of coaching advice, but it always boiled down to the same four words: *Have pride in yourself.*" Sweat ran off Dad's chin and dripped onto the floor as he looked at me piercingly. "What the hell?" he demanded. And then, with real fury: "I MEAN, JACK, WHAT THE HELL?"

"I'm sorry," I told him. "My friends do have pride in themselves, but they don't care about winning. Some of them even enjoy losing."

"How can anyone enjoy losing?"

"I guess they're in it for laughs," I admitted.

"Yeah," he agreed bitterly. "It was hilarious when Frank fell asleep in the goal. And your girlfriend also thought it was all one big joke."

"Becca's going through a tough time at home," I told him. "This is her release."

"We all go through tough times," Dad muttered. "But she's the one who came up with the idea of asking me to call Brian and get you your team."

"I already tried to apologize for that, but I'll say it again. I'm really sorry we embarrassed you. It's not what I wanted."

It was as if Dad hadn't heard me. He kept right on: "I had to stand next to Brian and watch that display that I had caused. It was stomach-turning for both of us. I understand that your friends want to make a mockery out of Fremont athletics. But what I don't understand is . . . why *you're* doing this."

"You mean why I'm doing this to you?"

"No," Dad said, "why you're doing this to yourself. I'm not surprised that you scored a goal. It was clear from the first whistle that you were the best athlete on the field."

"They had a couple of players who were way better," I said. "You're seeing something that's not there—"

"Jack, you have speed that's God-given. I think you might have a step on your brothers, and they were quick. Do you think Brian was putting you on his varsity just as a favor to me? He's no fool when it comes to football—he needs speed like that! You can burn. *You don't know what you could have done for them, or how far you could have gone.*" Dad's voice had gotten louder and faster, as if these thoughts had been tearing him up for weeks. "You earned a spot on varsity, and then you gave it away."

"I earned a spot in a hospital room," I fired back.

"I'm talking about pride," he said.

"And I'm talking about my teeth."

"Accidents happen in sports and in life. Part of becoming a man is facing them."

And that was when it suddenly got much more serious and personal. "So you think I'm a coward?" I asked.

My father stood next to the heavy bag he had been walloping, and when he spoke he let me have it as if putting his full weight into a right hook. "I think you got hurt and it spooked you and you walked away from a great opportunity. And now you're pissing away your senior year joking around with a bunch of jerks."

"Don't call them that. They're my friends."

"They enjoy losing. They don't care about what we care about."

"What *you* care about," I told him.

"You're part of this family, unless you make yourself not a part of it. The Logans aren't the smartest family in the world, or the richest. But we've always been proud athletes and that's our tradition. *Why do you have to make a joke out of it?*" He slammed the bag with his fist.

My first instinct was to back away, but now I was a little out of control and instead I took a step toward him. "You're absolutely right," I heard myself say. "Accidents do happen. You can't let fear take over or you're a coward. I'm sorry your knee got messed up and you missed your chance for a pro career—"

It was like a cold wind suddenly swirled through the basement. "That has nothing to do with this," he tried to cut me off.

"It happened years before I was born, but it was right there today on the sideline when you were standing next to Muhldinger looking so furious, like you wanted to kill someone—probably me. You've always been angry with me. What have I ever done to you?"

"*Stop,*" he told me in a warning tone.

But I stepped forward and slammed the heavy bag with my bare fist. "When I got my teeth bashed in you said I'd made you proud. That is the dumbest thing I have ever heard. Watching me get my clock cleaned makes you proud? If you want to talk about who's a coward in this family, why can't you face the fact that you're trying to live out the big-shot NFL career you never had through me and my brothers and the players on your stupid TV set—"

I'm not sure if he was trying to silence me or grab me and shake me, but he pushed me and I ended up flying backward. I crashed into a wall and went down hard, and lay there for a half second, stunned. He had never put his hands on me—or either of my brothers—before, and I couldn't believe he had done it. He looked a little shocked, too, and reached down to me, but I knocked his hand away.

Then I was running up the stairs, bursting past my mom, who must have been listening from the kitchen. She called out and tried to grab my arm, but I ran past her and sprinted out the back door. I heard my father coming after me, but I turned on the speed he was so proud of and even the fastest miler in the history of Muscles High couldn't catch me as I sprinted away into the darkness.

DARK STREETS TWISTED INTO EACH OTHER,
and the night shadows of houses flew by. I ran blindly, with
no idea where I was heading. I kept seeing the narrow
stairs to the basement, and hearing furious punches thud-
ding into the heavy bag. Those angry punches became the
desperate footsteps of my father running out of the house
after me, and even though I was already far from home I
imagined hearing his voice calling my name, and I sped up
to a wild sprint, my arms pumping madly.

I finally fell on my knees, gasping, before a big house.
After I caught my breath I looked around and realized
I wasn't far from someplace I really wanted to be. I got up
and started walking.

Becca's house was set back from the street, and above
the trimmed bushes I could see that the upstairs windows
were dark. I headed up the walk and climbed the steps.
When I pushed the doorbell no one answered, so I rapped
on the brass knocker. I turned and started back down the
steps, and then I heard the door open.

Becca stood in the doorway, peering out at me. "Jack?"

I walked up to her.

She took one look at my face and pulled me inside. The

door shut and then somehow we were standing in her kitchen and her arms were around me.

"Let me guess. Your dad was not pleased with what he saw at the game today."

"He wanted to use me as a punching bag."

"What! Did he hit you?"

"No, but he wanted to."

Her house was warm and silent.

"Where's your mom?"

"Upstairs in her room," Becca told me. "Watching TV. Sometimes it's hard to tell when she's awake or asleep. Want some cold water?"

"Sure," I said.

She got me a big cup of ice water, and one for herself, and said, "Come. There's something you have to see."

I followed her up a flight of stairs and we turned down a hall, past several closed doors. The upstairs was as neat as the first floor, and there were antiques everywhere. We passed an old grandfather clock, elegantly marking the hours. "Where are we going?" I asked.

"My room," she said, and pushed open a door. "Voilà."

I walked in after her and she pulled the door closed. There was a four-poster bed with a few stuffed animals on the pillows. School textbooks were neatly arranged on a shelf above her desk, and on higher shelves was an impressive library of novels, nonfiction, and plays, not to mention dozens of horse-riding ribbons and a photo of Shadow. I ran my eyes over the titles. "Have you read all of these?"

"No, I just looked at the pictures," she said.

I couldn't remember ever being in a girl's bedroom

before, not to mention alone and with the door closed. It smelled the way Becca's hair smelled—clean, sweet, and tempting.

"Did you get my texts about what's happening with the team?" she asked.

"You mean that we've been terminated?"

"Check it out," she told me, pointing to the laptop on her desk. I sat down and clicked the screen to life. Her browser was already open to a YouTube page. Someone had posted a video called "The Losers at Muscles High—America's Worst Soccer Team and Meanest Coach."

I pressed Play. It started off with a close-up shot of Muhldinger standing on the back of the bus, spewing insults at us. Someone must have secretly filmed him with their phone. His face was scarlet and he was jabbing his finger into the air as he vented: "That was the single most embarrassing thing I have ever seen in my entire life. The word 'losers' doesn't do it justice . . . The word 'vomit' comes a little closer."

The video cut to a quick shot of Pierre running after a ball and then pulling up suddenly and puking on the sideline while Marion girls shrieked. With background music added it was pretty funny to watch.

Back to Muhldinger: "You're wastes of your parents' genes. Spastics. Morons. Garbage."

Interspersed with his insults were quick shots of various players screwing up in horrible but hilarious ways. Chloe and Zirco's collision looked like a clown routine, and there was a great shot of Frank sound asleep in the goal, with Percy trying to wake him. It was more than just the ultimate sports blooper video—it was a "we're lousy and we don't care" statement, and whoever had made it was really good at editing. Taken all together, it made our team look hopeless but hilarious, while Muhldinger came across as the ultimate jerk.

"It's good," I told Becca, smiling for the first time that evening.

"We're not the only ones who think so," she said. "Look."

We'd gotten over ten thousand views in just a couple of hours.

She showed me how nysportsgod.com, one of the biggest sports blogs in the area, had already linked to the video and written a scathing post about Muhldinger and the insults he'd hurled at a bunch of high school students. When that blog post appeared, Becca said, the number of video views had jumped from the hundreds to the thousands in just fifteen minutes.

"Ten thousand people have watched us stink up a soccer field?" I asked Becca.

She glanced at the computer. "Four thousand in the last half hour. It's getting attention on Twitter, too. And the second most tweeted-about part of the clip is your goal."

It came near the end. First, Muhldinger thundered: "There's no room for improvement because I'm pulling the plug on this pathetic experiment in losing."

As if to contradict him, there I was, outrunning the defense and scoring the goal with a wicked low shot, and then turning to my team with both arms upraised.

"I hate to say it but you look just like your dad when he

scored that touchdown in the state championship," Becca told me. "Same eyes, same pose."

"Very funny," I told her. "So if I came in second, what's the most tweeted-about part of the clip?"

She found the end of the video where Percy's voice asked politely: "But we've made commitments to play five other teams. I realize you're disappointed with our effort, but isn't it in the spirit of Fremont High to honor those commitments?"

Muhldinger thundered back: *"I run this school, not you! To hell with those commitments. Those teams will be better off without playing us. You call this the C-team. C is for cesspool and I'm flushing you turds."*

After the video was a little message identifying our school and naming Brian Muhldinger as the principal and football coach. A message read: "If you enjoyed watching this team and would like to see them finish their season, let the Fremont School Board know." There was an e-mail address. "Tell them to honor their commitments and not to flush this team," the message continued. "And come out and support the lovable losers of Muscles High in their next match against the Midwood Tigers this Tuesday."

People from all over the state as well as Long Island, New York City, Connecticut, and Philly were tweeting that they planned on coming. They were posting back and forth to each other, as if making new friends, and a lot of them wrote that they'd had miserable high school sports experiences and horrible coaches like Muhldinger, and this was a chance to show that high school sports should be about fun.

I looked up from the screen at Becca. "What the heck is going on?"

"I'm not sure," she admitted. "We've tapped into something. We're a social media happening. Look, it's up to fifteen thousand hits."

"Isn't our season over?"

"Not if enough people e-mail the school board," she said.

"I don't think Muhldinger could care less."

"He said some things he probably shouldn't have," she noted. "He can't deny that he said them because thousands of people have seen it."

I thought it over for a second. "Who posted the original video? It had to be one of us."

"It's anonymous," she said. "There's no way to find out."

"It couldn't have been any of the players who appear in the video," I pointed out, "because they couldn't film themselves. And that's almost our whole team."

"Unless two or three people got together on this," she said. "Or maybe most of the filming was done by someone on the sideline."

"I didn't see anyone from our school there besides my father and Muhldinger."

"There were dozens of people on the sideline, and lots of them were filming the game," she noted. "I don't think there's any way to tell who's behind this. But I bet Muhldinger would like to know."

That's when her cell phone rang. She glanced at the screen. "It's your mom."

"Don't answer it."

Becca hesitated. Then she whispered "Sorry" and clicked

Answer. "Hello, Mrs. Logan? Yes, he's here. I'll ask him." She looked at me and whispered, "Wanna talk to her?"

I shook my head. Becca nodded and said, "He can't come to the phone right now. But he's okay. Can we call you back later?" She listened. "I understand, but trust me, he's fine. Yes, that's right, but I really don't think you need to." Then she clicked the phone off.

"Why did you answer?" I demanded.

"I knew she was worried about you."

"Is she coming over?"

"Probably," Becca said. "She asked me to confirm my address."

I stood up. "I'm out of here."

"Where are you going?"

"What was it you said when we drove down to the Jersey shore? Away."

Becca thought for a few seconds, and then asked: "How much do you weigh?"

"One forty. Why?"

"That puts us at a little over two fifty combined," she said. "He'll be able to manage that, easy."

"Who?" I asked, although I already knew.

Becca was heading for the door. "Come on," she said. "If you really want to get away, let's go."

I RODE BECCA'S FATHER'S BIKE, WHICH WAS

old and squeaked when I pedaled too fast. I would have thought a dentist could afford a better one, but Becca said he never rode it. The night had grown cool, and the stars were out above us. Becca pedaled next to me, not talking much, as if she understood my need for silence.

I was trying to stay angry at my dad, remembering how he'd called me a coward and kept saying my friends were pathetic, and then had thrown me against the wall. But the truth was that I felt increasingly guilty. He'd been right—my friends *were* pathetic, at least when it came to playing soccer. The video had nailed it—they were funny but hopeless.

It was strange that thousands of complete strangers thought that we losers were worth rooting for, but I guess there *are* a lot of people out there who had miserable experiences with high school sports. My father sure wasn't one of them. The more I thought about it, the more I was convinced that he had just been trying to grab me rather than punch me or hurt me.

We passed Wayne's Driving Range, shut up for the evening, and Pancho's Tacos with a half dozen cars still in the parking lot.

I sped up, gripping the rusted handlebars. In the distance, I saw the sign for Brookfarm Stables, but Becca turned off on a side road before we got to the main gate. We pedaled on gravel for a hundred yards, and then she hopped off and we walked our bikes on an overgrown path through the darkness. We were approaching the stable through a back route—one that Becca seemed to know well.

We reached a fence, and followed it to a small gate of chain mesh that was locked with a padlock. Becca hid her bike behind some bushes and fished a key out of her pocket.

"Where'd you get that?" I asked her.

"I gave riding lessons to beginners last summer, so they gave me a key," she said. "I made a copy before I gave it back."

"Have you ever snuck in before?"

She got the lock open, and we slipped through. "Once or twice," she whispered. She pulled the gate closed behind us and headed for the stable. "It's no big deal."

"I thought you were a rule follower," I whispered back.

"No way," she told me. "I'm just too smart to get caught."

She seemed to know the routines of this stable perfectly, and if she had done this before I figured we had a good chance of getting away with it.

We slipped into the low-ceilinged barn and passed the silent horses in their dark stalls. Shadow was standing motionless and didn't come to greet us as he had last time. "I don't think he wants company," I told Becca. "He looks zonked out for the night. Maybe we'd better leave him and go."

She swung the wooden door of the stall open and walked to him. The big horse didn't move a muscle as she ran her hand gently along his nose, but he opened his big black eyes and stared back at her adoringly. "Feel like some exercise?" she whispered.

"Sure," I said. "What do you have in mind?"

"I was talking to Shadow," she told me. "We're going for a ride."

"Don't go too far. I'll wait for you."

"You're coming," she informed me.

"I've never been on a horse in my life."

She was already saddling him up. "There's a first time for everything."

A minute later we were outside the barn, and she was leading Shadow by the bridle toward the back gate. I hadn't realized *how* big he was—the horse towered over both of us. He never seemed to question what Becca had in mind, and I figured if Shadow was willing to go along with her then I would, too.

The rear gate was unlocked, the way she had left it, and she swung it open. Shadow walked through and I followed him, more than a little worried. "Aren't we stealing a horse?"

"Technically he's my horse," she told me, closing the gate behind us. "And we're just borrowing him. But if this makes you nervous, don't come."

"Where exactly are we going?"

"Watch what I do, and get on behind me," she commanded. She stood on Shadow's left side, put her foot in the stirrup, and in one motion swung herself gracefully up and onto the stallion's broad back.

I grabbed onto the horn of the saddle and put my left foot in the stirrup. As if sensing that I didn't know what I was doing, Shadow stepped forward and I hopped after him, holding on for dear life. "Swing up," Becca encouraged me.

"I can't. Put on the brakes!" I half shouted.

Shadow stopped long enough for me to awkwardly pull myself up onto the saddle behind her.

"There are no brakes," Becca said with a laugh. "He's not a car."

"He's as big as a car," I muttered, getting used to the feel of sitting behind her on the saddle.

"Put your arms around my waist, and hold on to the reins with me," Becca ordered.

Pressed against her back, I held the reins where they came out of her hands. She must have stepped on the gas, because Shadow began to walk and then to trot. I was surprised at his speed and power—even at a trot we covered a lot of ground. Shadow didn't seem to notice that he had two people on his back—lucky for him Becca was slim and my father always said I was as skinny as a splinter.

That thought brought me back to the basement, and my memory of what I had said to him. I couldn't forget the look in his eyes after I'd mentioned the career he'd never had in the NFL. I wasn't sure where those words had come bubbling up from. I hadn't intended to say them, and I'd never thought of my dad as a coward or a failure. Muhldinger had suggested some of it, and the idea that he'd planted an evil seed and instead of rooting it out I had carried it home gnawed at me. What would happen the next time I saw my dad? How could we get past it?

Shadow sped up to a fast trot. I looked around, and for a long moment didn't recognize where we were. The trees thinned out, and I glimpsed open spaces and moonlight glinting on water. "Are we on the golf course?"

"The thirteenth fairway," Becca told me.

"How did we get on? I thought the course was fenced in and patrolled by security."

"Golf courses are too big to completely fence in," Becca explained. "I know three different ways in, and I've never run into any security after hours."

"I've always heard the Mafia owns this course," I told her. "I kind of believe it. No one I know from our town belongs."

"I'm sure the Mafia has better things to do than run a golf course in Fremont," she told me. "You said you wanted to get away. This is where I come to do it. It feels like being on another planet. Just enjoy the ride."

So I tried. It was more than a little otherworldly to be on a horse's back, cantering across fairways, picking our way through sand traps, and clop-clopping along the muddy banks of dark lakes. And I didn't mind sitting behind Becca, with my arms around her, feeling my thighs against the back of her legs, while her back pressed against my chest.

With each footstep Shadow took, Becca and I were thrown together in different ways, and I tightened my grip on her. Her sweet-smelling hair flew around my eyes, and when I couldn't stand it any longer I bent down and kissed the back of her neck. She twisted around on the saddle to look at me, and smiled, and just as we kissed I heard a shout.

I thought it was just a "Hey," but there might have also been a "you" added on. Shadow stopped walking and stood still.

"Did you hear that?" I whispered to Becca.

"It wasn't about us," she said, sounding nervous. "Someone was calling to someone else, far away. The wind plays tricks with voices at night."

A flashlight beam pierced the darkness, raking white channels of light across the fairway. It hadn't found us yet, but looking back along the beam I saw a guard in what looked like a golf cart, two hundred feet away. Something gleamed in his hand. It was either a flashlight or a gun.

"We have to go over and explain things to him," I whispered. "We're not doing anything wrong. He'll probably just let us go with a warning."

The beam licked closer to us, and instead of answering me Becca gave Shadow a little kick. He headed off down the fairway, moving swiftly and silently. "Do you want to get arrested for trespassing?" she asked. "I sure don't."

I heard the motor of a golf cart roaring at full speed, and I could see other lights zooming down a slope toward us as more guards joined the chase. "No, but I also don't want to get shot by a Mafia guard!"

"They'll never catch us," she assured me. "Hold on."

We burst through a curtain of trees to the next fairway, and suddenly we were flying as Shadow broke into a gallop.

Trotting had been rough, with every step tossing me up and down on the saddle, but now his strides were long and smooth. It felt like we were skimming five feet above the grass at a speed no golf cart could match.

I held tightly on to Becca and wondered if we would get out of this. I could hear the motors of the golf carts in the distance, and every now and then a searchlight beam shone through trees near us.

Shadow slowed as we entered a small woodsy area behind a tee box, and he picked his way carefully through dense underbrush. We reached the course fence with barbed wire at the top, and Becca guided us to where a large branch had fallen over and collapsed a section of it. Shadow stepped through the gap and immediately started trotting again. Soon we were on a path that led to a one-lane road, and I began to recognize a few landmarks.

"If they saw us, won't they call the stable?" I asked. "They'll see hoofprints and figure out where we came from."

"There are three other stables nearby, and lots of people keep their own horses," Becca said. "They'll never connect it to us. Did you enjoy the ride?"

"Till the Mafia started chasing us."

We brought Shadow back to the barn, and I kept expecting someone to catch us but we got him safely in his stall. The whole place stayed dark and quiet.

We rode our bikes back toward Becca's house, and it felt a lot slower than being up on Shadow's back at full gallop, but also much safer and more familiar. When we turned the corner of her block, I saw my mom's Chevy parked out in front. I was tempted to ride away, but I knew I'd have to face this at some point. So we left our bikes in the garage and Becca led me through the back door.

Our two mothers were sitting on the couch sipping tea and looking worried. My mom stood up when she saw me. She looked like she'd aged ten years in the past three hours. "Okay," she said, relieved and angry, "now I've found you. We just need to find your father."

21

MOM AND I WAITED TOGETHER IN OUR FAMILY
room, where there was a window that faced out toward the
street and the entrance to our driveway.

My father had driven away in his truck right after our
argument in the basement. He hadn't told my mom where
he was going, so we didn't have a clue when he planned to
come home. He usually kept his cell phone with him, but it
was lying on the kitchen counter where he had left it when
he went down to hit the heavy bag. So there was no way to
reach him and nothing to be done except to sit and watch
for his truck's returning headlights.

During those long night hours, surrounded by our family
trophies, Mom shared two secrets with me. First, she asked
me what I'd said to my dad when we argued. I told her how
I'd mentioned his college football injury and how he'd
missed his chance to play in the NFL.

She didn't seem surprised—I think she'd heard most of
what had gone on between us in the basement and guessed
the rest. "It wasn't really a football injury," she told me.

"What do you mean?" I demanded. "It happened in practice at the end of his senior year. A freak collision blew out
his leg."

"That's the story we always tell," she agreed with a sad

little nod, "and that's what your brothers think, too. But that's not what actually happened."

Headlights approached and we sat quietly and watched, but it turned out to be a passing car. When its taillights faded I asked her: "What really happened?"

"It did happen when he was away at college. Your father was a fanatic about staying in shape and he used to jog everywhere around the campus," Mom told me. "It was winter and he was running between classes. He turned to wave at a friend, and he slipped on a patch of ice."

I couldn't believe it. "He wrecked his knee on some stupid ice? Why doesn't he just tell the truth?"

"He was the Logan Express," she explained softly. "He'd never missed a game from grade school all the way through college. Nothing could ever slow him down. And then— when he had an NFL career right in front of him—he looked the wrong way for a split second and it was all gone. Can you blame him that it was too painful?"

The family room grew smaller—the trophies pressed in on me like trees in a threatening forest. From the framed black-and-white poster on the wall, Mickey Mantle seemed to glance down at me as he belted his tape-measure home run and smirk, as if suggesting: "It's all baloney, isn't it?"

"Could he really bust up his knee that badly wiping out on some ice?" I asked.

"The doctors didn't know if he would ever run again," Mom explained. "It was a few years before he could do more than just walk fast. He came home after college and he took the first job he was offered, in construction. It was right near my house. We started taking walks together, and he would go on for miles as fast and as far as he could, limping on his right leg. I could see how much he wanted to break into a run. He was like a tiger in a cage—it broke my heart, but it also won my heart. I knew within a week that I couldn't marry Brian, that your father and I would always be together."

"In some ways, I guess Dad was lucky," I told her. "I take it Muhldinger didn't let you go easily?"

"They almost got into a fight right outside the post office," Mom said. "It could have been really bad. But they knew that in the end it was my decision, and it was a fairly easy one for me to make."

"Muhldinger never got married, did he?" I asked.

"I think he married the Fremont football team," Mom said with a smile. "He's done very well. If you'd told me when we were dating that Brian would ever become the principal of a high school, I would have fallen over."

"But Dad's done okay, too," I pointed out, remembering some of the nasty comments Muhldinger had made in his office. "I mean, he likes his job and he works with friends."

That was when Mom told me the second secret of the night. I saw her hesitate, and then she leaned forward. "To tell you the truth, Jack, things haven't been going well for him at work lately."

"He hasn't said anything."

"He never would. But there hasn't been much new construction and his company has been downsizing. A few people in his crew have been let go, and they've cut his hours. He's worried about what may happen in the next few months. That's one reason I've applied to go on full-time at the library."

"They can't fire him," I said. "He's worked there over twenty years."

"Some of the men who were let go had worked there even longer. It's just a tough time."

I remembered the moment in the basement earlier that evening when I had told my dad that Becca was using our soccer team as a release because she was having a tough time at home. He had replied, "We all go through tough times." It hadn't occurred to me that he might be talking about himself. No wonder he'd been so tightly wound at my soccer game, and had gone down to pound on the heavy bag.

Just before two a.m. my cell phone rang. I thought it might be my father calling in from somewhere, but when I glanced at the caller ID I was surprised. "It's Becca," I told my mom.

"Isn't it late for her to call?" she asked.

"It must be something big."

"Go ahead and see," Mom said. "I'm gonna get some water."

She left the room and I answered the call. "Hey," I said, "what are you doing up?"

"Thinking about you," she said. "What's happening with your dad?"

"He's still not home. Thanks for the horseback ride. I needed to get away." I paused. "It felt good."

"I agree," she said. Then there was a little silence, and she said softly, almost like she was scared, "I love you."

I knew I should say it back, but I had never said the words out loud to a girl. I hesitated for a long moment and then whispered her name. I hoped she heard how I felt from my voice.

If she was disappointed she hid it well. She said, "Take care of yourself, Jack."

"I'm trying," I said. "It's really late. You should go to sleep."

"I don't think I can," she told me. "What's going on is too exciting."

"What's going on?"

My mom came back into the room holding a glass of water.

"I take it you haven't been around a computer," Becca said.

"No, my mom and I have been talking."

"ESPN and CBS Sports News have both picked up the Losers story and embedded the video on their blogs."

"You're kidding?" I asked.

"We hit a nerve. The video has gotten two million hits."

For a second I felt dizzy. "Did you really just say two million?"

"Two million people have seen Pierre throw up and Zirco fall in a lake."

"Wow," I said. And then, "Holy crap."

"Two million people have also seen you score your goal. Good night, you sports god. Call me if you need me. I'll keep my phone next to my bed."

I clicked my cell off and Mom asked me what was going on. When I told her about the video and the two million hits, she couldn't believe it. So I showed the video to her on my cell, and she stared at the little screen, smiling and shaking her head as my teammates screwed up and Muhldinger laced into us.

When it was done, she handed my phone back and said, "Your team may be inept, but I think you're going to be around for a while."

"Muhldinger said he was flushing us," I reminded her. "I don't see how he can go back on his word and unflush us."

"Something tells me he's not going to have much of a choice," she said. "And he may have to learn some better manners."

Another hour crawled by on the digital clock under the TV, and I was just starting to wonder if my dad would stay away all night when we saw familiar lights down the block. It was his truck, and he turned carefully into our driveway and shut off the engine. When his footsteps sounded on the back porch, my mom stood and walked out of the family room to meet him. I trailed after her, unsure what to do.

I heard the back door open and shut, and my mom say, "Where did you go?"

"Nowhere special," he answered.

"We were worried about you."

"I know you were. Sorry."

I gave them a minute or two together, and then I took a deep breath and stepped out of the family room.

They were standing together in the kitchen, holding each other. Dad was still in the black shorts and the T-shirt he had worn to hit the heavy bag. When he saw me, his arms fell away from my mother's back. I couldn't tell from his face if he was still angry at me or if he regretted what had happened. My best guess from the look in his eyes was that it was a little of both.

All night long I had felt sorry for him and guilty for what I'd said about his injury and missed pro career, but when I saw him in that T-shirt I remembered what it had been like when he had lost his temper at me.

My mother waited two or three seconds and then announced: "You two need to apologize to each other."

"Sorry, Jack," my dad said in a low voice.

"Me too," I told him.

My mother looked from one of us to the other. "That's the best you can do?"

"It's late," he grunted. "We should all go to bed." Without another word or glance at me, my father walked quickly to the stairs and started climbing.

SOMETHING HAD CHANGED AT MUSCLES HIGH.

I felt it when I first walked in the main entrance, past the trophy cases. The statue of Arthur Gentry still greeted us near the front door and the same impressive collection of gold cups and plaques glittered out at us, but the Losers story was all anyone wanted to talk about.

Frank and I were in the same homeroom, and I had never seen him so excited.

"You're looking at the most famous sleeping goalie in North America."

"That could be because you're the only goalie in North America who falls asleep during games," I told him. "Any idea who put the video together?"

"No one knows," he told me. "I just wish there were a few more shots of me. I don't think they got my best side."

"It's hard to get your best side when you're sleeping on your stomach," I told him. "You've gotta learn to fall asleep on your back."

"I can crash in virtually any position," Frank replied confidently. And then: "Did you see the *Star Dispatch*?"

"No," I told him. "I was up late and I barely made it to school this morning. Were we in the newspaper, too? What's the big news?"

"It wasn't exactly news," Frank said. "It was an editorial about Muhldinger using the words 'morons' and 'spastics' as insults. It said they weren't just politically incorrect but also hurtful. And his line about how if he were one of us he'd dig a hole and bury himself was not merely destructive and vicious, but—according to the editorial—it could encourage suicidal thinking among teens with poor self-esteem."

I laughed. "I have my low moments, but I've never thought of burying myself."

"I'm not sure if it's even physically possible," he admitted. "But it's still hurtful."

"Is Muhldinger in real trouble?" I asked.

Frank grinned. I think he hated Muhldinger as much as Becca did. "When he let loose at us on the bus he really screwed himself. The video's getting worldwide exposure and it couldn't happen to a nicer guy. Dylan heard from his mom that the school board is taking this very seriously. There's a clause in his contract as principal that relates to good conduct, so they can fire his ass if they want to."

In second-period chemistry, my childhood friend Rob Powers came over to me. He was moving slowly and gingerly, recovering from the rib injury he'd gotten in the Smithfield game. "Hey," he said, "I've been reading about your bozo team."

"You and three million other people," I said. "Isn't it freaky?"

"'Freaky' is the word." He nodded. "The football team is not amused."

"Amusing the Fremont football team isn't something I spend too much time worrying about," I told him.

Rob stepped closer. "I get that. Just be careful. Some people are pretty pissed off."

"I've done absolutely nothing," I told him truthfully.

"But you're the captain?"

"Because nobody else wanted the job."

He glanced around and then lowered his voice: "Hey, I'd like you to think about something a little radical."

I looked back at him over the orange flame of a Bunsen burner. "What's up?"

"I should be starting at quarterback," he whispered. "Instead Muhldinger put me on special teams, knowing I'd have to sacrifice my body. Every time I breathe now it hurts. That bastard set me up. He's always had it in for me. Because I do a little modeling he thinks I'm soft. He calls me Goldilocks."

"You'll get playing time at QB," I told him. "Everyone knows you have a gun."

"If I want it," he muttered. "Here's a thought. But don't tell anyone."

"Sure. What's up?"

"You got this really cool thing going," he said. "Soccer's not my sport but I could definitely contribute." He flashed me his ten-thousand-megawatt grin. "Not to mention I could enhance the team's, ah, social profile."

There was no doubt of that, but I couldn't understand what would be in it for him—Rob was one of the five best athletes at our school, and certainly one of the most popular kids, too. "Why would you want to join our lousy circus act?"

He glanced around warily, but no one was listening. "It might be fun," he said with a careless shrug. "I'm tired of getting my nuts busted by Muhldinger. I'd like to bust his nuts for a change. And maybe I could even help you guys win."

"My team doesn't want to win."

"How can they not want to win?"

"My dad asked me the same thing. I couldn't explain it to him, because I'm not sure I understand it myself. But they don't."

"So they want to lose? Isn't that easy? You just give up."

"Not necessarily," I told him. "They want to be what they are, which is a lousy soccer team. They don't want to play the game Muhldinger's way. And when they do lose, they want style points."

Rob thought that over for a few seconds and then glanced up at the front of the room. I could almost see him tense up and pull away from me. "Watch your back, captain," he whispered.

I turned to follow his gaze, and saw that Muhldinger's tall personal secretary with the orange hair had just walked into the lab and was talking to our chemistry teacher, jabbing one of her long, silver-painted fingernails in my direction.

A minute later I was following the secretary down the hall at power-walking speed. She was wearing heels and her steps clicked off the marble floor. She didn't say one word till we reached the administrative offices, and then the long silver nail of her index finger sliced out at me like a switchblade. "Sit," she commanded, pointing toward the waiting area where Coach Percy was already waiting, looking tense, his fingers knitted together on his lap.

I headed over, and he gave me a nod. "Hello, Jack. Sorry you've been called onto the carpet, too. I'm afraid this won't be much fun."

"What's going on?" I asked.

"I assume the principal's going to let us know once and for all that our season has been officially terminated."

I looked back at him, and remembered that I hadn't seen a TV or a computer in his apartment. Maybe Classics teachers are behind the curve when it comes to new technology. "You don't have a clue what's been happening?"

"When I arrived at school, I got a message to come here," Percy said. "I've been waiting for twenty minutes." He looked at my face. "Did I miss something?"

"You did," I told him. "You have a tiger by the tail. Or a lion. That would be the Fremont Lion."

"I still don't understand," he said. "Maybe you'd better start from the beginning."

I tried to explain to him what had happened, with our team's story exploding on the Web, but I didn't get through much of it before the secretary with orange hair told us to follow her. She ushered us into the conference room, where four people were waiting around a big table.

Dylan's mother smiled and said good morning to me—I assumed she was there because she was on the school board, not to mention the mom of one of my teammates. The president of the board, Mr. Bryce, was there, too, in a dark suit. He was an attorney in town and a big football booster. I think he had been a Fremont halfback three decades ago, and he had championed the idea of making Muhldinger the new principal. Mrs. Fritz, our school's athletic director, sat very erect with a black ballpoint pen poised over a blank notepad. And at the head of the table, sweating despite the fact that our school was air-conditioned, sat Muhldinger, looking uncomfortable in a jacket and tie.

The secretary with the orange hair left and pulled the door closed. Muhldinger cleared his throat. "Good morning, guys," he said to Coach Percy and me. "Take a load off."

We said good morning back and sat down. There was an awkward silence. Mr. Bryce nodded to Muhldinger.

Muhldinger swallowed and took a big breath. "When it comes to sports I'm a very competitive guy," he noted, "and sometimes I may take it a little too far." He focused his eyes at a point on the white wall between Percy and me. "We're used to winning at Fremont, but of course winning isn't everything. Even more important is . . ." His voice trailed off and his face showed baffled surprise, as if he'd had something in his pocket a minute ago but he'd somehow managed to lose it.

"Personal growth?" Dylan's mother prompted.

Muhldinger nodded slightly, as if there was no need to repeat the phrase. "So to cut to the chase, I've decided that your soccer team deserves to play out its season."

"Thank you," Percy said, and held out his hand.

Muhldinger shook it without speaking and glanced at me.

"Yeah, thanks," I said.

"Don't thank me," Muhldinger grunted. He forced a terrible smile, as if he wanted to bite something in half but could only flash his teeth. "I'm new to this job, and running a school teaches you a lot about yourself." He reached up with two fingers and pried his collar away from his stub of a neck. "In the heat of battle, I said some things that I regret." He looked like he would rather be chewing on glass, but he managed to spit out the rest of it. "Please let your team know that I hope everyone feels included and proud, no matter what it says on the scoreboard."

Dylan's mom nodded. "I think it's very important to get that message out."

Muhldinger glanced at Mr. Bryce, who told her: "We just *have* gotten that message out, Elaine." Then Bryce turned to Percy and me. "As I'm sure you know, this story has become a bit of a cause célèbre. A video was posted on the Internet that has attracted considerable attention." He paused, took a sip of ice water, and gave me a smile. "I assume the video was made by one of your teammates, Jack."

It wasn't a question, but everyone was looking at me. "No idea," I told him.

He studied my face carefully. "Whoever did it certainly has the right to free expression. But they should understand that there are limits to that, both legally and when it comes to our own school rules. Taping someone without their knowledge and posting it for the world to see exceeds those limits, in my opinion."

"If Jack says he doesn't know who did it, I believe him," Percy spoke up bravely. "This boy has a sterling character and I've never known him to dissemble."

"I agree," Dylan's mom said. "There's no reason to interrogate him, Paul."

Mr. Bryce smiled at her, took another sip of ice water, and set his cup down on a trivet. He turned his head and fixed his gaze on Percy and me. "This school system may decide to hire an expert to figure out who posted it. In the meantime, we have a long-standing policy at Fremont of not talking to news organizations about students and sports teams and what's going on inside our school family. We've always tried to keep a low profile because that's usually best for everyone. So if any members of your team are contacted by the press my strong advice is the less said the better. Mary?"

Mrs. Fritz tapped her pen on her blank notepad. "From now on your soccer team will be practicing and playing on the south field, where the grass is a little better."

Mr. Bryce added, "It's also more private. We've had a few requests from news organizations to film your practices, which we've turned down."

"Why on earth would anyone want to film our practices?" Percy asked.

Mrs. Fritz went right on. "Your games for the rest of the year will continue on the days and times previously scheduled. The five schools you're playing have been contacted and the dates reconfirmed. I think that's all. Oh, one more thing—the varsity cheerleaders want to perform at your home games, unless you have a problem with that?"

Percy glanced at me for help. Cheerleaders were clearly outside his level of experience.

"The more cheering the better," I said.

We all shook hands and Percy and I headed out of the administrative offices together. "That was damned decent of Muhldinger to give us our season back," he said. "I don't think it could have ended any better."

"He was forced to do it, but he still hates us," I told him softly. "This isn't over by a long stretch."

Coach Percy nodded. "I suppose you're right, but let's hope for the best. By the way, why do the varsity cheerleaders want to perform at our games?"

"For the same reason Bryce and Muhldinger don't want us to talk to reporters," I told him. "We're the hot story at Fremont High."

I'M NOT SURE THAT MRS. FRITZ WAS RIGHT about the south field having better grass, but it was certainly more private. The field was sandwiched between the swimming pool and the tennis courts, so there was no view of it from any street. The two TV news trucks that pulled into our school's parking lot in the early afternoon couldn't get close. Dylan heard from his mom that the reporters were brought to the conference room, denied permission to film on school grounds, and asked not to bother any Fremont students.

When we headed out for our afternoon practice, a school guard was patrolling the field, making sure reporters and strangers stayed away. But he couldn't stop other students from coming to watch, and more than twenty were waiting for us. They ranged from freshmen to seniors, from soccer fans to sports haters. The south field had no bleachers, so they sprawled on the grass and waited to see what all the fuss was about. I was surprised to see Rob Powers saunter over with two pretty girls and sit down gingerly. With his cracked rib and punctured lung it was clear that he couldn't run any football drills, but surely he had better things to do than watch our pathetic soccer practice.

We now had a nickname—the Losers—and my teammates seemed to be embracing their own breaking story with excitement and a weird kind of pride. It was as if they were thrilled at becoming famous for being lousy. When we circled up for our yoga stretches, they compared notes on how our story kept getting hotter on the Web.

Chloe was tracking our numbers. She claimed that more than four million people had seen us on different sites. "That's more than watched the president's press conference last week," she informed us.

"We're more entertaining than the president's press conference," Meg said.

"Yeah, the president never collides with anyone or falls into a lake," Dylan agreed. Meg smiled at him. I didn't think they were dating yet, but my shy friend was now relaxed around her and could even crack lame jokes, which was a big step forward.

Frank described a site that featured an unflattering photo of Muhldinger—his big bald head shiny under fluorescent lights—labeled THE MUSCLE-HEAD OF MUSCLES HIGH. The site was running a Meanest Coach contest, inviting students to post pictures of their own nasty coaches.

Becca stretched out next to me and asked softly: "Did you and your dad talk?"

"Not really."

"You don't look like you got much sleep."

"Just a few hours."

"I didn't get much either," she said, unable to contain her excitement. "I kept reading the comments of people who say they're going to come to our game on Tuesday. It's insane. They're carpooling from Brooklyn, and there's a group biking over the George Washington Bridge from Manhattan. There's even a weird men's soccer club in Hartford that claims they're worse and more out of shape than we are, and they may drive down in a van to prove it."

"We'll show them what it means to be out of shape," Pierre proclaimed. "I can boot again if necessary."

"I hope it's not necessary," I told him. "I doubt that's what they're all coming to see." Then I asked Becca, "How many people total do you think are really gonna show up on Tuesday?"

"Maybe a hundred," she guessed. "They sound pretty serious about it. They're mostly people who hated high school sports and felt pushed around and bullied, and they see coming out here and cheering for us as an opportunity to get some of their own back."

"Once a revolution starts, the real power rests with those who have been most abandoned," Shimsky contributed grimly.

"Who said that?" Meg wanted to know.

"Danton," Shimsky told her.

"Don't you mean Dante?" Becca asked.

"Georges-Jacques Danton," Coach Percy explained. "A leading firebrand in the French Revolution who was eventually guillotined. Let's take a lap around the field. It's not a race, so feel free to go at your own pace."

I'm not sure the Losers needed to be told that. We weren't exactly known for our team speed. I didn't want to show off, but even running slowly I couldn't help taking the lead and pulling away. I believe that most healthy teenagers could walk around a soccer field more quickly than our team ran. Becca and Meg practiced Latin as they jogged, conjugating verbs back and forth and not paying any attention to where they ran so that they swerved wildly. Frank and Pierre seemed to actually be moving backward, but that must have been an optical illusion because they eventually finished their lap and joined the rest of us by the goal.

"A few quick announcements before we start," Percy said. "First, as you may have heard, our season is back on."

There was applause and an explosive belch, which Zirco let loose. Everyone turned to look at him and he tugged at his right ear.

"Second," Percy continued, "the school authorities had a talk with your captain and me. They requested that all of you not speak to reporters about our team."

"Can't we talk to anyone we want?" Becca called out.

"Yeah, what about free speech?" Chloe demanded.

Percy looked at me for help.

"Go ahead and talk to whoever you want," I told them. "Just be aware that this story's getting big and Muhldinger's trying his best to contain it."

"He's the muscle-head of Muscles High," Meg shouted.

"Yeah, he needs to watch what he says a lot more than we do," Dylan pointed out.

"I understand your strong feelings, but let's try not to hold grudges," Coach Percy suggested. "Your principal gave us our season back. Suppose we repay his gesture with forgiveness and even a little rudimentary progress in soccer?"

There were boos and hisses from the Losers. They all looked angry, except for Shimsky who was smiling, as if enjoying the fact that once a revolution has started no one can control it.

"I'm not suggesting we plunge into Spartan training," Percy hastily explained. He glanced at Pierre. "But let's try not to launch any more shoes at the goal." His gaze swung over to Frank. "Or get tangled up in the net." He looked at Zirco. "And I'm sure we can all agree that we don't want anyone to drown."

"Why should we change the way we play for Muhldinger?" Becca demanded. Percy was her favorite teacher, so I was a little surprised by how sharply she confronted him.

"Yeah, he's only letting us finish our season because his job is on the line," Frank agreed. "We may be the Losers, but so far we're totally kicking his butt by doing what we do."

Percy looked surprised by the fury of the team's response. He knitted his fingers behind his neck and paced back and forth for a moment, the way I had seen him do in his apartment when Becca and I had asked him to be our coach. Finally he stopped pacing and nodded at us. "I take your point. I certainly don't want to change the wonderful . . . exuberance of our team. Let's do our best to . . . do what we do . . . and make sure we have fun."

Fun was a kind word for it—what we were good at was losing. As we ran onto the field, a chant went up from my teammates: "Losers, losers, losers forever!" It was picked up by a few grinning students sitting on the grass. "Losers, losers, losers forever," they chanted in a familiar rhythm that made a mockery of our most famous football chant: "Fremont, Fremont, Fremont forever!"

I joined the chant, but as I looked around I was also dreading what was to come.

Sure enough, everything that could possibly go wrong on a soccer field did. To the delight of the increasingly large crowds that came to watch us over the next few days, practicing seemed to make us worse and not better. Some of it was due to our genuine lack of sports talent, but as the week wore on I realized that several of my teammates were making themselves look lousy on purpose.

They must have been untying their cleats before shooting drills because the number of shoes that were launched at the goal kept growing. Frank dodged them and occasionally snatched one out of the air and winged it back. He fell asleep twice in the goal during practice that week, and it became a running gag that he managed to find new ways of getting tangled in the net. Once his head got snagged, and we had to cut the nylon mesh with scissors.

Our midfielders sprinted forward, backed up, and ran side to side at the same time, and frequently two or three of them collided in what looked like bad traffic accidents in the middle of the field. Bodies piled up, there were dramatic screams, arms and legs thrashed, and lots of laughter rang out.

The "Jenks" became our team's signature dribbling move, and was repeated with many creative variations. The move had been invented by our spectacularly uncoordinated defender—Alan "the Jinx" Jenks—who sometimes missed his head when he went to comb his curly brown hair. To perform a Jenks, a player whiffs on the ball completely while trying to kick it forward and then back-heels it blindly on the backswing. Great teams feature the Nutmeg, the Rainbow, the Maradona, and the Sombrero. We had the Flying Shoe, the Sleeping Goalie, and Jinx doing the Jenks.

Percy gave up trying to rein in the mayhem, and often contributed to it. His attempts at positioning drills were taken from ancient battles and frequently led to chaos. On Thursday he had us reenact the Battle of Gaugamela, and Meg led a "cavalry charge" into the fence of the tennis court. On Friday when the weather turned sunny Percy showed up in a pith helmet that made it look like he was ready for a safari. Kids on the sidelines laughed and filmed him with cell phones.

Every evening my mom asked me what was going on with our team, and I told her nothing much. Dad had no questions—he missed several dinners and when he was there he just wolfed down his food and excused himself. I couldn't tell if he was still mad at me or just pissed off at life in general. I decided to stay quiet for a while and keep a low profile, both at home and with our team.

I had never been involved in a breaking news event before, and I kept expecting the Losers saga to die down. Instead, our school's efforts to limit media coverage seemed to stoke the fires. We were featured on several TV sports and news shows, and every day I got more e-mails and phone calls from reporters and bloggers. I took Mr. Bryce's advice and deleted the messages.

But some of my friends were clearly doing a lot of talking,

although they were smart enough to ask not to be named. Articles and blogs came out with all kinds of inside information about our team. They described our goofy practices, our nutty coach, and our geeky players. A few of them even named me as the team captain and scorer of our only goal.

The media hype built through the week, as if our match on Tuesday against Maysville was some sort of watershed event. When I got home from soccer practice on Friday there were five messages on our home phone from different reporters asking me to call back. I erased them, but when the phone rang a few minutes later I picked it up out of habit. "Jack Logan?" a woman's voice asked.

"Yes?"

"This is Dianne Foster from the *Star Dispatch*. I left you two messages."

"Sorry but I'm not talking to reporters."

"Why not?" she asked. "I don't bite."

"I just don't want to."

"Well, then suppose I do the talking and you just listen," she suggested. "I think you'll want to hear this. Okay?"

"Go on," I said, curious despite myself.

"I'm writing an article about your soccer team that you may be very interested in," she said. "You see, I know who you are, Jack."

"I don't know what that means. I'm no one. Goodbye."

"That's very modest of you," she said with a laugh. "But you're Tom Logan's youngest son."

I gripped the phone a little tighter. "My father has nothing to do with this story."

"Doesn't he?" she asked. "The captain of the self-proclaimed worst soccer team in America that's challenging its own high school's testosterone-fueled sports ethos just happens to be the son of the best football player in the whole history of the school? To me that's a pretty interesting father-son story."

"Maybe," I admitted. "But please don't write it."

"I already have," she said. "I just want to confirm some of the details. Is it true that you were offered a spot on the varsity football team? They even wanted to give you your father's old number. And when you turned it down your principal put his fist through a door?"

"Who told you that?" I tried to think of who knew all the details of what had happened in Muhldinger's office. *Dylan? Frank?* I hesitated for a long second. *Becca?*

"And is it true that your father personally called Principal Muhldinger and asked him to give the Losers a chance to play, so in a way your team's challenge to your school is all his doing?"

I hung up the phone, and even though it was warm in our kitchen I shivered.

BECCA OPENED HER FRONT DOOR AND LOOKED
a little surprised to see me. "Hey, what are you doing here?"

"Just passing by," I told her. "Want to take a walk?"

She studied my face for a second and jumped to the wrong conclusion. "Are you okay? Did something happen with your dad?"

"Still just the silent treatment."

"You look . . . worried," she said.

"Just a little upset. All the attention our team is getting about our game on Tuesday is making me . . . anxious."

Her pretty hazel eyes glittered excitedly. "Yeah, it's crazy, isn't it? I think a couple hundred people may show up, and tons of reporters."

"You sound pretty happy about that."

"I love it that the truth about this stupid town's priorities is finally getting outed," she admitted, "and I think it's cool that so many people have been so appalled. And I *really* love it that Muhldinger and his minions can't put a lid on this story. No one can control social media."

"You seem to be controlling it pretty well," I told her. "I bet you'll get a great college essay out of it."

She studied my face. "Jack, what's going on?"

"How about that walk?"

"Okay," she said. "Let me grab a jacket."

She threw on a blue windbreaker and we walked along the sidewalk without speaking. It was late afternoon and starting to turn cold. Cars were pulling into driveways as people got home from work, and parents popped out on porches and shouted for their kids to come in for dinner. On a big lawn beneath some maple trees, a rough neighborhood football game was going on—tough-looking ten-year-olds tackling each other without pads as the next generation of Fremont warriors took shape. I watched three smaller boys stop one bigger kid, wrap up his legs, and drag him down like a pack of hyenas.

The houses and yards gave way to a nature reserve with marked trails. "Want to go for a little hike?" Becca asked.

"It's getting dark."

"I know the trails really well," she said, and her hand brushed my own. "Sometimes it's nice to get a little lost together."

"I'm already lost," I told her, sitting down on a bench near a streetlight.

She sat next to me, and we watched the last rays of the autumn sun filter down through the branches of the reserve's tall trees. "What's the matter, Jack?" Becca finally asked. "Why are you so mad at me?"

I described my conversation with Dianne Foster and the article she was writing, and how much she had known.

"You think I gave her that information?"

"Asking my dad to call Muhldinger was your idea," I reminded her. "You were the only one there—besides my parents—when we had that talk with him. After he made the call, I went up to my room and texted you the good news."

Becca nodded that this was all true, and then she stood up and turned away. "I can't believe you'd think I'd ever hurt you like that."

"Who else knows about that phone call?" I asked. "I didn't tell anyone. I'm sure my parents didn't, either."

"Lots of people know," she said softly. "Percy does. And I told the story to Meg, and that's like broadcasting it."

"Why did you tell Meg what happened in my house, with my family?"

Becca shrugged. "I told her the next day. She's my best friend. I was giving her a report on our date. Girls do that. I told her about the dinner, how nice your mother was, the walk home, and about our first kiss—and I guess I also talked about your dad and how we asked him to make that call. It was no big deal, I was just so happy the way the evening went that I gave her a full report."

"It's a big deal to me," I told her. "So Meg spilled everything to Dianne Foster and that's how this mess happened?"

"I didn't say that it was all Meg's fault. Reporters talk to lots of people when they write articles." Becca was wearing a coat zipped up to her neck, but she shivered. "Listen, I would never tell anyone private things about your family. I love you, Jack. I don't have anyone else I feel that way about right now."

An owl hooted, and its call seemed to circle through the gathering darkness like a warning. I was very angry, but I stood up and put my hand out for a fist bump. "Okay, teammate," I said, "can we agree to tell the truth to each other?"

She bumped me back and then came in for a hug. "We always should."

"Who locked the football team in the Keep?"

"Not me," Becca whispered. "I swear."

"But you know? And you don't trust me enough to tell me?"

She hesitated a second more. "Shimsky."

"I figured. And the video of our team? Did he post that, too?"

She shook her head. "That's not my secret to tell."

"You either trust me or you don't."

She looked up at me. "You really don't think we should keep secrets from each other?"

"They're poison."

"Okay," she said, "then here's a secret." She leaned so close that I could feel her warm breath. "I just want to be someplace else. I want to go off to one of the beautiful places I've read about in books and—and disappear. I even made a list: Togo. Madagascar. Fiji. Bali . . ."

She paused, out of breath, and her eyes were wet and shining.

"My father filed for divorce two days ago. My mom's on a heavy diet of antidepressants. She's like a zombie, walking around in silence, except when she talks to lawyers. I hate my life right now. Do you understand that? *I hate it*."

I held her tighter. "So what's happening with our soccer team is the only thing taking your mind off it?"

"It makes me smile and feel good about something. It's a lot more real than the two of us sailing away to Bali."

"The two of us? I thought you were getting ready to sail away yourself."

"Well, I wouldn't kick you out of the boat if you stowed away."

I ran my hand through her hair. "You posted that video of our team, didn't you?"

"No. But I helped," Becca admitted. "I filmed Muhldinger on the bus with my cell phone. I was aiming it between two seats and I was scared to death he would see me, but his anger made him blind."

"Who'd you give it to?" I asked. "Who put the video together and posted it?"

She kept silent.

"The school system may hire someone to try to find out," I told her. "Whoever did it needs to be on their guard. Was it Meg? I don't think she has the technical know-how. Dylan could do it but he wouldn't have the nerve. Chloe? Shimsky?"

Becca started trembling in a way that I remembered from her panic attack in the barn. She tried to shrug me off.

"Calm down," I said. "Just breathe."

"I'm fine," she gasped. "Go away, Jack."

"I'm not going anywhere."

"I told you I loved you. Why couldn't you say it back?"

There it was. I knew it was coming at some point, but I didn't know what to say.

"Well, maybe I need to hear it," she said, and started to hyperventilate. "I can't believe . . . you'd think . . . I betrayed you. That really hurts. *Go.*" She pushed my shoulder so hard I nearly fell over the bench, and she shouted: *"Get away from me!"*

I let her go and she sat on the bench, holding her stomach. I just stood there and watched, feeling stupid, but ready to help if she needed me.

She slowly came out of it and I sat down next to her. We stayed like that for about five minutes without speaking, and I listened to her breathing get more and more regular.

"My God," she finally said. "Worst ever." She glanced at her watch and stood. "I'd better go back. My mother notices when I'm not in the house and she panics. She called the fire department a few nights ago."

I stood also. "I'll walk you home."

We headed back up the block. The football game had ended and autumn darkness was knitting together tree branches and streets and empty yards. We walked silently. When we reached her house we stopped in the long shadow of the hedge, and she looked into my eyes. "Please don't make me tell you about the video."

"I'm not going to make you tell me anything, Becca. But I wish you would."

"Why?"

"Because I just do."

"Someone could get in a lot of trouble."

"Don't you trust me?"

"Of course," she said. "But there are things . . ."

"What things . . . ?"

Becca hesitated for a long beat and then said, "Sometimes

it seems like you're not like the rest of us. You are not a real Loser. You want to win."

So the truth was that she didn't completely trust me. I wondered if Frank and Dylan were thinking the same thing.

"Maybe I'm not like everyone else on our team, but I made a choice," I told her. "I know who my friends are, and I hope they know who I am."

She looked at me and finally said something so softly that it took a second for my mind to register it. "Percy."

I stared back at her. "No way. He doesn't even own a computer."

"He rocks on computers," she said. "He runs simulations of ancient battles on software he writes himself."

I was still skeptical. "He's too polite. He would never take on Muhldinger and our school."

"Don't be such a muscle-head, Jack. He's smarter than all of us put together. Muhldinger called him an idiot and Percy didn't like that. And he's going back to England next year. He's got a great teaching job lined up. So he can do whatever he wants."

I remembered meeting him in the principal's waiting room, and how he'd said he thought Muhldinger had summoned us to let us know he was ending our season. "But when the Web story broke he didn't have a clue what was going on."

"The English make the best actors," Becca told me with a little smile. "He certainly fooled you. Trust me, he knows exactly what's going on."

"Where did he get all that footage of our team playing its first game?"

"A friend of his from England is the coach of the Marion team. He sent Percy everything he needed."

"Becca?" her mother's voice called from the porch. "Is that you?"

"I was just taking a walk, Mom," she answered. "Go back inside. I'll be right in."

There was the sound of the screen door banging.

"It feels like he lied to me," I told her.

"Not telling the full truth isn't lying," Becca said. She took a deep breath. "But I don't want you to ever say I lied to you, Jack. So here's the full truth. You're right—I talked to that woman reporter at the *Star Dispatch*, too. Meg talked to her first, and I think Meg sent her to Dylan, and then she called me. I didn't know exactly what her article was going to be about and I *never*, *ever* intended to tell her any secrets about your family, but I did answer her questions about our team and how it got started. Maybe that was a mistake. I'm not sure."

We stood there in silence looking at each other. And then her mother shouted again: "Becca, Meg keeps calling you. It's some kind of emergency."

Becca hurried into the house, and I hesitated and then followed. I stood silently in the living room as she frantically hunted for her cell phone. "What's wrong?" she asked her mom as she ransacked the living room. "Did she tell you? Is she home?"

"No, she's at the hospital. She didn't tell me."

Becca was pulling cushions off the couch, searching for

her phone. "Is she hurt, is she sick, was it a car accident? She texts while she drives and I told her to be careful . . ."

"Calm down," Becca's mother said. "Meg's fine."

Becca found her cell phone under the couch and read something on the screen. "It's Dylan," she said. "Something bad happened."

AT THE EMERGENCY ROOM, WE TRIED TO GET
in to see Dylan, but the nurse at the front desk said he
was with his family and the police and pointed to the
waiting room.

Frank arrived a few minutes later, out of breath and
drenched in sweat. He'd gotten a text message from Meg
and had run two miles to the hospital. I believe that my big
friend had pushed himself as hard as any member of Fremont's track team could have done. "How is he?" Frank demanded, red-faced and gasping. "Did they catch the guys?"

"What guys?" I asked. "What happened? No one here
will tell us anything."

"Somebody beat the crap out of him," Frank told us.

I remembered Rob Powers's warning to me that the football team wasn't amused by all the publicity we were getting.
"Could it have been some of the football players?" I asked.

They looked at me.

"I hate our school," Becca said.

"I hope Dylan tells the cops everything," Frank said. "I
hope he names names."

"Why wouldn't he?" Becca asked.

"Because he has to walk through the doors of Muscles
High again soon," I told her.

"Things are going to change," she vowed. "Enough is enough."

I glanced down the corridor and saw two cops walk down the hallway to the exit. In a minute, Meg appeared. She didn't say anything but just waved for us to follow her.

In the ER ward, Dylan was the only patient. The curtains around his bed were wide open. Dylan's mom was usually a very calm woman, and I had watched her coast through three years of school board emergencies without ever once losing her cool. Now she looked worried and enraged at the same time. "Thanks for coming," she said in an unsteady voice as we entered.

Dylan's father—a tall and gentle guy who ran a small travel agency in town—was standing by the right side of the bed, and Meg moved to a spot on the left. Dylan was lying on his back with his neck in a protective brace and what looked like the biggest Band-Aid ever on his nose. There were cuts on his face, his left eye socket was badly bruised, and his right wrist had been immobilized in a splint. My friend wouldn't be hitting any killer Ping-Pong backhand slices in the near future.

"Hey, buddy," Frank rumbled, concern and anger clear in his deep voice. "You look awesome."

Dylan looked back at us, and I think they'd probably given him some pain meds because he smiled. "I feel pretty awesome," he said.

"What the hell happened?" Frank asked. "Who did this to you?"

"Dunno," Dylan told us. "After school, I was cutting through the Stevens." The Stevens is the nickname of a little patch of forest near the back of our school. A stream twists through it, and according to local legend a young solider named Stevens was drowned in it during the Revolutionary War. It still carries his name two hundred and however many years later. "They came from behind me, fast. I heard footsteps but I never saw who it was. The next thing I knew I was on the ground, they'd pulled my jacket over my head, and someone kept pounding on me and laughing."

Then he stopped talking and began to cry.

None of us knew what to do, as our friend lay there sobbing like a little kid. Tears squeezed out of his eyes and ran down his cheeks, and his nose started to run. His mother squeezed his hand, and his dad said to us, "Sorry, guys. You'd better go now."

We walked back to the waiting room and Meg came with us.

"Could he tell the cops anything?" Frank asked her.

She wiped away a tear of her own. "Just when and where it happened. The police are going to see if there are any footprints or other clues."

"He heard them laughing," Frank said. "Didn't he recognize their voices?"

"He said it could have been anyone," Meg told us.

"It was football players," Becca announced.

Meg looked at her.

"We don't know that for sure," I told Becca. "We shouldn't spread that around until there's proof."

"Who else could it have been?" she demanded. Suddenly the anger between us from earlier bubbled back up. "Dylan doesn't have an enemy in the world. Tell me who else it could have possibly been, Jack. A motorcycle gang? How about a Viking raiding party?"

Her sarcasm made Frank and Meg smile, but I said again, "You can't accuse people unless you know for sure that they did it."

"I can accuse anyone I want," Becca insisted. "You were the first one who mentioned the football team. They knocked out your teeth, too, remember? Why are you defending the people who just beat up one of your best friends?"

"Great, accuse anyone you want," I told her. "Maybe you want to call a newspaper reporter."

"Hey, guys, chill," Frank said. "It's not gonna help Dylan if you two go at it." And then he asked Meg, "What happened to his arm?"

"His wrist is broken. The doctor said it's a common injury when someone is knocked over and tries to break their fall."

"What about his nose?" I asked.

"They broke that, too," Meg said.

"Was that also busted in the fall?" Frank wanted to know.

"No, that was a punch," Meg told us.

We were all quiet for a long moment, and then Shimsky's voice rang out. He had stepped into the room behind us. "Those who make peaceful revolution impossible will make violent revolution inevitable," he said.

We turned to look at him. He was standing there nodding and almost looking pleased, as if he had always known this situation would flare up into violence.

"Who said that?" Becca wanted to know. "Danton?"

"Stalin?" I guessed.

"John F. Kennedy," he said. "You know what just happened, right? They just upped the ante and we have to hit them back even harder."

"What good will that do?" I asked him.

"It's not about doing good," he said, and I saw Becca nod slightly.

Percy arrived next, and two minutes later Chloe and Pierre showed up. Within half an hour, a dozen of our teammates were milling angrily around the waiting room. We might have been the Losers, but when it came to solidarity and friendship we were making a pretty strong team statement.

They operated on Dylan's wrist at about nine p.m. He had something called a distal radius fracture, and they had to use two pins to stabilize the bones.

"Remind me not to fly with him," Pierre joked. "Every time he travels through an airport he's going to be setting off alarms."

"I think these days they use titanium," Becca said. "It doesn't set off anything."

Suddenly Percy called out, "Everyone quiet down."

Dylan's mother had walked into the waiting room, with a young and athletic-looking male doctor in blue scrubs. "That's right, titanium's a nonferrous metal," the doctor said. "It doesn't set off any alarms. I just wanted you guys to know that your friend came through the operation okay.

His wrist is gonna be fine and his nose will heal up better than ever."

"They're going to keep him here overnight," Dylan's mom told us, looking and sounding a little better, "because he might have a low-grade concussion. He's resting now, but he wanted me to thank you all for coming and hanging out. It means a lot to him knowing you're here. He'll be out of the hospital tomorrow and back on the soccer field soon."

We all applauded the good news.

Dylan's mom paused and gave us a smile. "In the meantime, he's coming to watch the game on Tuesday, and he said he wants you to lose this one in his honor."

As if in response, a chant started that I doubt has ever rung out in a hospital waiting room before: "Losers, losers, losers forever!"

The young doctor looked around, a bit mystified.

"Let's lose this one big for Dylan," Meg called out.

"Not just big but ugly!" Pierre seconded.

Frank's deep voice boomed: "It's time to show the world just how bad we can be!"

26

THE NEWS ABOUT DYLAN WAS APPARENTLY exactly the kind of new fuel that was needed to keep our story roaring along as a trendy social media event. Internet loudmouths reacted with fury. Angry tweets and posts about the beating soon included Dylan's name and picture, and the rumor that the attacker had been a member of the football team.

It rained hard all weekend and there were no soccer practices, so I kept to myself and stayed far away from the media—and Becca. But I followed the chatter on the Web, and it felt strange that most of the people posting comments about us had never even been near our town. They still seemed to take our situation very personally, as if what was going on in Fremont touched something in their own lives, and what had happened to Dylan outraged them. Becca was right—there are a lot of people out there who hated the sports cultures of their schools and towns, and we had struck a nerve.

The *Star Dispatch* on Saturday had a news article about the assault on a Fremont student, with comments from our town's police chief that there was an investigation under way. On Sunday morning the paper's sports section ran a piece about our upcoming game against Maysville, and how hundreds of people were expected to attend. There was no sign of Dianne Foster's article about the Logan family, and I began to hope that either she hadn't written it or her story had been overshadowed by the attack on Dylan and would never be published.

I visited Dylan on Sunday afternoon. He was home from the hospital and enjoying his newfound fame. He was getting e-mails and texts from people he didn't know, and some of them were sending him flowers and chocolates. A fan in Greenwich Village with the username Jockhater had sent him two dozen cookies from a fancy city bakery. He had a black eye and his wrist was now in a plaster cast, but he was in high spirits. "I gotta get my wrist broken more often," he told me. "Do you want a white chocolate chip or a brown sugar butterscotch?"

I asked him about the police investigation, and he told me that he wasn't supposed to talk about it. But since we were old friends, he confided that the cops had searched the Stevens and found a few footprints.

On Monday the heavy rains continued. Two police cars were in the parking lot when I arrived at school, and rumors flew around about students being called in for questioning. I also heard that the school system had hired a private investigator to figure out who had posted the original video, and that Muhldinger was furious that his football team had been linked in unsubstantiated rumors to a vicious assault.

Becca didn't show up at school, and Meg told me she was a little sick and had stayed home to try to recover for our

Tuesday game. Our soccer practice was rained out so I went home right after school. I was feeling a little sick myself, so I headed up to my room and lay in bed watching the rain lash the windows.

I have a small room that looks down on our neighbor's garage. My bed faces the one window, and then there's just space for a dresser, a desk, and a chair. I've had this room my whole life, and a lot of the stuff in it is from when I was a kid. The Tonka fire engine my grandfather gave me when I was five is parked on top of my dresser. Above its ladder is a photo of my brothers tossing me back and forth across a leaf pile when I was seven. In the picture I manage to look both thrilled and scared to death, which pretty well sums up my relationship with my two older brothers.

Then there's some newer stuff. In computer club, Frank, Dylan, and I had built a robot with big hands that could navigate shoulder blades and spread suntan lotion on a person's back. We'd named him Sandy, and he'd won first prize in a robotics competition. Sandy waited on his treads on my night table, next to a framed photo of Becca. I had taken the picture of her on a windy day not long after school started and I liked how she was laughing and trying to push her hair out of her eyes.

Thunder shook the house, and lightning flashed so close to my window that it glinted off the metal frame of Becca's photo. I wondered where my father was—his crew couldn't work in such a storm. He hadn't said more than a few words to me all week. He'd spent a lot of time away from home and when he came back he either stayed in the family room watching the tube or went down to the basement and hit the heavy bag. On Saturday night he'd quarreled with my mom, which was very rare. I'd heard them shouting back and forth—him telling her that he just needed a little space, and her answering that he could take all the space he wanted, but he was also a husband and a father. There was real anger in their voices, and it made me think of Becca and what she was going through with her own parents.

I hadn't talked to her all weekend, and I was tempted to call or at least shoot her a text, but every time I glanced at my cell phone I remembered what she had admitted to during our walk, and how she had lashed out at me later in the hospital. She was the one who owed me an apology, and she wasn't exactly burning up the phone lines delivering it.

Thunder crashed, rain pelted the windows, and I lay there feeling dizzy and disoriented and wondering why this strange soccer season was splitting me apart from the people I loved the most.

Tuesday dawned bright and sunny. I came downstairs earlier than usual, but my father had already left for work. His crew likes to start early and he's always one of the first ones on-site. I saw that he'd had cereal and coffee—his bowl and mug were in the dish rack. And he'd read the newspaper and left it behind on the table.

Then I looked closer. Side-by-side photos of my dad and me filled up half of the front page of the sports section. The headline on the feature article read: "A Tale of Two Logans." The photo of my dad was from his playing days, and he was suited up and wearing number 32. The picture of me was from our first soccer game, and next to my dad in pads I looked ten years old and as thin as a pencil.

I sat in the silent kitchen and read the article from beginning to end. It was well researched and sharply written, but I thought it belonged on the Opinion page rather than the sports section because it had such a strong point of view. It painted a picture of an out-of-control school run by a bunch of sports lunatics who were trying to impose their will on a helpless student body. It noted Fremont's many sports championships but mediocre test scores, compared the school's whopping athletic budget to the relatively small amount it spent on the library and computer center, and contrasted the high number of athletes who won league and county sports honors with the few National Merit Scholars.

Muhldinger was described as a "nonteaching audiovisual specialist" who had been catapulted into the job of principal because he was a kick-ass football coach. According to the article, there was plenty of resentment among the Fremont faculty that a man who had no claim to being a serious educator had been promoted over their heads. The article described how he'd tried to pump up the sports culture even more by requiring seniors to join a team, and how some students really hated this. According to Dianne Foster, the school's sports-crazed policies had created a unique and dangerous situation at Fremont—what she called a school divided against itself.

That was where the article stopped talking about my school and started talking about my family. My father was described as the ultimate jock to ever come out of the ultimate jock school. She listed his records, including the most yards gained by a Fremont football player in one year, the most yards gained in a career, and his best-ever time in the mile run. If he hadn't been injured in college, Dianne wrote, my dad would have gone pro. Reading his achievements in the newspaper made me a bit proud, but it also filled me with dread at what was coming.

Sure enough, the article jumped to my brothers and their own impressive sports achievements. And then it started to talk about me, and how I had never played for any Fremont team. It described in surprising detail how I had been pressured into informally trying out for football and gotten my teeth knocked out. And it told how Muhldinger had met with me in his office, offered me a place on his varsity and even tried to give me my dad's old number—and when I turned it down, he'd socked a hole in his door.

I sat there wondering which of my friends had told the *Star Dispatch* reporter these private things. Did they think they were doing me a favor by giving her inside details? Muhldinger would think I was the one who'd provided this information to the reporter, and my dad would, too. I forced myself to finish the article.

> So the son of the best athlete to ever play for
> Fremont decided to fight back and start a very
> different kind of team than the one his father
> starred on. Ironically it took a phone call from
> Tom Logan to allow that team to be birthed.
> Apparently, the legendary star of the Fremont

*football dynasty had no idea that he was
stirring up an insurrection.*

*In just a few turbulent weeks his son's team
has called into question the values of a public
school system that chooses to glorify a sport
known to cause brain damage rather than
try to improve the minds of its students.
This afternoon, when the Losers take the field,
they will find themselves in the spotlight for
a very important reason. Fremont provides
a cautionary lesson in what happens when a
school loses its way—it's now a community
with wildly clashing values, an institution
divided against itself, and most intriguingly,
a tale of two Logans.*

CARS AND SUVS WITH OUT-OF-STATE PLATES

started arriving two hours before game time. They streamed into our school's parking lot, and friendly-looking strangers wearing a colorful assortment of hats, caps, and bandannas asked where the soccer game was going to be held. There were soon several hundred people milling around the south field, not to mention five TV trucks and a small army of reporters. Apparently our school could turn away strangers from practice, but it couldn't control who came to our games, which were open to the public.

Dylan joined us in the locker room in his uniform. He wasn't going to play but he had come to lead us out onto the field. Teammates signed the plaster cast on his right arm, and the bandage on his broken nose had a big red-and-gold letter on it—not an *F* for Fremont but an *L* for Losers.

I hadn't said a word to Becca in days, but as we prepared to run out she caught my eye. "Sorry about that article this morning. I know it hurt."

"Yeah, it wasn't good."

"None of that stuff about your family came from me."

I looked back at her and shrugged. "It came from somebody."

"How'd your father take it?" she asked.

"Haven't seen him. But I'm sure he wasn't too pleased."

"Time to go," Coach Percy told us, holding his pith helmet under his arm. "There are a lot of people out there today, so it's normal to be a little nervous. As Julius Caesar said: 'No one is so brave that he is not disturbed by something unexpected.'" He paused and smiled at us, and then lowered his voice as if preparing to share a secret. "But Caesar also said: 'If you must break the law, do it to seize power. In all other cases, observe it.'"

I wasn't sure what he was telling us to do, but I now knew who had posted the video of our team, and I was beginning to suspect that in his own polite way Coach Percy was much more of a dangerous revolutionary than Shimsky.

With his strange words of encouragement ringing in our ears, we hurried down the narrow basement corridor, out the side door, onto soggy grass. As our team approached the large crowd on the south field, I spotted the cheerleaders finishing a kick routine. Beyond them, in a corner near a goal, Muhldinger and Mr. Bryce were conferring with the referee and the Maysville coach, perhaps discussing how to handle this giant crowd.

We ran past a woman news reporter taping a stand-up. I heard her say, "Here come the self-styled Fremont Losers, whose claim to be the worst soccer team in America has captured—" but the rest of her words were drowned out by a roar.

The throng of students, townspeople, and strangers had recognized us, and a cheer went up. At that moment Dylan, who was leading the way, broke into a jog but seemed to get his legs tangled up with Frank, who was following close behind. They went down onto the wet grass, and Chloe and Zirco, who were trailing, skidded into them and joined the pileup. I was in the middle of the pack and was tripped up and knocked down myself. One after another the Losers fell onto the mosh pit of flailing bodies, and I heard the woman reporter shouting to her camera operator, "Stay on it, Gus. Make sure you get that! What an entrance!"

Mud-stained but smiling, the Losers untangled themselves and we ran to our bench as the big crowd laughed and cheered. I was a little worried about Dylan's wrist, but it was in a plaster cast and apparently suffered no further damage.

The Maysville squad was already on the field, all warmed up. Coach Percy sent me right out for the coin flip. We were playing a freshman team, and their captain looked about a foot shorter than me and kept peering around nervously. "How many people are here?" he asked.

"We're expecting more than five hundred," I told him casually.

"We've never had more than a dozen," he said, and gulped. "Do cheerleaders always come to your games?"

"They've come to all our home games so far," I said truthfully.

He blinked. "Hey, I think those TV cameras are shooting us right now." He ran a hand through his hair and threw his shoulders back.

I stood up a little straighter myself.

The ref walked up, and Mr. Bryce and Muhldinger were

trailing a few feet behind him. I heard Muhldinger grunt the words "ridiculous" and "travesty" to Mr. Bryce, who shrugged as if to say: "There's nothing more to be done."

"Guys, let's hold off on the coin flip," the ref told us. "We're moving."

Seconds later we were tromping across two hundred yards of wet grass toward Gentry Field. The football team, which had been practicing there, had just gotten the message, and they didn't look too thrilled at being kicked off their home turf. They walked past us, heading the other way—to the mud of the south field. They were griping among themselves as they watched the crowd filling up the lower levels of red-and-gold bleachers.

"Hey, Cathy, are you really gonna cheer for these geeks?" a helmeted player called out to a cheerleader.

"Watch me on TV tonight," she told him with an excited smile.

I saw Dylan studying the football players as they filed past, examining their faces as if he could tell by their reactions which of them might have jumped him. Most of them, busy complaining to each other that this was ridiculous, weren't even looking at us.

Soccer goals were rolled in through the gate and set up in front of the football goal posts. Within twenty minutes the football field was limed for soccer with a center circle, penalty areas, and eight-yard boxes, and we were ready to play.

It was a very strange thing to line up as the center midfielder in the heart of Gentry Field. This was sacred ground at Fremont—even our varsity soccer team had never played here. Around me, red-and-gold bleachers seemed to climb to the clouds. I'd guess at least seven hundred people must have been getting settled on those metal benches, with more trickling in. Gentry Field had been built right over the old football field where my father had set his records, and the track that circled the field was where he'd run his mile in four minutes and seventeen seconds.

I'd been looking for my father since we first ran out and hadn't spotted him. If he wasn't there, it was the first sports event in the history of the Logan family that he'd ever missed. It felt strange to not see him—from my first T-ball game at age five, to every swim race, junior rec basketball scrimmage, and town track-and-field meet he had always been there, shaking a fist and shouting encouragement from the sideline.

The ref blew his whistle and our game was on. The Maysville freshmen seemed intimidated at playing in a big stadium in front of TV cameras. They took two quick shots in the first five minutes, but one was right at Frank's stomach—which he saved, probably because he just couldn't get out of the way—and the other hit the top of the crossbar.

Strange things started happening when Fremont touched the ball, to the delight of the boisterous crowd. A few of the odd incidents were clearly set up by our players, but most looked unplanned.

Two minutes into the game Jenks tried to head a high ball that drifted out over the Maysville sideline. Backing up and watching the ball, he tripped over their team bench, flailed his arms wildly, and fell headfirst into a gray plastic recycling bin. The poor guy got wedged inside it, and I could hear his echoing voice calling for help like a kid stuck in a cave. We had to grab him by the feet and pull him out. When he emerged into sunlight he raised his hands over his head as if he had survived something horrible, and the crowd gave him an ovation.

Ten minutes into the game the ball was kicked out of bounds near our sideline. I guess somebody on our bench switched it for a ball that had been doctored, because when Shimsky threw it in to Pierre and the big guy stomped on it, he put his foot right through it. Pierre spun around with his foot inside the soccer ball while the crowd laughed and the TV cameras rolled. The sour-faced old ref stopped play, pried it off, and brought in a new ball that he checked himself. He gave Pierre a yellow card and scolded us all: "Whatever you guys are doing, knock it off. This isn't a comedy routine." But he was wrong—the big crowd was eating it up.

Maysville scored a nice goal ten minutes in. A few minutes later Zirco scored on our own goal when he tried to clear a ball out of danger, lost his balance, and miskicked it. The ball caromed off Frank's forehead into our goal as Frank staggered back like he'd been shot by a mortar. He got both his arms tangled in the mesh and flailed in front of the cameras like a giant squid caught in a net.

But then a freaky thing happened—we started playing the Maysville freshmen evenly. Half an hour into the game the score was still just two to nothing, and we were very much in the game, mostly because of me. I've never felt faster than I did that day. Maybe it was the article in the *Star Dispatch*, or playing on Gentry Field, or the knowledge that TV cameras might film me and my dad might see it. For whatever reason, I was flying around that turf field.

With five minutes left in the half their right wing dribbled by Becca, nutmegged Chloe, and had an open path to our goal. He angled in toward Frank, ready to score their third goal, but I raced back and made up about thirty yards. Just as he drew his right leg back to kick the goal I took the ball away from him.

I sped straight up the left side of the field and no one challenged me. I had distributed so many passes that the Maysville players kept expecting me to give it to one of my teammates. Instead I held the ball and crossed midfield. Pierre was wide open on my left, but I had already given him half a dozen passes that he had muffed. So when the Maysville midfielder stepped up to challenge me I tried a move I had seen on TV. I faked the pass to Pierre with my right foot, stepped clear over the ball, and pushed it with my left in the other direction. Before their midfielder could adjust I was racing past him, deeper into Maysville territory.

Their tough right fullback didn't mess around—he went for a sliding tackle. He had already taken down two of our players with that move, but I saw him leave his feet and scooped the ball over him. Then I hurtled above his outstretched legs.

Now only two defenders stood between me and their goalie—their sweeper and stopper looked determined to block me. They were standing in front of their penalty area, five feet apart. I knew I couldn't dribble around both of them, so I kicked the ball between them and tried to split them and accelerate onto it. Their goalie came out with his arms spread wide, but I put on a burst of speed, squeezed between the two defenders, and toe-poked the ball just before the goalie slammed into me. The impact knocked me flat, and I watched from the turf as the ball slowly rolled into their goal.

Normally when someone scores a nice goal on a solo run there's a roar of approval from the fans, but as I got up from the turf I heard only scattered applause. I figured that most of the people had come a long way to see us lose, so they weren't sure how to react to seeing us fight back and score a goal.

The ref soon blew his whistle for halftime. I jogged to our bench, and Frank was the first to unload on me. "Jack, what the hell do you think you're doing?"

I looked back at him. "What do you mean?"

"You're making us look bad," he said. "By making us look good."

"I'm just playing soccer," I said.

"Well maybe you should have gone out for varsity," Pierre told me.

That got me angry. "Look, I started this team," I told him.

"It belongs to all of us," Chloe Shin replied. "And this is our big day."

"Yeah, we were going to dedicate today's loss to Dylan," Meg reminded me. "Instead we got this!" And she nodded to the giant digital scoreboard overhead. The jumbo LED display was replaying my goal. There I was on the big screen weaving through Maysville traffic and out-hustling their goalie. "Maybe we'll even win," she said. "Wouldn't that be something?"

"Chill out," I told them all. "We're not gonna win. One goal is no big deal."

"Ego, ego, ego," Shimsky chanted back mockingly.

I actually felt my fists clench. "Shut up," I told him.

Becca stepped between us. "Let's all chill."

But several of my other teammates took up the chant. "Ego, ego, ego." I saw Frank mouthing the words, and even Dylan picked it up, looking right at me.

I turned and walked away from the team and stood by myself with my hands on my hips. I was tempted to walk out of Gentry Field and let them stink it up as badly as they wanted to.

Percy walked over to me. "Remarkable goal."

"Take me out of the game," I requested.

"Absolutely not," he said. "You're our best player."

"I don't want to be."

"You're doing what you should be doing," he told me. "As Shakespeare said: 'To thine own self be true.' We all have to act out our own part."

"Well, I'm not much of an actor," I replied, "unlike some people." He gave me a piercing look and walked back to the bench, and I stood there alone and tried to cool off.

On the field, the cheerleaders were wrapping up their big routine. One by one they were chanting for members of our team. Since they didn't know our names, I saw them glancing at cheat sheets. "Zirco, Zirco, he's our man," a willowy blonde shouted. "If he can't do it, Shimsky can." She cart-wheeled away, and a brunette ran forward. "Shimsky, Shimsky, he's our man, if he can't do it, Shin can."

I looked around the stadium, and the faces and shouts seemed to swirl. I imagined my father at eighteen, finishing his glorious mile and roaring down the final straight-away, taller and faster than everyone around him. And somehow that morphed to Arthur Gentry finishing his own final lap and sinking down onto his knees. I wondered what he had thought about in his last seconds, besides the pain and the fear. Had he regretted just going for it? Had he died feeling like a damned fool?

"Shin, Shin, she's our girl, if she can't do it, Logan can," a brunette cheerleader chanted.

The ref blew his whistle—halftime was over. I jogged back to join the Losers for the second half.

"Hey, buddy, I was just having some fun with you," Frank said.

"Yeah, we didn't mean anything," Dylan seconded, but I didn't say anything back.

They needn't have worried about us winning. In the sec-ond half Maysville started playing strong soccer, and the Losers lived up to their name. Our defense came apart and shot after shot whistled through Frank's legs or rock-eted between his arms. The goals mounted up against us, and the laughs from the bleachers came faster and louder.

Pierre's shorts fell to his knees but he somehow kept playing—to the delight of the roaring crowd—before his shorts fell to his ankles and tripped him up so that he fell flat on his face.

"Losers, losers, losers forever," our fans chanted. I saw Muhldinger and Mr. Bryce standing together, and they didn't look very happy at how their football chant was being mangled.

The strangest moment of the second half came when Chloe and Zirco smacked into each other in one of their defensive collisions near the top of our penalty box. Somehow when they fell to the ground her braces got snagged on the elastic of his shorts so that it looked like she was following him around. Zirco kept stepping away from her, flapping his arms like a bird trying to take off, while she followed closely behind him, pulled along by the elastic. The crowd roared and I saw hundreds of cell phones filming it. Even the ref couldn't help smiling as he whistled play dead so that we could get Chloe "unhinged."

True to his promise, with five minutes to go Pierre sank to his knees and vomited on the sacred turf of Gentry Field.

When the second half was finally over the score stood at eleven to one and the big crowd had gotten plenty of laughs. "Losers, losers, losers," they chanted, and I saw some of them holding up signs for the TV cameras:

I STILL HATE MY GYM TEACHER

FOOTBALL KILLS BRAIN CELLS!

We shook hands with the Maysville players, and then most of my teammates stayed together near midfield as fans came over and reporters tried to get interviews.

I walked off alone. I heard Becca calling my name, but I ignored her and started to jog away. Suddenly a well-dressed woman stood in my path.

"Beautiful goal today, Jack," she said. "I know you don't

like to talk to reporters, but my name is Dianne Foster and I wondered if you had any reaction to my article this morning."

My parents brought me up to never be rude to adults, but I looked her in the eye and heard myself say, "Yes. Go to hell."

28

I DROPPED MY MUDDY CLEATS ON THE FRONT
porch, slipped into our house, and heard my dad talking on
the phone in the kitchen.

"Hey, Jack," he called, "get in here a minute." He hadn't
said a word to me in four days, so I was a little surprised
and headed right in. He was sitting at the counter, the
phone in his hand. "How'd the game go?"

"We got massacred," I told him.

"And you?"

"I played okay."

"Sorry I wasn't there to see it," he said. "Work."

"I figured."

"There's a man on the phone who wants to talk to you."
He held out the receiver.

"It's just a reporter," I said, and suddenly there was
plenty of anger in my voice. "I don't talk to them, and just
so you know, I never have. Tell him not to bother us anymore and hang up."

My father looked back at me, a little surprised. "It's not
a reporter. His name is Jan and I think you might want to
talk to him."

"I don't know anyone named Jan. What does he want?"

Dad gave me a strange little smile and again offered me

the phone. Given how cold things had been between us lately, I couldn't figure out the reason for that smile, but it looked to me like my dad was proud of something. I took the receiver. "Hi, this is Jack Logan."

"Jan Brent," a man's voice said. He had a slight European accent, maybe German or Dutch. "Great goal today."

"Thanks," I told him. "I got lucky."

"I wouldn't call it luck," he said. "You took them on and ran through them. Your father says you can run a hundred meters in under eleven seconds."

"That's unofficial," I told him. "I haven't been timed in years. What's this about, anyway?"

"Jack, I coach a soccer team in Warren."

Warren is a large town about ten miles from Fremont.

"A youth travel team?" I guessed.

"We have youth teams, but I run the club's men's team," he said. "We're pretty strong, but we've aged a bit and we lack speed up top. Our fastest striker just tore his meniscus. We need someone young to replace him, who can make runs like the one you made today."

"I'm flattered," I said, "but I never played organized soccer before a month ago."

There was a moment of silence. "That's a little hard to believe," the voice said. "I saw that run you put together in that first YouTube video. And you pulled off a pretty fancy move today to set up your goal. Where did you learn to step over the ball like that?"

"I've got two older brothers who are much bigger than I am," I told him. "I had to learn to dodge them or I'd get crushed."

Jan laughed. "That's a very unorthodox soccer training method but it seems to have worked. Jack, I've seen you shoot with your right foot. How's your left?"

"Not real good."

"We practice early on Saturdays. I gave your father the information. No guarantees, but would you like to work out with our team?"

I hesitated and glanced at my father, who was looking back at me. "Okay," I said. "I guess I'll try it once. Thanks."

I clicked off the phone and Dad raised his eyebrows. "You've been playing this sport for a month and men's teams are calling you up to join?"

"It's just a tryout. They had an injury and they need someone fast. They're probably calling every soccer player in the county."

"It's pretty damn impressive, is what it is," Dad said, and this time he didn't hide his pride. "Especially for the Logan who doesn't like sports."

I couldn't tell from his face if he was angry or just teasing me. "Look, I'm sorry about that article. They should have left you out of this. I want you to know I never said a word to that reporter."

"I had some stories written about me back in the day that I didn't appreciate," Dad told me with a nod of understanding. "But I haven't had my picture in the sports section in a long time. The guys I work with got a kick out of it, and so did I. Especially today."

"What happened today?" I asked.

"Nothing I didn't expect. Want to take a ride?"

Five minutes later I was in his truck, headed out of town

at ten miles over the speed limit. He switched on a sports radio talk show, and three baseball experts dissected the Yankees' playoff chances. I listened for a while, and then zoned out and just looked out the window.

He drove to Highland Lake, a mountain lake near Fremont. Dad had been going there for years to fish, and I knew he'd helped build several of the luxury houses on the north shore. He pulled his truck over to the side of a dirt road near a beach, and we both got out. "Let's take a walk," he said.

The banks were spongy from all the recent rain. The day had been sunny and hot but it was clouding over now and starting to get a little chilly. A late afternoon breeze rustled the scrub bushes on shore and stirred the lake's surface. We passed a secluded cove where lily pads rippled as they rode the waves. Wild rosemary with small lilac flowers sweetened the air.

"Nice spot," I said.

"I always liked it," Dad told me. "My father used to bring me here to fish. I caught my first lunker bass where those lily pads are. I was eight years old and it was a toss-up whether I pulled it out or the bass pulled me in."

"You still come here a lot?" I asked.

"Helps me relax. See that blue house? We did a total knockdown rebuild on it—ripped down an old wooden wreck on a big view lot and put up that new one that's easily worth more than a million."

"It's pretty sweet," I said.

"Yeah, when I worked on it I used to eat my lunch up on the roof. You can see the whole lake from up there."

I imagined him sitting alone on the roof of a nearly finished lake mansion, eating his ham and cheese sandwich, sipping from his thermos, and looking out at the million-dollar view.

"Check out that white one, with the observation tower," he said, pointing with a finger. "That's my favorite. Been here since I was a kid. It's still the only one with a pool."

I heard something in his voice that I couldn't identify, but I knew we were getting close to talking about something private and powerful that meant a lot to him. I figured it was why he had brought me here, and I didn't want to rush him. "I don't see why they need a pool if their house looks out on a lake."

"They don't need it," Dad agreed. "But it wouldn't be a bad thing to have, just for a little evening dip."

"Sure, why not," I agreed carefully, studying his face.

Dad bent and picked up a rock and threw it far out over the dark water. "I was going to buy that house," he told me, watching the rock land.

"What?" I asked. And then, "When?" I was smart enough not to ask how.

"I used to come here when I was in college and I was working my butt off to make myself into pro material. In those days top draft picks wouldn't get nearly as much as they do now, but if you went in the first round you could easily sign for a million or more. I used to swim across the lake to that house and stand in the sand in about three feet of water and check it out close up. They had parties almost every weekend, and I could hear the music. I felt like a spy, but I knew what I wanted."

I didn't have a clue what to say, so I just kept silent.

"If it had worked out, you would have grown up there," he went on. "Your brothers would've played football on that lawn. Mom would've read her books while sunbathing by the lake." He said the words as if he had thought them a thousand times.

"I like the house we live in now," I told him.

"Sure," he said, still gazing across at the white lake house. "Funny thing is I almost bought it, and now I can't even work on it."

"You got fired today?"

"They don't like to use that word. Nothing personal. Just tough times. Thanks for twenty-three years."

"You'll get another job," I told him. "You're great at what you do."

"It will probably work out in the long run. I've put in calls to lots of guys I've worked with over the years. The problem is nobody's hiring right now. But these things go in cycles, so . . ." He stopped talking and his hands clenched into fists. If there had been anything nearby to punch I think my dad would have demolished it, but we were standing on a grassy bank and there wasn't even a nearby tree for him to hit. So he just stood there helplessly with his fists hanging down at his sides.

"I'm sorry," I told him after a while.

He shrugged his big shoulders. "Life is funny, but I never thought I'd be out of work." And then: "Feel like a swim?"

"I didn't bring a suit."

In a second he was in his boxers wading out into

Highland Lake. I stripped down and followed him. The water was cold, and when I dove in, it was a shock to my system. Then I got used to it and even started to enjoy it. Dad was a strong swimmer, and I think he got some of his aggression out by racing me across that cold mountain lake. I stayed right with him, and we ended up standing side by side on the sand about thirty feet from the white house.

It took me a while to catch my breath. "If they see us out here they might call the police," I said.

"It's not a crime to be swimming in a lake," he noted.

I took a few more breaths. "It's not so nice up close," I finally told him. "It's too much. I really do like our house better."

"Maybe you're right," Dad said. "It's probably hell to keep clean." His eyes moved over the lakefront mansion with its pool and observation tower and big windows facing out on the lake. "It's a strange thing that a man can make a million dollars a year running with a football around a grassy field, but he can't save that much money in twenty-three years working ten-hour days building homes. Your mother told me she let you know how I busted up my knee."

"Yeah, she did."

A few seconds passed. "Was that the dumbest thing you ever heard?" he asked.

"No," I told him. "The dumbest thing I ever heard is that she almost married Muhldinger."

My father grinned. "She dated him but I don't think she ever would have married the guy."

"Stuff happens you can't predict," I said.

"That's for sure," Dad agreed, and we were quiet as the breeze kicked up and small waves splashed us. "I think I tried every sport with you. Swimming. Track. Baseball. Football. Basketball. You really sucked at basketball."

"Thank you," I said. "I appreciate the honesty."

"Who ever thought I would have a soccer player for a son?"

"We also didn't try volleyball," I pointed out. "I might be good at that."

"To hell with volleyball. You're a soccer player. It makes perfect sense. You've always had speed and balance. You just never had any hand-eye."

"I'm getting cold," I told him. "We've gotta swim back soon or I'm gonna turn into an ice cube."

"Cold water's good for you," he said. "Listen, I don't know anything about soccer but I'm proud you're gonna give this men's team a try."

"It probably won't come to anything."

"You gotta grab your opportunities while you can," he told me, casting one last long look at the white house. Then he finally turned to face me. "It's a harder world than you know, Jack." His voice thickened. "Senior year is one foot out the door. You're the last of my sons. Gonna be a big change for everyone." He broke off, took a quick breath, and said, "Sorry I pushed you the other night, son."

"We pushed each other," I told him. "Maybe it was for the best."

"How do you figure?" he asked.

"If it didn't happen, we wouldn't have gotten to freeze together in this lake."

"Good point," he admitted. We stood for a long minute more, looking at each other as the numbing lake waves slapped us. Then he said, "Cold water's good for you, but I can't feel my feet. Let's go home."

I WAS IN CHEM LAB WITH ROB POWERS,
trying to make a battery out of two lemons connected to
zinc and copper electrodes. We'd plugged the electrodes
into a digital clock, but so far the only juice we were pro-
ducing was lemon juice. Rob's ribs were healing fast, and
he kept bugging me about joining the soccer team. "Why
haven't you at least asked them?"

"Because I know they won't go for it," I told him.

"I'm not good enough?"

"You're too good. You're one of the best athletes at this
school. They don't even want me on the team."

"That's ridiculous," he said. "Tell them I've never played
soccer before in my life and I'll probably suck worse than
they do. I'm not doing this to win the World Cup. I just want
to have some fun."

"How come our battery doesn't work?" I asked.

"I don't know," he admitted. "You must've plugged the
electrodes into the wrong part of the lemon."

"That's ridiculous," I told him. "You must've bought
the wrong kind of lemons."

Suddenly flashers turned our school's parking lot blue
and red, and three police cars sped up and made their own

spaces right by the front entrance. Half a dozen cops piled out and I saw Police Chief Duggan leading the charge.

"What's this about?" I asked Rob.

"Don't have a clue."

Ten minutes later the same six cops emerged from our school with two students in handcuffs. Everyone in the lab left their experiments and stood silently at the window. One of the handcuffed students was a backup lineman on our football team named Davis. He was clearly scared and looked like he might burst into tears. The other was the co-captain of the Lions and starting running back, Barlow. His face held no fear at all—it was just hard and angry. For a moment he seemed to glare right at me, and I remembered when he had knocked me flat at Founders' Park, and how it had tasted to have blood and teeth washing around inside my mouth. The cops pushed down their heads, loaded the two of them into the back of a cruiser, and sped away.

By the time we changed periods fifteen minutes later, the school was buzzing with news. A third football player, Lowry, had been arrested earlier that morning, at his home. Everyone figured he must have given the police the names of Davis and Barlow. The two of them had been in study hall in the cafeteria when the cops had marched in, yanked them out of their chairs, announced that they were being charged with assault, and read them their rights.

I wasn't completely surprised when seventh-period classes were canceled and we were led to the gym for an unscheduled assembly. We were seated by grade, with the seniors at the front. I hadn't exchanged more than a few words with Frank, Dylan, or Becca in the two days since the Maysville game, but Dylan was seated in front of me. His black eye and the bruises on his face were healing fast but his wrist was still in a cast. He was looking around the gym nervously, as if he couldn't quite believe that his beating had triggered this chain of events.

"Hey, Jack, what do you think's going on here?"

"It's not a pep rally," I told him.

He nodded. "Becca was right. She kept saying it was guys from the football team."

"I'm glad they caught them. How's your wrist?"

"It just itches a lot. Can't wait to get this cast off. Listen, after practice today we're all getting together in my basement."

"Thanks, but I have to head home," I told him.

"Come on," he urged. "If Frank and I pissed you off at the soccer game, I'm sorry. I apologize. You can't hold a grudge against your two best friends."

"Why not?" I asked, remembering how they'd looked into my eyes and chanted "Ego, ego, ego" with the rest of the team.

"Because I bought two giant bags of your favorite barbecued potato chips for the team meeting and if you don't come Frank will eat them all."

Before I could respond to that, the auditorium quieted as Muhldinger walked to the mic. At the rally when they'd retired my dad's number he'd seemed completely at ease and in control, but this afternoon he looked uncomfortable. Police Chief Duggan, the assistant principal, and several school board members sat behind him—I saw Mr. Bryce watching carefully.

"Hey, everyone," Muhldinger began with a friendly smile. "As a lot of you know, there was some police activity at our school this morning. First, I'd like to assure all of you that our school is completely safe."

"The hell it is," somebody called out from a few rows behind me.

I thought I recognized the voice. Could it have been Shimsky? I twisted around to look, but everyone was shifting and craning their necks so it was impossible to tell who had shouted.

Muhldinger broke off and stared hard at the crowd as if he, too, was trying to figure out who had just challenged him. He took a breath and tried to act as if nothing had happened. "For the next few days, just to reassure everyone, we're going to have a couple of policemen at our school. They'll be in front when you come in, and walking the halls, and just making sure that everything stays calm. We're a family and we're going to pull together and be just fine, but it's good to be extra careful. I'd like to thank Police Chief Duggan for helping us out."

Duggan raised a hand as if to let us know that his men were at our service.

Muhldinger took a sip of water and continued. "Now, it's not appropriate for me to comment on legal matters that haven't been decided yet," he said. "This is of course a serious matter. Some of the students involved are on my team, and they're fine young men, but . . ."

Scattered boos and hisses sounded. They weren't loud

and it wasn't as if the whole crowd was turning against him, but they caused Muhldinger to break off again and blink. He planted his hands on the podium in front of him, with his big arms angled to either side. It looked like he was anchoring himself, and I realized, with a shock—no, he's not just nervous and angry, he's also scared. He couldn't seem to figure out what to say next, and seconds dragged by.

I noticed Mr. Bryce watching closely, as if he was taking the pulse of the whole situation. The boos and hisses ended, and the gym fell eerily silent.

"The point is," Muhldinger finally went on, "what's important is that we are a family. And in a family there can be no room for cruelty or violence to any family member. I want to make it very clear that we simply will not put up with bullying or intimidation at Fremont High. I have no tolerance for it. Zero." He thumped the podium with a big fist for emphasis, and lots of people clapped.

He should have quit right there. He could have cut his speech short and used the applause to turn the mic over to the assistant principal or Mr. Bryce, or just let us go back to our classes. If he'd sat down with that loud "Zero" as his last word on the subject he would have been fine.

But Muhldinger glanced up at the American flag and the dozens of championship pennants hanging down from the rafters, and they seemed to inspire him to keep talking. He lowered his gaze back to us. "Some have suggested that there is a culture of bullying at our school, and that it's linked to our long sports traditions." He gave a little smirk. "Sure, we've won our share of championships and we're rightly proud of them." It was as if he kind of knew better but he still couldn't stop himself from slipping into his pep rally speech. "They're part of who we are. That doesn't mean we're not also a respectful and tolerant school. And that's exactly why we're going to pull together as a family and defeat Lynton tomorrow, and I hope all of you will make the trip to the game and come support our Lions . . ."

This time the boos and hisses that interrupted him were noticeably louder, and I even heard mocking laughter. One voice called out loudly: "Give it a rest, Muhldinger!"

Other students clapped for him, and a girl I recognized as a varsity cheerleader stood and yelled: "Go Lions! Fremont forever."

Muhldinger couldn't continue over the noise so he just stood there with his big arms on either side of the podium, as if he were trying to wrestle something unexpectedly tough back into a box. No question about it—he definitely looked scared.

Dylan turned to me and asked, "Can you believe this?"

30

DYLAN OPENED THE DOOR TO HIS BASEMENT
and flashed me a grin. "Was it the barbecued potato chips
or did you miss us?"

"The chips," I told him, looking around. "This place is
becoming party central."

At our first team party everyone had looked restrained
and a little uncomfortable, but now they were letting it all
hang out. Heavy metal was thrashing from the speakers—
I was pretty sure Shimsky must've chosen it. He was standing at the foosball table with Chloe, beating up on Pierre
and Becca. I watched our revolutionary and our ace statistician work the foosball back and forth between offense and
defense, and suddenly rip in goals. They gave each other
flying high fives when they scored, and while they seemed
to me like an unlikely couple, maybe Muhldinger was right
and there was something going on between them.

Becca was concentrating on trying to defend against
Shimsky and didn't see me come in. Or maybe she was just
ignoring me. We hadn't exchanged a word or a text since
the Maysville game. I couldn't help noticing that she was
wearing tan shorts and a red V-necked top—the same
outfit she had worn on our first date. She looked great, even
though she was getting annihilated at foosball.

This wasn't easy music to dance to, but Zirco didn't care. He danced too close to the Ping-Pong table and almost collided with Jenks, who was in a heated match with Frank. As I watched, Jenks tried to slam the ball and let go of his paddle, which clipped Zirco on the side of the head, knocking him over the black leather couch. He got up, rubbing his scalp, and went right on dancing.

It was pure Losers mayhem, but everyone was having a good time. Dylan's mother carried a pitcher of lemonade down the steps and I saw her smiling at her son, who had his right arm thrown carelessly around Meg's back. My friend had lost his shyness in record time, and looked very comfortable in his new roles as boyfriend and host.

A hand touched my shoulder. "Good to see you, Jack." Coach Percy hadn't come to our first soccer team party, but he was at this team meeting—or whatever it was—dressed fairly normally for him in jeans, a white shirt, and a blue jacket.

"Good to see you, too," I said. "Strange day at school. Muhldinger could have used your quote."

"Which one?" he asked.

"The one from Caesar about how no one is so brave that he is not disturbed by something unexpected. Our fearless principal looked a little off his game."

"It wasn't his best day," Coach Percy agreed with a smile. "American schools are turning out to be more dramatic than I thought." We were alone for a moment and he lowered his voice. "Jack, at halftime in the Maysville game, you mentioned that you aren't much of an actor—unlike some people. Were you referring to anyone specific?"

I looked back at him. "I just think people should be straight with each other."

"I agree," he said. "If you ever want to talk about this further, let's have a chat just between the two of us."

"Fine," I said. "But I think Dylan is calling this meeting to order."

Our host was banging a Ping-Pong paddle on the table.

We gathered around. "I got a call a little while ago from Chief Duggan. They connected Lowry to the beating 'cause they searched the Stevens and found his shoe prints in the mud. The goon wears size fifteens."

"Done in by canoe feet," Frank called out, and people laughed.

"They brought Lowry to the station and put a scare into him, and it wasn't long before he cracked and gave them Davis and Barlow. Lowry told them exactly how it all went down, and who did what. They're going to charge all three of them as adults with aggravated assault, which is a felony."

There was applause, but no more laughter. I guess everyone understood that there was nothing funny about the word "felony." "Was it really serious enough to be 'aggravated'?" Chloe asked.

"They broke his wrist," Meg said protectively.

Dylan gave her a smile. "Because of the seriousness of my injuries and because three ganged up on one, they think they can make the felony charges stick. Chief Duggan told me not to talk about the legal stuff with the press"— he broke off for a moment and glanced at his mom—"and I won't. But he didn't say anything about talking to my friends. And I don't think the Losers should let themselves be gagged. Especially not when we have the forces of darkness on the run."

There were shouts of "They're going down!" and "Muhldinger for janitor!"

"A word of caution," Percy cut in. "This school has been run by certain . . . elements in the same way for many years. It would be a mistake to think they won't strike back."

"Every revolution has its counterrevolution," Shimsky chimed in ominously.

"That's exactly why we shouldn't back off or be afraid," Becca said. "We should all go to the football game tomorrow and sit as a team, wearing our soccer shirts. Let's make a statement."

"Yeah," Meg agreed. "Losers for Lynton!"

Lynton was the town the Lions were playing tomorrow. They were competitive with us in basketball and baseball, but when it came to football we always beat the crap out of them. I guess they were willing to take their lumps on the gridiron, because I'd seen us dish out some pretty ugly thrashings and they kept coming back for more, year after year.

I spoke up: "We can go and sit together but I don't think we should cheer for Lynton."

"Why not?" Meg asked.

"Because we go to Fremont."

"So we should cheer for the people who broke Dylan's wrist?" Meg demanded.

"The three guys who did that have been arrested," I

reminded her. "We can't keep whipping this up." I looked around at Frank, Dylan, and Becca, and I could tell they didn't agree with me, but they held their tongues.

Coach Percy walked next to me. "I happen to agree with Jack. You should listen to what he's saying."

"Making this bigger and angrier and more violent won't help anyone," I said. "Dylan got hurt, three guys were arrested, and that's enough."

"It won't be enough for Muhldinger," Pierre called out. "He likes dishing out pain."

"You really want to get him?" I asked. "I have a way."

They all waited.

"Most of you know Rob Powers. The backup quarterback."

"Meathead," Shimsky called out.

"Misogynist," Becca added.

"I don't even know what that is," I admitted. "But I've known him for years and he might've gotten a meaty head from being on the football team, but deep down he's a good guy. Muhldinger's always had it in for him, and Rob hates Muhldinger as much as anyone in this room. He wants to join our team."

I could tell from their faces they didn't like the idea. Chloe said loudly, "We don't need anybody else. Especially a football player."

"We've never turned anyone away," I pointed out. "One of the best things about the Losers is we've had an open door. I don't see how you can slam it on Rob just 'cause he's a good athlete." I paused and added, "And if you want to push things without violence—this is a great way. I know

Muhldinger, and if his backup quarterback quits to join us, that will piss him off more than anything else you could do."

They put it to a team vote, and to my surprise it narrowly passed. I got the feeling most of them didn't want Rob on their team, but my friends knew they had treated me badly and owed me one.

I ate a last handful of chips and was on my way out when Becca appeared right in front of me. "Leaving without saying goodbye?"

"You didn't say hello when I walked in."

"I didn't see you walk in," she said.

"You weren't exactly looking."

We stood there glaring at each other. I wanted to turn my back on her and walk out of the basement, but I also wanted to grab her and kiss her. "So what's a misogynist?" I asked.

She gave me a little smile. "Don't play dumb."

"I just don't study vocab words all the time."

"It's someone who hates women."

"Are you kidding? Rob has more girlfriends than anyone at this school."

"And look at the way he treats them," she pointed out.

"They seem to like it."

"It's a technique some guys use to take advantage of girls with low self-esteem," Becca explained. "Sometimes girls don't know what they want. But that doesn't mean he's not a jerk. C'mere."

There was a back room in Dylan's basement, really just a giant closet, filled with the water heater and the electricals for the house. Becca drew me into it and pulled the door closed. The little room was hot and stuffy, and when the door was shut the only light was from a partially blocked window and the illuminated dials on the machines.

"You were right about my college essay," Becca admitted. "In fact you were so right that you made me feel guilty. I owe you an apology."

"So you are writing about the Losers?"

She nodded. "My college essay is now called 'Revolution and Counterrevolution at Fremont High.'"

"It sounds a little more impressive than 'Knight and Shadow,'" I told her. "Not that I have anything against your horse."

"To get into Stanford or one of the top Ivies you need a story, and I think I've found mine."

"You definitely have. Just don't start a civil war and burn our school down to impress the admissions people."

"I don't think that will be necessary," she said. "But, Jack, I didn't know that any of this would happen when we were floating on our backs on Hidden Lake and I first mentioned joining the team."

"You were so nervous that day about asking me out for a date that you couldn't have been thinking about anything else," I told her.

"Don't flatter yourself," she said. "Seriously, it's also not why I talked to that reporter from the *Star Dispatch* about our team. I don't want you to think I'm super calculating and that I'd been planning this all along, or that I used your family and your father—" She broke off. "'Cause I swear I didn't. It all just sort of happened."

"Okay, I believe you," I said. "My dad and I had a talk the other day and things are better between us."

"I'm glad," Becca said. "Things are a little better with my father, too. I had lunch with him and he was really trying not to be a jerk. He's full speed ahead with the divorce, but he's making it as painless as possible. He's giving my mom the house and the car, and pretty much everything she wants. It's uncontested, and moving ahead at record speed."

"Well, isn't that good?" I asked. "At least it's not a bitter fight."

"I suppose." She nodded. "Except that it makes me feel strange. Doesn't he have any feelings for our house where I grew up? It's like he's trying to escape from everything we shared. Part of me wishes that it was a little more contested. And he wants me to meet his new *friend*, Emily." Becca fell silent for several seconds. "At lunch he kept stressing the word 'painless,' as if he was going to inject us all with Novocain, like one of his patients. But maybe you're right and painless is better than the alternative."

"I preferred painless when they were gluing my teeth back together."

"I know you don't like dentists," she said with a little smile. "And I also know how much you care about your old friends. I said some stuff at the hospital I regret."

"Me too," I told her. "And you were absolutely right that it was guys on the football team who beat up Dylan."

"Actually, you were the one who said it first. So you were right."

There was a machine in the little room that suddenly made a *thwump-thwump* sound, like a racing heartbeat. I looked into Becca's hazel eyes and waited for it to finish thumping, but it kept going and even seemed to speed up. "Is there anything else we need to apologize to each other about?" I finally asked.

"I don't think so," she said. It was hard to tell in the low light, but I thought she'd started blushing. "I missed you," she whispered. "A lot."

"Me too."

"Really?" she asked. "That's a little hard to believe. Because you couldn't say you loved me. And you've been completely ignoring me."

"I wasn't ignoring you, I was pissed off at you," I told her. "But I guess I couldn't have gotten so angry if I didn't care about you so much."

No, she wasn't blushing. It was something else. Her eyes glowed.

Becca stepped toward me and I put my arms around her, and then the electrical room suddenly got a lot hotter.

31

THERE WERE FIFTEEN OF US NOW—ROB
Powers had wasted no time in letting Muhldinger know
he was leaving the Lions for the Losers. "I told him in his
office before first period. His face turned so red I thought
he might explode," Rob told me almost proudly. "He kept
repeating: 'You'll regret this, Powers. Your father will
be ashamed of you. I guarantee you'll regret this.' But the
only thing I regret is that I didn't do it long ago. I hate
that son of a bitch and I'm glad I'm not down in that pit.
Now, where's that bag of chips?"

We were sitting together, all wearing our home soccer
jerseys. Instead of a tailgate party we had brought lots of
snacks. The Lynton Mud Pit, as it was known in Fremont,
was much smaller than Gentry Field, so we had a good view
of the marching band playing "Fremont Forever" while the
cheerleaders built a three-story pyramid. Several thousand
Lions fans had made the short trip, and they sang as if in
one voice: "Fremont High will rise to the sky, to be number one."

I picked out my dad ten rows down, standing with his
old high school cronies, including Rob Powers's father. I
wondered if Muhldinger was right about Rob's father being
ashamed, or if our principal's threats were now all empty.

On the field, the Lions were fired up and ready for battle. They circled around Muhldinger, who thumped a playbook the way a preacher pounds a Bible. He was going over last-minute strategy, but I could tell he was also ordering them to keep their heads in the game. Three of their teammates had been arrested, and their backup quarterback was watching from the stands.

Not that any of it mattered, because the Lynton Foxes were outnumbered and too small to put up much of a fight. There were more than sixty Lions on our sideline, and when they broke the circle with a loud cheer they looked like red-and-gold giants. Across from them stood thirty or so maroon-and-white Lynton Foxes, and when they ran out onto the field, they looked pint-sized. Their kick returner, who waited alone in the end zone, couldn't have been more than five-five. He was going to get stomped on, and the Foxes were going to be buried in their own mud pit, as usual.

The short Lynton returner caught our towering kickoff deep in his end zone. I thought for sure he would down the ball and take it at the twenty, but he never gave it a thought. Instead, he ran it out—straight up the center of the field—and the little guy was a maroon-and-white blur against the green grass and brown mud. The home crowd roared as his blockers formed a flying wedge to protect him. At the fifteen a ferocious red-and-gold wave smashed into the Lynton wedge and dissolved it.

But the kick returner wasn't hiding behind the wedge any longer. He had danced sideways, and he was so short and moved so fast that the Fremont tacklers hadn't picked up his cut. By the time they gave chase the Lynton speed-ster was streaking down the right sideline with only the kicker to beat. He gave our kicker an inside fake and darted by him. It was a footrace to the end zone, and our fastest guys couldn't catch him. Their kick returner high-stepped over the end line like he was seven feet tall and raised his arms, and the Lynton fans let him know just how sweet it was to draw first blood after decades of being blasted by Fremont.

Next to me on the bench, Rob whispered, "Holy God. That's a hundred-and-five-yard runback!"

It's a dangerous thing to give the home crowd of an un-derdog team some hope. I could almost feel the Lynton fans begin to rally behind their Foxes and start to believe that maybe, just possibly, this might be their day.

Fremont tried to shrug it off. Our band played, our cheerleaders twirled, and the Fremont faithful chanted: "Fremont number one. State champs, state champs. Bury Lynton in their pit." But their defense stopped us at mid-field, and we had to punt it away. Down they came in half a dozen plays, and their short runner made a slick out-side move, took it around the end of our line, and dove right through the legs of the last defender to score again. Almost before we knew what was happening it was four-teen to zilch.

Good football teams respond to falling behind by getting physical. Fremont had been trained for this moment by practicing line drills, hitting the tackling sled, and power-lifting in the weight room. We didn't need big plays—we needed to assert ourselves and start pushing them around.

Whatever Muhldinger said about how we didn't have a culture of bullying at Fremont, when it came to football that was definitely our style. The Lions tried to take over the line, stuff their runners, and grind out yards on the ground. But Barlow's replacement fumbled deep in Lynton territory, and their quarterback uncorked the longest pass of his life to their tallest receiver, who somehow caught it and ran it in. Fifteen rows of Fremont fans fell silent, and Becca whispered to me, "They're going to lose to Lynton."

"Can't happen," I told her. "Not Lynton."

"Lynton," she said. "They're spooked."

"She's right," Rob Powers agreed from my other side. "They're toast. They just don't know it yet."

It was twenty-eight to three at halftime, and I kind of wondered what Muhldinger was saying to the Lions in the locker room. He had fired them up for a comeback against Smithfield, and I was sure he was screaming and punching the walls. If Lynton could score twenty-eight points in a half, then in theory Fremont also could—especially since we were projected to be state champs and the Foxes always finished near the bottom of our league.

My teammates passed chips and pretzels around during halftime. Most of the Fremont fans were sitting in silent shock, and I was a little worried about how obvious it was that our Losers section wasn't dejected.

Frank and Dylan started laughing it up, and I went over and suggested they tone it down.

"I was just saying, we might have to start calling the football team the Losers and find a new name for our soccer team," Frank told me.

"Instead of the Lions how about the Kittens?" Dylan suggested.

"Say anything you want later," I told them, "but for now, chill."

"This is not a good thing for anybody," Rob Powers agreed, sounding nervous. "People around us are taking this pretty seriously."

They sure were. I could see my father's face, and he looked like he was going to the funeral of an old friend.

One of the Fremont cheerleaders sat alone on the end of a bench, her hands clasped, as if whispering prayers.

Now that the game was on break, other Fremont fans had started watching us. I could almost feel their attention swinging our way. Maybe it was because the Losers had become school celebrities, or they could have been pointing out Dylan as the guy who'd been beaten up, or possibly Rob Powers was drawing their stares. News travels fast, and he wasn't hiding having switched teams. Whatever it was, I could feel lots of eyes on us.

When the Lions ran back on the field for the second half, the Fremont band played the loudest charge of the day. The cheerleader who had been seeking divine intervention jumped up and screamed for all she was worth. A white-haired lady everybody called "Ma Bell" who hadn't missed a Fremont game in twenty-two years rang her large cowbell over her head, and my father shook his right fist in an encouraging and demanding way that I remembered from when I was a kid.

The Lions dug in and tried to claw their way back, but the old Fremont magic fizzled that fall evening and the rout became a debacle. Our most sure-footed defenders tripped over their own feet. Reliable runners fumbled. Our All-League quarterback threw passes that bounced short or sailed right into the opponents' arms.

Lynton kept pushing. Soon it was forty-two to ten, and our cheerleaders stopped yelling and sat silently. Our band quieted, too, as if the mouthpieces had been taken from the brass section and the tips of the drumsticks were wrapped in cotton. Even my father, who never gave up, stopped shaking his fist and sat with his elbows on his knees, as if he was ashamed of something.

It ended forty-nine to ten—the most points scored against Fremont in fifty years and the most lopsided loss that anyone could remember. When time ran out on the scoreboard, the Lynton fans gave the victorious roar they had been waiting to let out for decades.

Muhldinger walked quickly across the field and shook hands with the Lynton coach, and then he turned, stuck his hands in his pockets, lowered his head, and didn't look up once all the way to the team bus. It was strange given how much I disliked him, but I actually felt sorry for the man.

32

THE WARREN SOCCER CLUBHOUSE WAS A
one-story brick building that looked out on a beautiful
pitch. There were two other ragged-looking fields, where
their youth teams played, but the men's field had grass so
thick and carefully trimmed it looked almost hand mani-
cured. Several hundred blue and red plastic seats in rows
faced down on it, and the trophy case in the Warren clubhouse held numerous silver soccer balls and even a golden
boot.

"They seem to take their club pretty seriously," Dad
noted appreciatively as we walked in. "Don't tell any soccer jokes."

"I'm the soccer joke around here," I muttered.

"You'll do fine," he said. "They asked you to come this
morning for a reason."

"Yeah, they're desperate."

Jan Brent was older than I would have guessed—at least
in his midfifties. He was a friendly man who looked like
he had once been a superb athlete but in the last few years
had eaten too many desserts. He had a big potbelly and
thinning white hair. "Jack, thanks so much for coming
out so early," he said, hurrying up and giving me a firm
handshake.

Then he turned to my father and offered his hand. "Don't worry, Mr. Logan, we'll run him hard but we won't run him into the ground."

He had the wrong Dad. As my father shook hands he growled: "Go ahead and run him into the ground all you want."

Jan smiled as if my father was joking, but I knew better.

After warm-up drills with the squad I found myself wearing a yellow pinny over my shirt and lining up at right wing. The men's team was going to play a practice scrimmage, and they had divided into two squads. There were only three other guys on the field who looked like they might possibly be teenagers, while the rest of the players were grown men with beards, wedding rings, and decades of soccer experience.

When the coach, playing ref, blew his whistle, I knew in about five seconds that it was a completely different game from anything I'd played before. One team would keep the ball and probe for an opening, moving it around from side to side but also kicking it up and dropping it back. It wasn't so much about trying to score as possessing the ball and doing the right things with it.

I didn't have a clue where I should run to or what I should do with the ball if I got it. Our center midfielder, Diego, was the best player I'd ever been on a field with. He kept trying to position me: "Jack, stay wide. Show for the ball. *Hold your run*—don't let them catch you offsides."

But they caught me offsides again and again, till I was afraid to go across the midfield line for fear the coach would just blow his whistle. The few times I did get the ball I didn't know who to pass it to, and when I finally completed a pass and stood there proudly Diego shouted at me: "After you pass it, Jack, move! That's the moment to run and you'll get it back! Don't stand still."

At halftime I suggested to Jan that he should take me out. "I'm just hurting my team."

"You're fine," he said. "But you're not running at them. That's why we brought you here."

"Yes, take them on," Diego urged. "Make them defend you." He spent the rest of halftime explaining to me that when we started to break on a counterattack I should check the defensive line to make sure that I was onside and then wait an extra second before starting my run.

In the second half I tried to have fun and do what they said. I was more careful of offside traps and stayed wide. When the ball was kicked to me I tried to take on my defender. Their left fullback who was guarding me was a guy in his thirties named Manny, and he didn't seem inclined to let an eighteen-year-old novice show him up. He played me tough, and twice when I almost got by him he took me down with tackles that were more leg than ball.

With just a few minutes to go in the scrimmage and the other team leading four to three, they threatened to score and put us away for good. They passed it around our penalty box and then their center forward cracked a whistling shot that our keeper snatched out of the air. He looked around quickly, took two giant steps, and hurled the ball thirty yards to Diego, who chested it down in the direction of his run. He dribbled past a defender and looked up quickly, and our eyes met. I checked their defensive line, and sure enough, they were stepping up to try to pull me offside. So I moved up with them half a yard and raised my hand to Diego. He swung his leg back and just as he kicked the ball I started my run.

He lofted a perfect pass down the right sideline. Their left midfielder read it and came swooping in on a sharp angle, trying to beat me to the ball. He was pretty fast, but I had a gear he didn't have. I flew into full sprint and managed to get there first and touch it by him.

Manny came roaring up for a challenge the same way he had several times before, lowering his center of gravity till he looked more like a wall than a man. His feet were close enough together so that I couldn't nutmeg him but wide enough apart to cut in either direction to stop me.

I couldn't go through him and I hadn't had much luck dribbling around him, so I decided to try going over him. I stopped my dribble, got my toe under the ball, and scooped it. The ball flew two feet over his head and took a nice bounce toward their goal. Then it was a test of pure speed. Manny tried to keep his body between me and the ball but he couldn't match me stride for stride. I whipped around him and touched the ball forward.

I saw the goalie coming out, arms spread to his full wingspan, making himself as big as possible. I heard someone—I think it was Diego—yelling, "Have one, Jack! Shoot!" I had no time to get the ball to my good right foot, so I tried to kick it solidly with my left.

The goalie dove and his fingertips grazed the ball, but I had kicked it with enough power to get it by him into the net.

I raised my arms and turned, and saw my dad. He was

sitting in the front row of blue plastic chairs, and just when I looked he punched the air so hard he lost his balance and nearly toppled over the rail. He caught himself and laughed, and I laughed, too.

Diego slapped me hard on the back. "That's what I'm talking about!" My other teammates congratulated me, and a minute or two later the coach blew the whistle and the game was over.

"Who says you don't have a left foot?" Jan asked me.

"I couldn't do that again if I tried," I told him. "Most of the time out there I didn't have a clue what I was doing."

"You are a work in progress," he agreed. "I can't play you in games yet, but I also can't not play you. Your speed makes you a real terror."

"I could have caught him," Manny grunted, walking off the field behind us.

"In your dreams." Jan laughed, and then he said to me, "It's up to you, Jack. If you want to practice with us next Saturday, we'd like to have you. I can't start you in a game yet, but once you learn your position and refine your skills we'll work you in as a sub. I've seen plenty of good college players and you definitely have the potential to play at that level. I could even make some calls for you if you'd like."

"He'd like that," my dad said, and then shut up and looked at me. "I mean, wouldn't you?"

I hesitated for a long second, but I had to admit the breakaway run had felt pretty terrific. "Sure," I said. "Let's try it."

33

WHEN DAD AND I GOT HOME FROM MY
soccer tryout, Mom had made us brunch and we all sat
together around the kitchen table eating and reading the
morning newspaper. The *Star Dispatch* reporters hadn't
held back: "Lions Lay an Egg," the front page of the sports
section blared in a big headline, with an embarrassing
photo of our quarterback fumbling the ball. "State Champ
Dreams End Early as Team Loses and Three Players Are
Arrested."

Lowry, Davis, and Barlow had been charged with aggravated assault as adults and let out on bail. I was starting
to learn how much a news story is like a fire. If it runs out
of wood, it sputters and dies. But give it a little new fuel
and a puff of wind and it roars up again, much bigger than
before. When our story began, the TV and newspaper coverage of the Losers had been mostly local and regional.
When Dylan's wrist was broken, it had swelled. But as word
got out that three football players had been charged with
a felony, the national press came racing in as if all suddenly
scenting the same trendy story.

Bullying in schools was a hot-button topic, and I guess
our story had other things going for it. Soccer was becoming more popular all over America, while high school

football was in retreat because of the controversy over head injuries. A football powerhouse run by people with screwed-up values made our story even juicier. Muhldinger was a villain right out of central casting. Finally there was our team—the Losers. There's a saying that everyone loves a winner, but actually I think most people prefer to hear about likable losers.

On Monday morning a network news reporter whose face I recognized was doing interviews right on school grounds. It was funny because she was trying to ask questions and kids kept coming up and asking for her autograph. When we jogged out to the south field to practice on Monday afternoon, the guards had given up trying to shoo away reporters. Maybe our school authorities had realized that the more they tried to keep a cap on this the hotter the story got. Fifty students and fans were waiting for us, and three news crews filmed our pathetic soccer practice as if something important were taking place. It was a little hard to see how fifteen lousy soccer players preparing to play another school's JV team deserved such attention.

Coach Percy told us to ignore the fuss and concentrate on our upcoming game against Pine River. That's a little like being in the middle of a tornado and someone telling you to please disregard the fact that your house just got sucked into the air.

Rob Powers came to Monday's practice and immediately made his mark. He'd never played soccer before, and he wasn't trying to be competitive, but he was a natural athlete and he couldn't turn it off. During a scrimmage he always seemed to be at the right place for passes, and while he toed the ball his kicks were still rockets compared to the rest of the Losers'. He kept dialing back his sports ability and trying not to show off, but it was clear that he could run rings around our other players.

It was fun for me to have another good athlete on the team. Rob's dad had played on the same Fremont football team as my father, and we'd spent grade school tossing all different kinds of balls around. We were both new at soccer, but with Rob playing stopper I remembered how it felt to play ahead of Diego—the sense that there's someone behind you who can make stops and feed you passes.

But there was also something about Rob's joining our team that was all about his showmanship. He always seemed to be diving in front of TV cameras, getting up slowly and flashing his million-dollar smile. I knew he had a modeling career, and I started wondering if he'd wanted to join the Losers for the same reason the varsity cheerleaders wanted to do their routines at our home games. I told myself there was nothing wrong with a little self-promotion—Becca was using our weird season to help her get into college. And every time I saw Rob acrobatically flip in front of a TV camera and get up smoothing out his hair, it kind of cracked me up.

Our Internet followers quickly embraced our new team member. "New Loser Is Hot Hunk!" came the tweets, and soon pictures of Rob were posted on our fan sites, and not just soccer photos but also shots from his modeling gigs, including one of him in a bathing suit.

Becca saw what I saw, and at first she was hostile to Rob. But as he goofed around and got to know everybody, he was soon accepted by the Losers. I was surprised to see how much Becca hung out with him. She laughed at his lame jokes, and stretched out next to him, and while I wasn't really jealous I was a little curious how he had persuaded her so quickly that he wasn't the misogynist she'd pegged him as.

Rob might have been having fun on our team, but he paid for it in school and in the town. I heard people say things behind his back, and to his face, that I wouldn't have known how to deal with. "Traitor" was the word most commonly used, but there were plenty of nastier names.

Rob just looked the other way and walked on by.

The Fremont football fans were hurting, and they needed someone to blame. Every afternoon the Lions practiced on Gentry Field, but their season was in shambles and few came to watch them. The bleachers sat largely empty, and the statue of Arthur Gentry with his motto "Just go for it" seemed to mock them. Every afternoon we practiced nearby on the south field and drew TV trucks and crowds.

The media hype built all week, till on Wednesday night, before the Pine River game, a network news show ran a big feature spot on our team and what was going on in Fremont. There were interviews with students, two TV psychologists who specialized in school violence explained how misguided our town's values were, and Mr. Bryce even appeared to say Fremont was taking this seriously and cleaning its own house and would people please just give us some space.

By the time we got onto the bus for Pine River I didn't

know what to expect, but I knew things were getting a little out of control. It was clear from the spike in our hits online and all the new posts and chatter that this was no longer really about the Losers at all—we'd plugged into a much bigger national issue. A high school girl had recently committed suicide in Connecticut because she'd been teased mercilessly, and a ten-year-old boy in Pennsylvania was in a coma after a beating. Somehow our story had been adopted and embraced by people who cared a great deal about school violence, and we had become a flash point for them.

I sat on the bus behind Becca and Rob, who laughed and kidded each other the whole ride to Pine River. Rob was a natural athlete for sure, but he was even more naturally gifted when it came to getting pretty girls to like him.

Pine River High is just what it sounds like—a fifty-year-old brick school in the bend of a river, surrounded by pitch pines. It's a small school that serves a farming community, and they weren't prepared for what descended on them that October afternoon. The date and time of the game had been posted online by what my teammates had taken to calling "Loser Nation," and many of our fans had promised to show up. By the time our bus chugged up to Pine River High School, there was nowhere to park. The lot was jammed, and the backup lot near the sports fields was also full. A guard directed us toward a grassy field a few hundred yards away, and when we got off the bus the press was waiting for us.

"Losers, look over here! Can we get a team picture?"

"Where's Dylan? The attorney for one of the arrested football players said his client can't get a fair trial because of all the publicity. Any comment?"

"Guys, do you think being victims makes you Losers or are you really winners?"

Some of us shouted replies and mugged for the cameras, but I kept my mouth shut and followed Coach Percy to the field. It had no bleachers so all the people who had driven to see the game were standing around it in a steadily growing crowd. The mob parted to let us through and then re-formed, so we were surrounded by staring, screaming strangers who felt like they knew us. I saw lots of signs against bullying and school violence, and activists were handing out leaflets. There was even a state politician shaking hands and giving interviews.

"What a circus," Frank said, staring at a woman who had wrapped herself in bandages and was wearing a gag.

"We used to be the circus," Dylan agreed with a nod, "but now I think we're the sideshow."

Coach Percy tried to get us to calm down. "It's not luck that you are where you are right now," he told us when we huddled up. "As Seneca said: 'Luck is what happens when preparation meets opportunity.' Have fun out there and play your own game."

"Who's Seneca?" I asked Becca.

"He's not on my list of two thousand important people to know for the history AP," she said.

When I went to midfield to meet the Pine River captain for the coin flip, he kept asking me what was going on.

"I don't know," I told him honestly. "It's out of control."

"No kidding," he said, and ran a hand through his short hair. "But what's going on?"

Before the game started the ref had the cops push the crowd back fifteen yards from the field's perimeter so the line judges could run the sidelines. That gave us a feeling of a little breathing room, but within a minute our fans had edged back toward the corners, and the TV crews were practically standing on the field.

The ref blew his whistle and the game started, but the crowd was so distracting that it was hard to concentrate. Pine River was barely mediocre, and I had the same strange feeling I'd had against Maysville—Losers or not, we were actually just as good as they were. Rob was trying not to be too intense, but he kept stopping their attacks and feeding me the ball. Pine River scored three minutes in, and I quickly tied it. We might have actually played a fun, close soccer game but after twenty minutes it came to a surprising end.

Rob fed me a pass and I was dribbling the ball up when the ref blew his whistle. I knew I couldn't possibly be offside, so I turned to him and shouted, "Come on, look at their defenders—I'm on!" He looked back at me and pointed.

A dozen protesters carrying signs with messages like MY SON WAS A VICTIM and ENOUGH PAIN—START THE HEALING NOW! had walked out onto the field and were chanting slogans in front of the TV cameras. The police tried to lead them away, but they sat down, linked arms, and refused to budge.

People from the crowd shouted at them to leave: "We drove an hour to see this game, you idiots."

The protestors kept chanting, the crowd yelled back at them, and even though it was a protest against bullying, things started to feel a little hostile and threatening.

We gathered at the sideline where Coach Percy told us to drink water and not get involved. The Pine River coach hurried over with their athletic director and talked to Percy, who nodded. Then the athletic director told us, "Guys, I love a good soccer game, but I think it might be better for everyone if we just pulled the plug on this thing and went home."

We walked through the crowd to the bus and drove back to Fremont, and my last view of Pine River was of the cops putting wrist restraints on protestors, picking them up, and carrying them off the field.

"OF ALL THE STUPID IDEAS MANKIND HAS
come up with for wasting time since the dawn of history,
I'd have to say bowling is at the top of the list," Becca
complained as she watched her third gutter ball of the
afternoon get swallowed by the ball return. "I'm positive I
told you on our first date that I hate bowling." She was
tense and even a little angry, but since I understood what
was really bothering her I cut her some slack and tried to
tease her out of her mood.

"Your problem is that you're watching your ball instead
of keeping your eyes on the pins," I told her. "Trust yourself that if you focus on the target, the ball will roll where
you want every time."

"I trust myself that I'd like to roll my way out of Fremont Lanes and never come back," she responded. "How
can you possibly enjoy this idiocy?"

"What's not to like about bowling? I've rolled four strikes
so far and there's root beer and french fries, not to mention a game room."

"Greasy fries," she noted. "And there's a birthday party
for a seven-year-old going on in the game room."

I took a sip of root beer and gave her a smile. "Well, I'm

sure Rob would find something more sophisticated and romantic."

Becca shot me a look. "What's that supposed to mean?"

"I've been listening to his bad jokes since we were five years old and they're not that funny, but you always seem to be laughing."

At least that got her to stop complaining about bowling. "Are you jealous?"

"Should I be?"

"No," she said. "Don't be ridiculous."

"One minute you're calling him a misogynist and the next you're the leader of his fan club."

"Hey," she said. "You *are* jealous."

I picked up my bowling ball and stepped out onto the polished wood of the lane. I took a three-step approach and rolled a late-breaking power hook. The ball hugged the right side and at the last second broke sharply into the pocket. All ten pins went flying like someone had just tossed a grenade at them.

I walked back. "Turbo pin action. Watch and learn."

Becca didn't look particularly impressed. "Of all the useless, pointless, irrelevant skills to learn in life, you've mastered *numero uno*."

"I didn't know you spoke such good Spanish," I told her. "Your turn, novice. Eyes on the pins. Try to avoid that giant gutter."

Becca picked up a fry and, greasy or not, popped it in her mouth and chewed. She clearly wasn't in a hurry to roll another gutter ball, and I could tell she also wasn't looking forward to the second part of our date. I noticed she hadn't dressed up for it. I, on the other hand, was wearing a button-down shirt with a collar, which is a lot nicer than what I usually wear to Fremont Lanes. "So what's your big news?" she demanded. "Who called you?"

"Just a soccer coach."

"From where?"

"I can't remember the name of the school. I think it started with an *R*."

She grabbed a handful of my hair. "Out with it or I yank."

"I thought you were against bullying. Ouch! Let go. Rutgers."

She released me and looked impressed. "A coach from the state college is recruiting you?"

"Actually he was just an assistant coach and he isn't recruiting me. He just wanted my personal information."

"And how did this assistant coach hear about you?"

"The manager of the men's team I've been practicing with called him."

Becca thought that over. "Why did Rutgers believe this guy?"

"It turns out the manager—Jan—used to play for Ajax."

"Since I seem to be asking all the questions this afternoon, what's Ajax other than a cleaning product?"

"The most famous professional soccer team in the Netherlands," I told her. "So Jan's word carries weight in soccer circles, and I guess he said a few nice things about me."

"I guess so," Becca said. "Wow. That's pretty incredible."

I shrugged. "It's not as if the Brazilian national team has been phoning."

"You just picked up the sport," she said. "I've been jumping horses since I was seven and nobody's trying to recruit me."

"I don't think Rutgers has a horse jumping team."

"It's called an equestrian team, for your information."

"I don't think they have one of those, either. And for your information, it's your turn. We only have the lane for one hour."

"Thank God for that," she said, and rolled another gutter ball.

When we were done we walked out of the mall and headed toward Main Street and the Olympus Diner. It was nearly seven, and I was a little nervous. Becca wasn't exactly nervous, but she was clearly dreading this meeting. As we neared the diner she started walking more and more slowly.

"We're going to be late," I warned her.

"That's the idea. They'll wait."

"He's not going to drill my teeth or anything?" I asked.

"He doesn't usually bring his tools with him to dinner," she said, and took my hand. "Listen, I owe you one. I'm glad I'm not doing this alone. And for what it's worth, you don't have to be jealous."

"About Rob? I wasn't really. But he's always been a magnet for cute girls."

"I just think he's fun," Becca said, squeezing my hand a little tighter.

"And that's why I shouldn't be jealous?"

She stopped and kissed me on the lips. "That's why you shouldn't be jealous," she told me.

The Olympus Diner, with its gigantic sign in the shape of a fake mountain, was only a half block away.

"Are you ready?" I asked.

Instead of answering Becca tensed and then waved her arm. "There he is. And there she is. Oh, she's wearing a lovely outfit."

On the steps of the Olympus Diner a man in a brown jacket waved back. Standing next to him was a pretty blond woman, noticeably younger, in a short yellow skirt.

Still holding my hand tightly, Becca sped up and walked straight to them. "Hey, Dad," she said. "This is Jack."

"And this is Emily," he told us.

"Hi," his young companion said, making the one word sound perky.

"Hi," Becca echoed with all the enthusiasm of an old tennis ball bouncing off a wall.

"Hey." I tried to vary things a little bit.

"You're late," Dr. Knight scolded, glancing at his watch.

"We were bowling," she told him.

"I love bowling," Emily announced brightly. "I was in a league."

"That's terrific," Becca replied, and Emily caught her tone and gave her a look.

"Let's go eat," I suggested, trying to keep the peace. "I'm hungry."

We were seated at a window table with a view of the cars going up and down Main Street. Becca's father was an intense man who didn't seem to know when to take his foot off the gas. "So, any word from Harvard?" he asked as soon as we sat down.

"Applications aren't due for a while yet," she told him. "And Harvard's not my first choice, anyway."

"That's ridiculous. If you get in, you're going to Harvard. They must know who they want by now. This whole process is ludicrous. Jack, where are you thinking of going next year?"

I was about to name the three podunk colleges I was going to apply to when Becca cut in: "Jack is being recruited for soccer by Rutgers in a big way."

"Really?" her dad said. "I thought your team was lousy. I thought that was the whole point."

"Jack is from a family of superathletes," she told him. "When you've got his genes, the normal rules don't apply."

Dr. Knight looked me over, as if he could somehow scrutinize my genes and didn't spot anything special. "I'd like to see you play," he said. "I hear your games have gotten a little controversial lately."

"This week's turned into a political rally," I told him. "And because of that our next two games have been canceled. The schools we were supposed to play didn't want to deal with the hassle. So all we've got left is our final game against Lynton, if it's still on."

"I'll try to come to that one," he said. "If I can free myself up at the office."

We ordered our dinners and after the waitress took our

menus there was an awkward silence. "So, Emily, what exactly do you do?" Becca asked.

"I'm a party planner," Emily explained. "I threw your dad's office party. That's how we met."

"Emily's great at what she does," Dr. Knight said, and touched her arm.

"I'll bet," Becca said. "Excuse me."

She left to go to the ladies' room, and I was alone with her father and Emily.

Emily gave Dr. Knight a look and told him softly, "I should go."

"Give it time," he said to her. "We knew this wasn't going to be painless." He turned to me and smiled. "Jack, I gather you've been a real friend to Rebecca over the last few months, when things have been difficult."

"I've tried my best."

"Thank you for that," he said. He peered at me, and one of his eyes seemed to narrow. "Hey, what happened to your front teeth?"

"Nothing," I told him, covering my teeth with my lips. "Just a little sports accident."

"Give me a big smile and let me see. Maybe I can fix you up . . ."

Just as it seemed he was going to reach across the table and start prodding my mouth with a knife and fork, Becca came out of the bathroom and announced: "Dad, my stomach's kind of messed up. Jack and I have to go."

"But we just ordered," he said.

"Sorry. I'm feeling nauseous."

"Becca . . . sit down in that chair." He snapped it out as an order.

"Dad, don't tell me what to do," she shot back, and the people at nearby tables all looked over. And then she smiled and said, "Nice meeting you, Emily. Come on, Jack. We're out of here."

35

"CAN YOU BELIEVE SHE'S A PARTY PLANNER?"
Becca demanded. "Isn't that perfect?"

"What's wrong with party planners?" I asked.

"Your job right now is to agree with everything I say," Becca informed me.

"Right. I can't believe that she's a party planner."

We had turned off Main Street and were walking toward Becca's home. It was a cool night, and I put my arm around her.

"That yellow skirt was halfway up her thighs."

"Outrageous," I agreed. "Shameful."

"And she likes bowling!"

"Ridiculous sport," I agreed. "It's really not a sport at all."

"Oh, and she was in a league," Becca said. "Did you hear the one question my father asked me? Have I heard from Harvard? Because if I get in that's where he thinks I'm going. No way in hell—I'm getting as far away from Fremont as I possibly can. And he might come to see us play if he can get time free from his office. Don't do me any favors, Dad."

"He wanted to fix my teeth," I said.

Becca looked a little surprised. "At the diner?"

"I think he was tempted. He said I should come by."

"Maybe you should let him. He's a good dentist."

And that was when I first heard the siren. It was a distant wail that cut through the gathering darkness like the cry of a giant dinosaur.

"I'm not looking for a good dentist," I told her. "Go back to ranting about dinner. You were on a roll."

"Did you like how he greeted us? 'You're late.' As if they've got so many better things to do together. And did you hear him snap at me to sit down?"

"Yeah, I noticed."

"The commander in chief issuing a command. At least he didn't use the word 'painless.'"

"He did while you were in the bathroom," I told her.

"He 'painlessed' behind my back?"

Then the wail came again, and this time it was picked up by other dinosaurs till a whole herd of them seemed to be shrilling in the night, heading our way. "That's a fire," I said.

Lights flashed on the dark tarmac and lit up the trees as fire trucks sped toward us. We watched three of them zoom past. They cut sharp turns around Cedar Lane, and I could see their lights converge with other lights a block or two away. There were loud clanging sounds and people shouting. "It's close to us," I told Becca.

"The big excitement of a fall night in the New Jersey suburbs," she said. "Let's go watch someone's house burn down."

We walked toward the lights, and the sounds of the fire grew louder. When we turned onto Coover Street I realized that all the action had converged on the big white house in the center of the block. "That's Rob's house!"

"You're kidding," Becca said, but I was already running. She followed me up the block and we joined the crowd that the police were keeping back. I didn't see flames, but I could smell smoke, and two hydrants were pumping water. There were firemen all over the place, but their hoses weren't pointed at the house. Instead, they were dousing Rob's car in the driveway, which was a smoldering wreck.

Becca and I moved closer, and I spotted Rob's parents talking to the police and the fire captain. Rob's father looked calm, but his mom was extremely upset and holding her toddler daughter with both arms.

"Jack," Rob said from behind us, and we spun around. He was a very laid-back guy, and I'd never seen him look so furious. His face was tight with anger, and he kept glancing from the house to his ash pile of a car.

"Hey, Rob," I said. "What happened? Is everybody okay?"

"Yeah, yeah," he said. "We were just hanging out watching a movie and saw the flames through the window."

"You think it was an electrical fire or something?"

"Don't bet on it," he spat out. "People have been saying stuff to me all week."

"You really think someone would do that?" Becca asked.

"Sure." He stared at his mom, who was holding his sister protectively. "And I'll be damned if I let them get away with it. See you guys later." He walked back to his family and took his sister from his mother. The little girl might have been sleeping when the fire broke out, but she was now wide awake and having lots of fun. The commotion was just a big game to her and she kept smiling and waving to the crowd. Rob hoisted her up onto his back, and she shrieked delightedly at being up so high.

"Let's go," Becca said.

I walked her home, and we didn't say much. The run-in with her dad no longer seemed very important compared to what we had just seen. Someone had targeted Rob, and setting his car on fire in front of his home had pushed things to a new and very dangerous point.

ROB'S THREAT TO STRIKE BACK WORRIED ME, because I was afraid he might escalate things and end up getting hurt. But nothing much happened in the next few days, except that the fire department found some evidence that the fire might have been intentionally set, but it was inconclusive and there were no witnesses.

A week later I woke up early to study for a math test and came downstairs to gobble some cereal. I was surprised to find my father on his way out the door dressed up in gray pants and a blazer. "Hey, fashion plate," I kidded him. "What's up?"

He looked just a little embarrassed. "Probably nothing."

"Nice outfit for 'nothing.'"

"There's a possible job," Dad admitted. "I don't want to shoot off my mouth because I'm sure I won't get it."

"Must be pretty fancy construction work."

He hesitated and then told me: "It's another kind of job."

"What kind is that?"

He was reluctant, but I sensed he really did want to talk about it. "There's a junior college in South Jersey that's looking for an assistant athletic director. They need someone who can step in right away and help coach their football team this fall."

"That's perfect for you."

He shrugged. "Except that I don't have any experience."

"You led the state in rushing."

"Back in the Dark Ages."

"You coached my teams, and all my brothers' teams, and you were by far the best coach any of us ever had."

"That was kids' stuff," he said. "And you always said I was too much of a hard-ass."

"You were. But we've got a room in this house filled with cups and ribbons, and they didn't come out of nowhere."

I think he appreciated the shot in the arm. "Well, I'm going to give it a try." He hesitated. "There is one reason I might get this."

"Because you're the most qualified person in New Jersey?" I guessed.

"No," he said, "because it pays peanuts and nobody else may want it." He glanced at his watch. "I'd better head out. Got a long drive ahead of me and I want to get there bright and early. You should read the paper today, Jack."

"What's going on?"

"To me, it's kind of a sad day for Fremont. But you'll probably look at it very differently."

Mom came down the steps then, and asked, "What's a sad day for Fremont? Hey, who's sneaking out early? Look at you!"

Dad glanced from her to me. "Am I really usually such a slob?"

"No," Mom and I said at exactly the same moment.

"She just means you look like a coach," I told him.

"A college coach," Mom agreed, walking over and fixing

his collar. "You'll knock 'em dead. Want some coffee for the road?"

"Already had two cups," he said, and kissed her good-bye. Then he headed out to his truck, and Mom and I looked at each other.

"Great job for him," I said.

"He's worried they'll give it to someone younger, who's just starting out," she told me.

"He's not that old."

"Let's hope." She poured herself a cup of coffee from the pot my dad had brewed. "So what's a sad day for Fremont?"

"I don't know yet." I walked to the kitchen table where the newspaper was waiting. Since the sports section was sitting on top, I flipped through it. There was a golf tournament going on, but nothing about Fremont. Mom pointed to the news section, where there was a big front-page feature article by Dianne Foster titled: "The Dark Side of a Sports Culture." I sat and held the paper with both hands, and Mom read it over my shoulder.

> *For many years, Fremont High was known as "Muscles High" and gloried in its long string of championship seasons. But this year, a cycle of escalating violence has plagued the school. There has been a pattern of bullying and intimidation, leading to an assault on a student, the recent arrest of three football players, and a possible case of arson at a soccer player's home this week. Shocking new revelations from a source very familiar with the football team*

place the responsibility for that attitude, and
for several of the specific incidents, squarely at
the feet of the school's football coach and new
principal, Brian Muhldinger.

"Wow," I said.

"Poor Brian," Mom whispered.

The article linked a string of things that had happened in the last five months to Muhldinger, starting with his policy that all seniors had to join sports teams. It explained how nonathletes had felt caught in a bind, and that our relaxed soccer team was an attempt to deal with his new rule.

> *From the start Muhldinger saw this soccer*
> *team as an embarrassment, and as it gained*
> *popularity he soon came to look upon it as a*
> *threat. He let his football players know that he*
> *wanted the team harassed and that he intended*
> *to find a way to break it up. He called it the*
> *"cesspool" and its players "wastes of genes." In*
> *early September he told a handful of seniors to*
> *lead the football players on a run straight*
> *through the first soccer practice and "Show*
> *them what contact sports at Fremont is all*
> *about." Soccer players, including several girls,*
> *were knocked down and terrorized when the*
> *football players came charging through.*

I flashed back to when the football stampede had hit our practice, and I'd intuitively tried to protect Chloe. Rob

Powers had almost slammed into me, and for a moment we'd caught each other. He'd looked very guilty, as if he knew he was doing something he shouldn't have been doing.

Suddenly I realized who Dianne Foster's new source, the one "very familiar with the football team," must be, and that Rob had chosen his own way of striking back.

The article described how the football team had been locked in the Keep and almost missed its first home game. A few days later, in the football coaches' office after practice, Muhldinger had told several seniors that our soccer team was to blame, and that we should pay for that outrage. According to Dianne Foster's source, all three seniors who had been arrested for beating Dylan had been present when Muhldinger voiced this opinion.

The article ended by explaining how Rob had left the football team for our soccer team and been insulted and threatened.

> *Less than one week later, his car was set on fire right in front of his family's home. The police are still investigating, and may never be able to identify who set the blaze. But it's clear that the culture of bullying at Fremont High that created this firestorm is directly attributable to one man and his policies.*

I lowered the paper and looked at my mom, who had finished reading a few seconds before me. "It's over for him, isn't it?" I asked her.

"Unless that reporter has it wrong."

"I doubt that she does."

School that day was weird. Everyone knew what was going on, but no one talked much about it. Even my fellow Losers seemed to sense that some sort of turning point had been reached, and the moment was a little too serious for words. Nobody saw Muhldinger all day, but several school board members were spotted around the halls. Sports practices were all canceled, so I headed home after school. I was cutting through the parking lot when a familiar voice called out in a British accent, "Hallo there, Jack."

"Hey," I called back.

Coach Percy had been about to drive home. Instead he walked over to me and said, "Strange day."

"Sad," I agreed, repeating the word my father had used.

"We talked about having a chat. Is this a good time?"

"Sure," I said.

"Let's take a stroll," he suggested, and off we went. We walked behind the school, and soon entered the wooded area where Dylan was jumped.

Coach Percy looked around at the trees and the brook that spilled down in a waterfall over sharp rocks. "A pretty spot for cruelty."

"I guess Muhldinger's gonna get what he deserves," I said.

"I take no pleasure in that," Percy told me. "We all make mistakes."

"That's for sure," I muttered.

He looked at me sharply and said: "I've certainly made

my share." He paused, as if hoping I'd say something to help him out, and then continued: "I assume that we're now discussing something Rebecca told you. Is that correct?"

"That's right."

"You realize this is a rather serious matter? One that could get me fired."

I thought to myself that it could have gotten him fired up till this morning, but Muhldinger wasn't in a position to fire anyone now—even the teacher who'd put together the video of him shouting at our players on the team bus and posted it on the Web for the world to see. "I guess you knew you were taking a risk."

"To tell you the truth," he admitted, sounding a little embarrassed, "there are times when a man acts without thinking about the consequences."

"In any case, it's over now," I said.

"Absolutely," he agreed. "In fact it never really was there at all. I mean, nothing consequential happened. I just wanted to make sure you understand that."

Actually, his posting the video had had lots of important consequences. "I'm not sure I agree," I said.

Percy rubbed his hands together, as if trying to clean them. "I suppose she showed you the sonnet."

I looked back at him, but before I could ask what the heck he was talking about he went on. "I should never have written it. But she is a wonderful girl, as I know you'd agree. By far my best student. And I've been a bit of a stranger in a strange land. Anyway, we took a walk together, and held hands once, and I wrote her the sonnet, and that was the extent of it. You came along, and I'm so glad that you did. It was certainly best for everyone. You're a lovely couple and I'm heading back to England to a job I'll relish, and—"

He broke off and took a breath. "I'm grateful we finally got everything out in the open. I hope you won't hold it against me." He held out his right hand.

I shook hands with him and looked him in the eye. "Good luck in England."

"Thank you, Jack," he said. "Good luck with soccer. I have a feeling you may have stumbled onto something. And if I may say so, good luck with Becca."

We walked back through the Stevens toward the school, and there was a very uncomfortable silence. I found myself thinking how a crisis like the one in Fremont brings out so many different kinds of secrets. I guess when you stir up a school and a small town hard enough, all kinds of hidden things rise to the surface.

I finally broke the awkward silence by saying, "So do you think this is it for Muhldinger? He can't survive this mess, can he?"

"He's gone," Coach Percy said.

"Don't you mean that he will soon be gone?"

Coach Percy hesitated. "Since we're exchanging confidences, I'll share with you that the faculty received word just before school let out that Muhldinger has resigned as principal, effective immediately. Mr. Anderson is going to be taking over as acting principal till they find a permanent replacement."

Mr. Anderson was the gentle and scholarly head of the history department who had been teaching at Fremont for forty years.

"I think he's a good choice," I said.

"Superb," Coach Percy agreed as we reached the parking lot. "Well, I'd better be heading home. Are we square, Jack?" He held out his right hand again.

"All square," I told him, and we shook one more time. He turned, walked quickly to his little red car, and sped off. I walked away alone, past the parking lot and alongside Gentry Field, where the only thing moving was an old black crow that had landed on the turf and was hopping around, perhaps looking for bugs.

MUHLDINGER DID NOT RETURN TO DELIVER
a goodbye speech to the student body, and Mr. Chester, a
phys ed teacher, took over coaching the football team.

I noticed that the unusual nameplate on the door to
Muhldinger's office—BRIAN MUHLDINGER—PRINCIPAL/HEAD
FOOTBALL COACH—stayed up for a few days. He was no longer either one, but maybe now that he was gone it didn't
seem necessary to remove it right away.

Mr. Anderson wasted no time in making the obvious
first change at Fremont High. He rescinded the rule that
all seniors had to join a sports team, "effective immediately." I knew what it meant for the Losers. We had only
gotten enough players because all seniors were required to
play a sport. Without that rule, the cesspool team would
dissolve after our last game against Lynton.

Frank, Dylan, and Becca agreed it was sad that our
team would only exist for one season. "I kind of hoped the
Losers would become a dynasty," Dylan said. "Decades of
mediocrity. A tradition of glorious failure!"

"Yeah, and we would go down in school history for found-
ing it," Frank added.

"Actually, Jack founded it," Becca pointed out.

"It served its purpose," I told them. "And it was fun while it lasted."

The last practice of the Losers took place in late October, on a Friday so gray and cold that not one person came to watch us. When Muhldinger resigned, our story grew instantly less compelling and our following in the news and on the Internet quickly fell off. It had been a struggle between David and Goliath, and once Goliath toppled over, people lost interest. Now it was just our team out on the south field, which felt like a big wind tunnel as blasts of wintry air whistled down from the cloudless sky and rustled the branches of nearly leafless trees.

We were wearing sweats, fleece hats, and gloves, and the only way to stay warm was to keep moving. Our team jog around the field was noticeably faster than usual—even Frank and Pierre chugged along, banging their hands together. It was too cold for yoga stretches on the grass, so we stretched standing up and jumped right into our drills. The soccer ball felt like a rock each time somebody kicked it, and when Zirco headed a high ball he fell to the ground as if he'd been bashed in the forehead with a brick.

Coach Percy ended practice early, and we circled around him beneath the branches of the same oak we'd gathered under for our first practice. "Given the blustery weather," he said, "I won't keep you long. But I have two announcements. The first is that I've accepted a position at the Westmount School in Shropshire, and they want me to start teaching in the spring term, which begins after Christmas holiday. Your new principal was very understanding, so I'll be heading back to England in a few weeks. May I say that coaching this team has been one of my most enjoyable experiences in America. For a team that calls itself the Losers you've accomplished quite a lot, and I daresay had a bit of devilish fun doing it."

There was silence for a moment, and then Zirco shouted out "Stegosaurus."

"Yes, that's exactly what I'm feeling," Coach Percy told him with a smile. He looked out at us. "Forget all of what I just said. Let's leave it simply at Stegosaurus."

"Stegosaurus," we repeated back.

Becca spoke up loudly: "Hey, Losers, we never would have had a team if Percy hadn't agreed to coach us." She gave him a sad smile that made me just a little jealous, and said, "Three cheers for Coach Percy."

We gave him a trio of hip-hip-hoorays and he tipped an imaginary cap to us, and then shivered. "Before we all freeze, my second announcement is that Lynton initially canceled our last game of the season. As you know, it was supposed to be here at Gentry Field this coming Monday. They read about what happened at Pine River and decided to skip it."

There were boos and shouts of "Cowards."

"But a few hours ago their coach called to see if they could still play us. Apparently they're having a perfect season—seven wins and no losses. Seven matches their most wins ever for a JV season in more than fifty years. If they beat us they'll be eight and zero, and they've decided they want the record."

"Let's summon the Loser Nation for one last game and make a mockery out of their record!" Dylan shouted. "It won't mean anything if they beat us twenty to zip! We can humiliate them with our awfulness!"

"Or we could play the first half and then refuse to play the second," Shimsky suggested. "So they win on a technicality because we walk off the field, and they always have an asterisk next to their stupid record."

"Or we could beat them," I said.

That shut everyone up for a long moment. "Why would we do that?" Frank asked.

"It's our last game," I pointed out. "We've already lost in every possible way. We were destroyed by the Marion girls and massacred by Maysville. Once you've been obliterated, what fun is another rout? And we already had a game cut off at Pine River. I don't know about you, but I didn't enjoy walking off the field early."

"He might have a point," Becca said.

"Don't let him hijack our revolution," Shimsky said angrily. "We're Losers, not winners. Let's go out in a glorious blaze of failure."

"It seems to me your revolution's already over," Percy told him. "Muhldinger's gone. You may be Losers, but like it or not you've already won."

"That's right," I agreed. "This is our last game, and we should try something new. Suppose we prove that Muhldinger was wrong and we're not garbage? Lynton beat up on our football team and our whole town. Let's win one for Fremont, and wreck their chance at a perfect record."

"I agree," Rob Powers jumped in to support me. "Someone torched my car, so I have more anger than any of you except maybe Dylan. But my anger was about Muhldinger, and he's history. Fremont's where I live, and I didn't enjoy seeing Lynton whip our butts. If you let it be known that the Losers are going to try to snap their losing streak, you can probably get one last burst of publicity."

"Let's put it to a team vote," Percy suggested. "All in favor of trying to actually win our last game?"

Seven players raised their hands.

"And how many want to go out Losers?"

There were seven more.

"Who didn't vote?"

"Zirco," Chloe said.

We all looked at him. "Xander, do you think we should try to win or try to lose?" Coach Percy asked him.

Zirco scratched his head, and we waited. "I want to live in a blue house," he finally said.

"Yes, we're aware of that," Percy told him, "and I have no doubt you'll accomplish that worthy goal. But do you want to win or lose against Lynton?"

"Wind," he said as a chilly burst blew through our huddle. "Wind, wind, win, win, win, win, win!"

And so it was settled, and several of my teammates already had their phones out to broadcast our new agenda out to "Loser Nation."

I came home and took a hot shower, and then I called the *Star Dispatch* and asked for Dianne Foster. "She's gone for the day," someone told me. "Would you like her voice mail?"

"Sure," I said. When it beeped, I left her a short message.

She called five minutes later. "Jack? This is Dianne Foster."

"Hi," I said.

"I thought you weren't talking to me."

"Things change," I said, echoing Coach Percy. "And for what it's worth, I thought you did a good job with that last article about Muhldinger."

"That's very generous of you. You mentioned a new story?"

"Since you've been covering Fremont and our soccer team, I thought you might be interested in a story about our last game, which is coming up on Monday against Lynton."

"That game was canceled," she said.

"It's back on," I said, and I told her the plan.

"PASS ME THAT PIPE WRENCH." DAD WAS ON
his back, fixing our kitchen sink's pop-up drain. "Do you
really think you guys have a chance?" The Sunday morning paper was spread out on the floor beneath a plastic
bucket to catch any water that leaked. A small headline
on a sports page read: "Losers Vow to Go Out Winners—
America's Self-Styled Worst Soccer Team Throws Down
the Gauntlet in Final Game."

I handed him the pipe wrench and he removed the trap.
There wasn't much that could go wrong in a house that
my dad couldn't fix. "We have a slim chance," I told him.
"Some of our players aren't half bad. And it helps a lot
having Rob."

"His dad's not happy about him playing with you guys,
but the football season's a washout anyway. Ed's never seen
a soccer game in his life, but I told him they're not so bad,
except for the scoreless ones." Dad glanced up at me. "And
with your defense you're not likely to have any of those.
Hold this trap for a sec."

I held it as my father lifted the old pop-up drain from
the top of the sink. I looked down past him at the article
on the floor. Dianne Foster had done a good job of making
the fact that we'd decided to try to win our final game

sound newsworthy and fun. In seconds Dad had put in the new drain and connected it up underneath. His hands were a blur as he tightened the nuts. "All done," he said, gathering up the newspaper and bucket. "I told Ed to show his face on Monday and I'd explain the finer points of soccer to him."

"Now you're bringing football fans to our soccer games?"

"I don't have that many better things to do on my unexpected little vacation."

"Your vacation will be over really soon," I assured him.

"Unfortunately, you're wrong," he said. "They gave it to a young guy who's done some coaching for them already. I can't blame them—it's always better to work with people you know."

I was shocked. "Sorry," I told him. "They're fools."

"The good part is I've got the bug now," Dad said. "There are two Web sites that list coaching jobs in the area, and I've been checking them out. One job in Bergen County sounds particularly interesting. I don't want to shoot my mouth off because I probably won't get it, but they want to interview me next week."

"Keep applying," I told him. "You'll get one and you'll love it. And I'm glad you're coming to our last game. It felt weird to play and not see you on the sideline."

"I'll come," he promised, and then glanced out the window. "If there's not a blizzard."

It was a cold gray morning and snow seemed a definite possibility. But the sun peeked out in the early afternoon and Dylan, Frank, and I went to Founders' Park to toss around a Frisbee. The park is usually mobbed on weekends, but it was so chilly that the moms and young kids had stayed home. Only two players were on the public tennis courts, hitting yellow balls into cold gusts.

Dylan was in great spirits. "They're putting me in charge of set-building for the Christmas play," he told us. "It's gonna be *Scrooge* and I've started meeting with the director and drawing sketches." His right wrist must have completely healed because he was hurling the Frisbee on long line drives that bit into the wind.

"Let's cut this short and go grab some pizza," Frank suggested. "My face is freezing. It's too damn cold for soccer, too. They should just call our game off tomorrow and save us the frostbite."

"No way," Dylan said. "Loser Nation is psyched to see us try to win."

"We'll never win and we shouldn't try," Frank grumbled. He had voted against us trying to beat Lynton.

"With you in the goal, big guy, I don't see how Lynton can score," I said.

"Under me, around me, and through me," Frank suggested.

"Here comes an airmail!" Dylan shouted, and took advantage of a gust to throw the Frisbee over my head. I chased it, but the wind caught it and it sailed an extra thirty yards. It finally came down on a paved walkway by the duck pond and rolled in a big circle. I ran over to it and saw a man sitting on a bench beneath a willow tree. As I reached the Frisbee, I glimpsed his face—it was Brian

Muhldinger. He was wearing a Fremont football jacket and a blue Giants cap pulled down over his ears, and he was looking out at the icy and deserted pond. I bent to pick up the Frisbee and as I straightened he turned his head and saw me.

He didn't react. Instead, he sat completely motionless, his big arms folded over his chest, hands tucked into the pockets of his jacket. His small black eyes fastened on my own. Probably we both were remembering he'd been sitting on this same bench with my dad the afternoon I'd tried out for the football team and gotten my face broken. It seemed like a long time ago, but it was less than five months. I licked my tongue down over my teeth and remembered the pain and how my blood had tasted.

But now the park was cold and empty, and Muhldinger was sitting by himself. He spat once on the ground and looked away from me, back out at the frozen duck pond.

I grabbed the purple Frisbee and ran back to Dylan and Frank. If we stayed another few minutes they might spot him, and for some reason I really didn't want that. "Hey, guys," I said, "I'm freezing. Let's go for pizza."

"The wind's dying down. We've got all afternoon for pizza. Let's play a little more," Dylan said.

"Let's go now," I told him. "My hands are so numb I can't feel the Frisbee. Come on, I'm treating."

"Big spender," Frank said enthusiastically. "Did I mention I'm feeling like three slices?"

"Fine," I said. "As long as you don't eat so much that you can't save goals tomorrow."

"My eating ability and my goaltending skills are not linked," he assured me.

I glanced quickly back toward the duck pond at the sad figure sitting motionless under the willow tree, and then I said, "Let's put that to the test," and we headed off to binge on hot pizza with sausage and mushrooms.

IT WASN'T THE BIGGEST CROWD WE HAD
ever played in front of, but for a cold November afternoon
it was still pretty impressive. More than five hundred fans
sat in the bleachers of Gentry Field, waiting to see if the
Fremont Losers could actually win a game. License plates
in the parking lot included some out-of-staters, but when
we ran out onto the turf to warm up I scanned the crowd
and saw plenty of faces that I recognized.

My dad and mom were sitting with Ed Powers and his
wife, Stephanie, in second-row seats. It was a little strange
seeing them there because I was used to seeing them
together at football games, cheering for the Lions. As I
watched, my father leaned over to Ed and gestured toward
the field, and I knew he was explaining something about
soccer to his old teammate. Who would have ever thought
my dad would become a soccer expert?

A few rows back I spotted Mr. Knight with Emily. He was
wearing a dark suit, and glanced at his watch as if wondering whether the game would start on time. Emily wore a
light-blue ski coat with a hood trimmed in white fur. She
saw me looking and waved, and I found myself waving back.

"Your dad's here," I told Becca.

"Yeah, I saw. Must be a slow day at the office for dentists

and party planners. My mom's here, too. On the other side of the field, thankfully." I followed her gaze and spotted Mrs. Knight sitting with Meg's mom and dad.

Jan Brent filed in with a tall man I'd never met, but I knew his name was Sam Magee. Sam was an assistant soccer coach at Rutgers, and he'd told me he'd be coming. I'm pretty sure this was the only time Sam had ever scouted a team called the Losers, and knowing that he would be watching gave me a little extra jolt of excitement.

There was only one camera crew on hand to film our last game, from a local news station. A guy in a leather jacket was taping a stand-up while the scoreboard clock ticked down to start time. When there were five minutes left the ref blew his whistle and shouted, "I need the captains."

I walked out to midfield where the Lynton captain was waiting. He was an inch taller than me, with a heavier build and a super-confident smile that could also be read as a sneer. "Last game of the season," he said. "Ready to go?"

"Let's play before we freeze," I said. "I hear you guys are undefeated."

"Undefeated and untested. We've been coasting. We need better teams to play."

"That's a good problem to have," I told him. "We've been getting crushed."

"Yeah, it sounds like you guys have turned losing into an art form. I can't wait to see the show." He was smiling the whole time he said it, but it clearly wasn't meant as a joke. Right then and there I decided that we would have to beat Lynton that day.

"Lynton, call it in the air," the ref ordered. He flipped

the coin and their captain called heads. Sure enough it was heads, and he took the side of the field that didn't face the afternoon sun.

"Shake hands, guys," the ref said.

"Good luck," I told their captain as we shook. "Congrats on your great season." I looked him in the eye and added: "But it's not over yet."

"It's over," he said, and then turned away, and we walked back to our teams.

"Which side do I have?" Frank asked when I approached our bench.

"Facing the sun. Maybe it'll keep you warm. By the way, try not to let the Lynton captain score."

"Jerk?" Frank asked.

"Total jerk. Thinks we're garbage."

"We are garbage," Frank said. "Dump us into the truck and turn on the compactor."

"Buddy," I told him, "I know you voted against trying to win today, and since you're our goalie you can screw this game up single-handedly. But I'm asking you as a favor not to do that."

"Why is a stupid soccer game so important to you?" Frank wanted to know.

"My dad's here, with my mom," I said. "First one she's ever seen." I hesitated. "There's a scout here, too."

"Like an Indian scout?"

"No," I said, "like a scout from Rutgers."

It's hard to surprise Frank, but I'd managed it. "You're being recruited at a Loser game?"

"Please keep it to yourself. And I guess the last reason

I'd like to win is that Lynton thumped Fremont so badly in football. They crushed our whole town in their stupid mud pit. It doesn't make you a jerk to want to win one back for the place you grew up."

"Not sure I agree," Frank said. "That actually sounds to me like the place where all the stupidity starts. But we've been friends since I ate your lunch in kindergarten and made you cry." He shot me a grin. "I might be able to save a few today, if they're not kicked too hard."

"Keep us in the game," I told him. "That's all I'm asking."

The countdown clock showed two minutes. Coach Percy called us in and we circled around him. He was wearing his weirdest outfit of the season: plaid pants, a yellowish tweed coat that zipped up to his chin, and a black fedora that looked like it belonged in a Mafia movie. "Well, team," he said, "we've climbed the Alps. It's time to descend into Italy and lay waste to Rome . . . or at least to Lynton."

"It's cold enough to be the top of the Alps," Becca complained, shivering.

"My feet are frozen, so how can I kick a soccer ball?" Meg asked. "Not that I can even when it's warm."

Coach Percy looked around at us and smiled. I think he genuinely liked this team, with all our grumbles and goofiness. "When Hannibal reached the crest of the Alps, a blizzard blocked all the paths down," he told us. "His generals came to him and said they were within sight of Italy but there was no way to descend. He told them: '*Aut viam inveniam aut faciam*,' which means, roughly: 'I will either find a way, or make one!' I don't expect you to win this game the way a normal soccer team wins, but I'm sure you'll find a way or make one! Losers forever, on three."

I wasn't sure I wanted to be a loser forever, but we put our hands in the middle and counted: "One, two, three— Losers forever!" and ran out onto the gleaming emerald turf of Gentry Field.

I LINED UP AT CENTER MID, WITH ROB BEHIND
me at stopper. "Just to be clear, Jack," he said, "we're trying to win today, right?"

"This is the famous Logan-Powers partnership, second
generation," I told him. "Take no prisoners."

"You got it." He glanced over at his father in the stands.
"I kind of owe Dad something to cheer about. I guarantee
the defense will hang tough today." After that promise he
turned toward the one news camera that was filming us
and flashed a thousand-megawatt smile.

The ref blew his whistle, and our final game was on.
Pierre kicked the ball to Jenks, who tripped over it like it
was a giant mushroom that had suddenly sprouted in his
path. A speedy Lynton forward scooped the ball up and
sliced through our midfield before we knew what was happening. Rob stepped up to stop him but he slid a pass
sideways to their tall captain, who was making a parallel
run. The captain one-touched a whistling shot from thirty
yards away right through Frank's upraised hands into our
goal. Lynton had scored in under ten seconds—I'm not
sure the ref had even had time to lower his whistle.

Their captain did a little victory dance and tapped his
wrist as if saying, "Check your watches. Record time!"

Frank dug the ball out of the back of the net and bounced it twice, angrily, before handing it to me. "Even I'm embarrassed by that one. I swear I was trying to stop it."

"It wasn't your fault," I told him. "We all fell asleep."

"There's still plenty of time to get back in this game," Rob assured us.

"There's still the whole game to get back in the game," Dylan pointed out. "That took about three seconds."

Pierre kicked off again, and this time he passed it to Becca who kicked the ball back to me. I took one touch and instantly three Lynton players swarmed me and got the ball away. One of them passed it to a short striker on the right wing, who made a darting run down our sideline. Chloe and Zirco ran to intercept him and when he swerved they collided so hard I could hear their bodies smacking together thirty yards away. Zirco flipped completely over Chloe, and it looked like a clown routine except that they both went down painfully hard.

The Lynton striker didn't kick it out of bounds at the possible injury—instead he lofted a cross over our goal toward the long corner. Frank jumped to punch it away, but vertical leaps were never his strong point and he barely got off the ground. The ball grazed his fist and when it came down their tall captain was in the perfect spot to snap his head and bang it into the netting.

This time he rotated three hundred and sixty degrees while holding up two fingers. Then he tapped his wrist again to let us know he had drawn blood twice in two minutes.

Zirco got to his knees but he looked shaky. Chloe lay on

the turf, pressing her hands to the right side of her face. We eventually helped her to her feet, and she put an arm around Percy and an arm around Meg and hobbled off the field. The Fremont fans clapped for her, but not one person in Gentry Field was laughing.

The collision hadn't been funny and neither was the score—two to zero in record time. Something had changed on this cold autumn day, and our gags and screw-ups that had amused people in late summer sunshine now made them shake their heads and cover their eyes.

I tried my best to get us back in the game, but a Lynton defensive specialist had been assigned to mark me all over the field, and he stayed with me like a shadow. Whenever I touched the ball he was quickly joined by a second teammate and even a third. They bumped and banged me and I couldn't shake them. When I tried to dish out quick passes, there was no one nearby.

Our defense got mad after Chloe limped off the field, and we held Lynton for a while. But they scored their third goal on a penalty kick after Zirco used both hands to stop a shot. Then, just before halftime, their short striker sensationally nutmegged Rob and kicked a screamer into the right corner for their fourth goal. He celebrated with a front flip and a victory yell: *"Perfect season!"*

The ref blew his whistle for halftime and we walked over to our bench.

"Sorry about that last one," Rob said. "That little guy made me look like a chump."

"Don't worry about it," I told him.

"I don't like it that my dad saw it," Rob muttered. "And I didn't appreciate the gymnastics routine."

"What does it matter?" Dylan asked. "We all suck. This was much more fun when we were trying to lose. They're pounding us."

"That's because we're trying to be something we're not," Shimsky said. "What you've forgotten is that it's okay to suck. We used to take pride in being pounded. What happened to feeling the thrill of defeat and the agony of victory?"

"I feel more pain than pride right now," Chloe told him, holding an ice pack to her bruised cheek.

"One of their players called me lard-ass," Pierre reported. "I'm not sure exactly what that is, but it doesn't sound like a compliment."

Frank walked by, shaking his head. "Out of my way, lard-ass." He clearly wasn't happy about the way things were going, either. He said to me in a low voice, "Sorry about the college scout. Maybe you'll get in on your grades."

I glanced over at Sam Magee. I was surprised to see that he and Jan were both still sitting there, given how little I had done. Every time I'd touched the ball, I'd been mugged. It wasn't just that Lynton was covering me tightly—they were being rough, knocking me off the ball any way they could. When I tried to pass, it was like being on a raft with sharks circling and nobody around to help.

I walked over to Coach Percy, who was standing with his hands in the pockets of his tweed coat. "Not much to be done, I'm afraid," he said.

"Probably not," I agreed, "but here's a suggestion. Let me play striker and bump Rob up to attacking midfield."

"He's the only thing holding our defense together," Coach Percy noted.

"Every time I touch the ball I've got three of them on me," I said. "I need an option. We're going to lose anyway."

Coach Percy thought it over for a moment and then gathered us in for his final pep talk. "Don't look so discouraged," he told us. "We wanted to win today, but if we lose you all have a lot to be proud of."

"We suck and we're not funny anymore," Meg said. "What else is there?"

"We never have to play soccer again," Becca called out, as if that was a positive thing. Then she looked at me and said, "But, okay, let's try to avoid total disgrace."

"Yes, let's hitch up our shorts and give it a last run," Percy encouraged. "If Lynton can score four goals in the first half, there's no reason Fremont can't do it in the second half."

"The reason could be that we blow chunks," Dylan said. "We haven't even had one shot on goal."

Coach Percy glanced at me and then announced: "I'm going to make a little offensive readjustment. Rob, move up to midfield, and help Jack with the attack. Jack, you're a striker now. Let's get that shot on goal. Okay, Losers, all the paths to Italy are blocked. Make your own way down the Alps. On three—'Fremont number one!'" We all looked at him in surprise.

"No way," Shimsky said. "I'd rather chew broken glass."

The ref blew his whistle, summoning us back out.

We put our hands in the middle, and looked around at each other. Shimsky stayed outside our team's huddle and glared at us. "One, two, three—Fremont number one," we shouted. It came out sounding weird, but then everything had gotten a little strange. We ran out for our last half of soccer.

I was now playing striker up top, with Rob behind me at attacking center mid. That should have given our attack some extra punch, but we couldn't get anything going. Meanwhile, it left our defense exposed, and ten minutes into the second half, Lynton pounced.

Meg gave the ball away deep in our end, and Rob and I were too far up to run back and help. Their short striker picked up the loose ball and zipped between Zirco and Jenks. He probably could have scored an easy one himself, but he made a beautiful pass to their captain who was alone at the top of the box and all ready to get his hat trick. He let loose a thunderous shot at the right corner of our goal and raised his arms in victory.

Then a strange thing happened. Suddenly a large body got horizontal in a hurry, as Frank threw himself side-ways. I can't say it was a graceful dive—it was more like an old tree toppling. But when Frank stretched out his long arms they seemed to cover the whole goal's mouth. The shot was a bullet headed for the right upper corner, but at the very last second Frank's big hand swatted it a few inches over the crossbar.

The Lynton captain lowered his arms and looked

puzzled, as if something had just happened that defied the known laws of physics.

Frank lay on the ground for a second, dazed. Then he got to his knees and pumped both fists in the air. Our team gathered around him, congratulating our goalie on his first hard save of the entire season.

It's strange in soccer how one save from a goalie can turn a game. If Lynton had scored their fifth goal, I'm sure we would have cracked apart and been humiliated by ten goals. But Frank's diving save got us going. Zirco headed out Lynton's corner kick, and Dylan passed it to me at midfield. Instantly my shadow was on me, and two other Lynton midfielders came running over to help him. I looked desperately for an outlet, and saw Rob ten feet away.

I got off a quick pass to him. For a moment I flashed to Diego on the Warren club's field, shouting at me that when I made a good pass I shouldn't stand still admiring it but that that was the exact moment to make my move. So I took off toward their goal, and because I'd just made a pass and had been standing still the three Lynton players who were marking me were caught ball-watching. Rob was enough of a natural athlete to understand what I was trying. He gave me a nice lead pass back, and suddenly—for the first time that day—I found daylight.

I've seen soccer plays on TV when a striker outruns his entire offense and has no one to pass to. He either has to hold the ball up or take it all the way in solo—one man setting off to war alone. When I sprinted onto that lead pass from Rob I was several steps ahead of our other forwards.

I didn't make a conscious decision to go in the rest of the way alone—I just found myself flying toward their goal.

A whole gang of Lynton players appeared in front of me—four or even five of them. There was no time for me to plan anything, no way around them. I just wove right into them like a skier attacking a mogul field—slalom left, swerve right, cut left again—and they all seemed slow, terribly slow. I glimpsed desperate and frustrated faces, heard grunts and curses, and saw feet that kicked out at me too late, and then I was through them and on the other side.

There's nothing like a breakaway run—despite the gray clouds all I saw was daylight, pure golden open daylight, as I locked in on their last two defenders. Their stopper raced up to challenge me, but he was too eager. I waited for his legs to slide open like a gate and then I nutmegged him—touching the ball between his ankles—and burst past.

Their sweeper was the last man back, and he was smart. He knew I was too fast for him, so he tried to buy some time by mirroring me—staying between me and their goal till more help arrived. Every time I moved, he moved, not to try to steal the ball but just to keep me blocked. Out of the corner of my eye I glimpsed their tall captain sprinting over to help. I only had two seconds.

I faked left and then powered hard right and got a step on their sweeper. I took a second step and he tried to run with me, but with every stride I gained an inch of separation. I took one final touch, teeing the ball up for my right foot.

Their goalie stayed on his line, protecting his near

corner. I told myself "far corner," but just as my right leg started to swing forward their goalie read my mind and dove sideways across the goal. He managed to cover the long corner, and I think he might have saved my shot. But before he dove I saw his weight shift and I winged my shot at the near corner, so that he launched himself away from the ball. It flew into the unprotected near corner for our first Fremont score.

I started to pump a fist and then the Lynton captain smashed into me. He didn't hit me as hard as Barlow had at Founders' Park—I never blacked out or lost any teeth. But his elbow went into my chest, and suddenly I was lying on my back and I couldn't breathe. I gasped and panicked as the team surrounded me—it's scary not to be able to breathe. The ref hurried over, with Percy behind him. "You just got the wind knocked out of you," the ref told me. "Easy does it. You'll be okay." Then he turned and flashed a yellow card at the Lynton captain.

Becca knelt next to me, her hand on my shoulder. "Short breaths, just like you always tell me," she whispered. "Relax. You'll feel better in a second."

It actually took a minute or two for me to start breathing seminormally. I was still gasping, and my sense of panic at not being able to breathe wouldn't go away. Coach Percy took me out of the game, and as I walked off the field the Lynton captain ran over and said, "Sorry, man. Couldn't jam on the brakes in time. Hell of a goal."

I saw my parents watching me carefully as I headed for our bench. Mom looked worried but my dad gave me a thumbs-up, and Mr. Powers shook an encouraging fist. I glanced over at Jan Brent and Sam Magee, who was busy writing something on a notepad.

The game started up again, and I stood next to Chloe. "Great goal," she told me. "Best I ever saw."

"Thanks," I said. "How's your head?"

"The ice helps. Check it out. We're starting to dominate."

It was true. Even without me on the field, the momentum was shifting. Lynton's confidence had cracked, and the Losers were battling for loose balls and making smart passes. Ten minutes after I came out Rob passed the ball to Becca on the wing. She had always been fast and athletic, but she'd never given a damn about soccer before and I don't think she'd ever really tried. When she got Rob's pass she faked out a defender, and for a moment she looked completely surprised at what she'd just done. Then she dribbled the ball for twenty yards and kicked a decent cross into the middle where Rob was waiting to blast it into the net.

Four to two. I shouted, "Way to go, Becca!" and she smiled and shrugged as if to ask: "Did I really do that?"

I walked over to Coach Percy and said, "I feel better. Put me back in."

"Sorry, Jack. I can't."

"Why not? We're only two goals behind. We can come back on them."

"New school rule. Principal Anderson sent it around to all the coaches. When a player is taken out of a game for an injury, you can't put him back in."

"That's to protect kids from concussions," I said. "I just had the wind knocked out of me. My head didn't get banged at all."

"You were hit hard, Jack," Percy said. "Anyway, it's beyond my control. Mr. Anderson's here watching the game, and it's his rule." He pointed to a group of teachers sitting behind our goal, and sure enough I spotted old, white-haired Mr. Anderson, leaning forward, looking excited.

Lynton didn't like it that the score was getting close, and they tried to put the game out of reach. Their skillful little striker lashed in a dangerous cross. This time Frank didn't jump—he sidestepped over to catch it, and immediately hurled the ball out to Dylan. Dylan couldn't dribble to save his life, but he knew exactly what to do with it—he fed a good pass to Rob.

Rob was new to soccer but he was a superb natural athlete, and he had something to prove to his dad. He made a slick turn, dribbled past a Lynton midfielder, and toed the ball from more than forty yards out. In baseball terms it was a high fly ball, a cloud scraper. The Lynton goalie backed up step by step as he waited for the white ball to come down out of the gray clouds, and at the last minute he stumbled and the ball glanced off his fingers into their goal.

Four to three. Something weird was happening at Gentry Field. The peaceful fans of Loser Nation were now all cheering for us to kick ass and score. People holding signs that read FAIL WITH FLARE and LOSING IS AWESOME! were now screaming for us to win. But it was looking doubtful that we could even tie the game, because we were still one goal down and the minutes were ticking away fast.

Lynton wanted their undefeated season, so they gave up trying to score and packed their midfield and defense. They killed time dinking useless passes back and forth, and knocked ten- and fifteen-second chunks off the clock by kicking the ball far out of bounds. It was legal but it was cowardly. Twenty minutes shrank to ten, and then dwindled to five. We couldn't get the ball, and the few times we did, we couldn't penetrate the defensive wall they had built in their own half.

I saw our players trying hard, and realized that some of them had actually gotten in better shape during the season and learned a thing or two about soccer. Pierre's face was red and he looked like he might vomit at any moment, but he never stopped running during those final ten minutes. Zirco for all his nuttiness was pressing hard and challenging every pass. Even Meg and Becca, who made so much fun of soccer, were trying to steal the ball, but they just couldn't.

With three minutes left, I glanced at my dad. He saw me looking and raised his hands, demanding wordlessly why I wasn't on the field. I pointed to Coach Percy, and Dad shook his head—he still didn't get it. When he had needed to score the winning touchdown, the Logan Express hadn't taken no for an answer. For a moment I recalled that clip of him refusing to go down, and carrying five players into the end zone.

I walked over to Coach Percy, who was pacing up and down, glancing at his watch. Lynton had just kicked the ball far out of bounds, wasting another precious twenty seconds.

"I'm afraid it's not going to happen today, Jack," he said. "There can't be more than three minutes left."

"Put me in."

"I can't," he said. "We already discussed this. When you get taken out for an injury, you're out. No exceptions."

"Since when do you follow school rules?" I asked him.

He stopped glancing at his watch and focused on me. "What does that mean?"

I kept my voice low. "I know you're the one who put together that video of Muhldinger screaming at us on the bus."

Percy looked a little shocked, but he didn't say anything back.

"And then you posted it on the Web, even though you pretended to be clueless. That's why I said you were such a good actor."

He tried to interrupt me, but I talked right over him. "Muhldinger called you an idiot and you brought him down. You broke every rule in the book doing it. In your quiet way, you're much more of a revolutionary than Shimsky. What does one new rule matter now? Put me in."

"Things have changed," Coach Percy told me. "It's a new day here at Fremont. Principal Anderson's been very kind to me. He's letting me go to England early for my new job."

"Well, that's great for you, but what about the rest of us?" I demanded. "You're the coach of this team." Our eyes locked. "I may not know a lot about Hannibal or Caesar, but I do know that you can't only break rules when it serves your purpose." I couldn't stop myself—I stepped a little closer to him. "And for what it's worth, no matter how lonely you were, you probably shouldn't have been writing sonnets to seventeen-year-old girls. Show some character here in New Jersey before you go back to England. Put me in the damn game now."

I could tell that he didn't like any of what I'd just said. His face tightened up like a hand was clenching the skin from the inside, and his sharp black eyes glittered like two sword points. I thought to myself that he was very smart and in his own way extremely dangerous. I couldn't predict what his reaction might be to what I'd just said. He hesitated two or three seconds and then looked beyond me to the ref. Lynton had kicked the ball out of bounds again, and Coach Percy yelled, "Ref, sub. Meg, come out."

I ran onto the field and asked: "How much time left?"

The ref checked his watch. "Less than two minutes."

One hundred and twenty seconds don't last long on a soccer field when you're losing. I felt every second tick away as we chased Lynton and they played keep-away. I was just about ready to give up when Jenks got lost on the field and blundered far out of his position. He popped up unexpectedly at midfield and his total cluelessness allowed him to steal the ball. The Lynton player he'd taken it from hurried to win it back, which would have sealed the game. Jenks was desperate to kick it upfield, but he whiffed on his first try, and that colossal miss threw the defender off. Jenks connected on his second kick, and the ball dribbled to Rob.

"Powers," I shouted, and started my run. He heard me, and even though there were two players on him he somehow got off a long pass into their left corner. The tall Lynton captain chased it with me, matching me step for step. He was fast and determined, and this was by far my best footrace of the season. I knew there couldn't be more than ten seconds left, and I switched into that extra gear that my father had given me as a birthright. The Lynton captain looked like he couldn't believe it as I started to pull away from him, and we both realized that I would get to the ball first.

It had rolled to a stop near the corner flag, and when I reached it and turned I saw five Lynton players between me and the goal. There was no way I could dribble by them all, and any second the ref would whistle the game over.

There was only one chance—I had to cross the ball and trust that one of my teammates would knock it in. I picked up my head and saw Rob waiting in the penalty area, and Pierre and Dylan running up. The Lynton captain tried to tackle me, but I pushed the ball to the goal line and got off a hard cross with my right foot. A split second later he knocked me off my feet, and we both went down.

I lay on the grass and watched my cross sail toward their goal. Rob jumped for it, but it went two feet over his head. Pierre might have gotten to it if he was just a little faster. I thought for sure Dylan would head it in and turn out to be the team hero who had gotten his wrist broken and came back to score the wonder goal. But he mistimed his header and the ball flew by him. It finally came down right in front of the smart Lynton sweeper who did exactly what he was supposed to do—he booted it as hard as he could upfield.

His attempted clearance traveled about five feet on a line drive, smacked into the side of Shimsky's head, and rebounded toward the Lynton goal. Their goalie dove at it and managed to push it with his fingertips. The ball rolled sideways along the goal line, hit the side of the post, and rebounded slowly back. It crossed the goal line by a quarter of an inch before their goalie frantically grabbed it.

The ref blew his whistle several times and I wasn't sure if he was announcing the goal or the end of the game. It turned out to be both. "Four–four tie," he shouted. "Game over. Well played, both teams."

The Lynton players protested that the goal shouldn't count. They were still undefeated but the last-minute tie had destroyed their perfect season. They surrounded the ref, who shouted for them to back off.

The ball to the head had knocked Shimsky to the turf. I reached him first, and he looked up at me, a little confused. "What just happened?"

"You won it for us," I told him.

"But I wanted to lose," he said.

The rest of the team arrived, and we picked Shimsky off the grass and hoisted him to our shoulders. I saw Becca standing next to me helping to hold him up and we shared a smile. "I didn't want to score," he protested loudly. "It shouldn't count. It was an accident. Put me down! I want to go out a Loser!" But he was high up on Pierre and Frank's shoulders, and we carried him around the field in a wild team victory lap as our fans cheered. Somewhere along the way Shimsky stopped fighting us and just went along with it. I'm not positive, but I might have even seen him smile.

DAVID KLASS

Giselle Benatar

What did you want to be when you grew up?
For a long time, I wanted to be a baseball player. I was a pitcher, and then, as I got older, a first baseman. Later on, I considered being a doctor and volunteered in a hospital during college. But telling stories seemed to be what I was best at.

When did you realize you wanted to be a writer?
I started writing short stories in my early teens, and midway through college, I began to consider it as a career.

What's your first childhood memory?
When I was four, my parents took us to India for a year. My father was an anthropologist who was doing a study of a small village there. My earliest memories are of India: the smell of the spices, the festivals, going to a missionary school, hearing about President Kennedy's assassination over the radio, and being bitten by a rabid dog. I still remember a little Bengali.

What's your most embarrassing childhood memory?
When I was in second grade, I stuck a paper clip in a wall socket and nearly electrocuted myself.

As a young person, who did you look up to most?
I was blessed with wonderful parents. My father was a wise, gentle, funny man who loved us dearly and read to us every night. My mother is a novelist who is probably responsible for the fact that her three children all grew up to be writers.

What was your worst subject in school?
I didn't like algebra, and I struggled with physics. It's strange, because these days, I find theoretical physics to be fascinating. I still don't like algebra.

What was your first job?
My first full-time job was selling a book called *Basic Wiring* over the telephone. I couldn't believe anyone would actually buy it, but every day, I managed to sell a dozen or so copies. I truly hated calling complete strangers during their dinner hour and trying to sell them a book that I would have never read myself.

How did you celebrate publishing your first book?
I sold my first novel, *The Atami Dragons*, to Scribner when I was twenty-three years old. I was living in a small town in Japan, and I celebrated by going out that night with some friends for a Japanese feast.

Where do you write your books?
I used to write at home, or in coffee shops or libraries, but now that I have two small kids, I rent an office in midtown Manhattan.

Where do you find inspiration for your writing?
I wait for a story to grab me. Sometimes, I hear the voice of
the main character and try to let him tell his story through me.
That's what happened when I started to write *You Don't Know
Me* and *Firestorm*. Other times, I become interested in an issue and slowly flesh out a story around it. An example of this
is *California Blue*.

When you finish a book, who reads it first?
My father used to read my books first. He read at a great
speed and caught all spelling and grammatical errors. I miss
him terribly.

Are you a morning person or a night owl?
I'm a morning person. I get up in darkness, and do some of
my best writing while the rest of my family is sleeping.

What's your idea of the best meal ever?
A three-hour dinner in the Italian countryside with good friends
and a nice bottle of wine or two.

Which do you like better: cats or dogs?
I like dogs—the bigger the better. I married a woman with a
cat, and now we're stuck with two of them. One doesn't get
everything one wants in life.

What do you value most in your friends?
I like friends who are smart and funny, genuine and loyal,
interesting and a little quirky, but at the same time, rock solid
when it comes to the most foundational qualities.

Where do you go for peace and quiet?
I write alone in an office, so finding peace and quiet is not a
problem. When I need noise and to be around other people

during the day, I go to a gym and play pickup basketball. I enjoy coming home in the evening to two kids who want to sword fight and play hide-and-seek.

What makes you laugh out loud?
Both my son, Gabriel, and my daughter, Madeleine, are very funny. I laugh out loud when they make fun of me, which they do quite often.

Who is your favorite fictional character?
I loved John le Carré's character Jerry Westerby. And when I was younger, I liked Edmond Dantès from *The Count of Monte Cristo*.

What are you most afraid of?
I'm most afraid of not being able to protect my kids in what I see as an increasingly dangerous world. We live in Manhattan, and September 11th is a very powerful memory.

What time of the year do you like best?
I love autumn. I lived in Los Angeles for ten years and I missed the change of seasons. It didn't rain for two years after I moved there. Then I decided to throw a barbecue party. As soon as I lit the grill, a downpour started. I knew I'd better move back east.

If you were stranded on a desert island, who would you want for company?
If I was stranded on a desert island, it would be the perfect time for a family vacation.

If you could travel in time, where would you go?
I would like to accompany Hannibal on his march over the Alps. I would also love to go back to Athens just before the Peloponnesian War.

What's the best advice you have ever received about writing?

I remember an essay by Rudyard Kipling where he talks about following his Daemon—an inner voice that was infallible in telling a story well. I am the least mythical person around, but I do believe that somehow, in some way, a writer must try to be led by his characters rather than force them to do his will.

What would you do if you ever stopped writing?

I think I would shift from one writing form to another. I also write screenplays, and I would love to try writing plays for the stage. I directed a bit of theater years ago, and it would be a dream to write and direct my own play.

What do you like best about yourself?

I guess what I like best about myself is the time and energy I devote to my kids. They are a true blessing.

What is your worst habit?

My worst habit is probably wasting so much time watching sports on TV that I really don't care about. A football game can gobble up three or four hours.

What do you wish you could do better?

There are many things I wish I could do better. Here are a few, in no particular order: Sing, draw, dribble a soccer ball, write crisper dialogue, speak better Italian and Japanese, understand string theory, shoot jump shots from three-point range, and devote more of my time to good causes.

What would your readers be most surprised to learn about you?

Many of my YA book readers are surprised to learn that I have a double career, and that I spend most of my time writing action movies for Hollywood. It's a big jump from a novel like *Losers Take All* to a movie like *Walking Tall* or *Kiss the Girls*.

What do you consider to be your greatest accomplishment?

Probably the hardest thing I've ever done is go to Hollywood without connections and become a successful screenwriter. It took seven years of struggle and near-starvation. But my greatest accomplishment is building a family.

FRESHMAN DANIEL PRATZER AND HIS FATHER
have been invited to compete in a prestigious chess tournament
as a team. It's Daniel's chance to prove himself to his peers, but
then he finds out his father has his own dark past with the
game. Suddenly, there's much more at stake for Daniel and his
father than just winning the competition.

READ ON FOR AN EXCERPT.

1

Chess club was done for the day, and so was I. I had played three games that afternoon, two of which I'd managed to lose in the first fifteen moves. I tried to remind myself that I had just taken up the game six months ago and was still learning the basics, but there were times when I wanted to heave the nearest chess set out the window and never touch another rook or pawn again.

I pulled on my coat and headed out the door. Suddenly a hand yanked me back into the empty room and I found myself alone with the two senior co-captains of the chess team, Eric Chisolm and Brad Kinney. "We need to talk to you, Patzerface," Eric said as Brad locked the door.

A "patzer" in chess speak is a beginner who barely knows the moves and is a pushover to beat. It's like being called a combination of chump, rookie, and dufus. Given the unfortunate similarity of my name to "patzer," I had been called it many times since I first walked in the door of the chess club. But "Patzer-face" was a new twist by the co-captains that I didn't particularly like. "Actually my name's Pratzer," I stammered, glancing from one to the other to try to figure out what was going on.

Eric Chisolm was senior class president, a turbo-charged student and a superachiever with intense black eyes who had never gotten less than an A in his life. He was a grind—maybe not brilliant but he outworked everyone else. He literally could never sit still—even when Eric played chess he was always fidgeting, getting up for water, and pacing behind his chair, probably doing his calculus homework in his head while figuring out a next move that would destroy his opponent. He was the son of a heart surgeon, and everyone knew he was going to be the valedictorian, go to Harvard, and discover the cure for cancer.

Brad Kinney was less intense but more naturally talented. He was tall and rugged, with a grade point average that glittered as brightly as the huge trophies he won as captain of the swimming team and contributed to our school's trophy case. For fun, and maybe to make us all even a little more jealous, he dated the prettiest girl in the freshman class. He was the best chess player in our club—a master at eighteen who regularly won local and regional tournaments.

At another school the two of them probably wouldn't have been caught dead on the chess club, but Loon Lake Academy had the oldest and strongest chess team in New Jersey—the

Looney Knights—and it was cool to be on it, especially if you were Eric Chisolm or Brad Kinney.

I was not Eric or Brad—I was Daniel Pratzer, apparently also known in certain circles as Patzer-face. I was not tall or brilliant or rich. The admissions office must have accepted me because it was a weak year and my combination of mediocre scholarship and undistinguished extracurriculars was just enough to pass muster.

My grade average hovered above C+, resisting all my attempts to lift it into the B range like an airplane that has reached its operational ceiling and can't gain a few more feet of desperately needed altitude. I could play a bunch of sports reasonably well, but the electrifying soccer run and the diving baseball catch forever eluded me. I had decided to join the chess club on a whim. The school sports teams practiced for more than two hours every day, and since I was still struggling with the homework load I didn't have enough free time or ability for them. Chess met every Tuesday, and I thought the club might be a good way to make some new friends.

"We know what your name is, Patzer-face," Eric said. "That's why we need to talk to you."

"What about my name?" I began to ask.

"Sit down and shut your trap," Brad advised with his usual charm.

I sat at a desk and waited nervously. Was this some kind of freshman chess club initiation? Would they do something awful to me with rooks and bishops, leaving scars that would last for the rest of my life? I had only been at Loon Lake Academy for seven months, and had so far managed to fly under the radar of the cool-and-cruel crowd.

I glanced from one senior co-captain to the other and tried to figure out what these two towering school icons could possibly want from me.

"What are you doing this weekend?" Eric asked.

"Nothing special," I told him. "Staying home. Watching some junk on TV. Rethreading my sheets."

"Rethreading your what?"

"It was a joke," I explained.

"His sense of humor's worse than his chess playing," Eric grunted to Brad.

"You're not going to be rethreading anything this weekend," Brad told me. "Don't make any plans."

"What's this about?"

Brad plunked his big frame down on the desk next to my chair and folded his arms, staring at me with his bright blue eyes. It didn't seem fair that a guy who could swim fifty meters in thirty seconds and had the physique of a Viking raiding-party chieftain was also a chess master, with a rating well above the 2200 norm. "We know about your father," Brad announced.

"Huh?" I gulped. What was there to know about Morris Pratzer except that he was the shortest, baldest, and no doubt poorest father to ever send a child to Loon Lake Academy? He was practically mortgaging our house so that his only son could go to this fancy private school.

I don't mean to be critical—my dad's a good guy who works

long hours at his accounting firm and sacrifices everything for his family. He also has a lighter side and some notable hidden talents that he sometimes reveals at parties: he can wiggle his ears, arch his eyebrows in opposite directions, and do a half-decent Elvis impersonation, but he's not the sort of "A-Lister" that people suddenly dig up revelations about.

"There's a chess tournament this weekend in New York," Eric said, as if that explained everything.

"Didn't see it on our schedule . . ." I replied cautiously. The truth is I rarely looked at the tournament schedule because I wasn't on the five-member travel team. Nor was I on the seven-member backup team. I was on the euphemistically titled Regular Reserve Roster, which meant they would use me when necessary—which was no doubt never unless a comet struck Loon Lake and killed the dozen players ahead of me.

"That's 'cause it's not a regular school tournament," Brad cut me off. "It's a new kind of tournament. A father-son tournament. Each team needs six players to enter—three fathers and three sons. It's at the Palace Royale Hotel in New York City. There's twenty thousand dollars in prize money. Ten grand for first place. Do you understand now?"

No, I didn't understand. Eric and Brad were strong players and I knew their fathers were both experts, but I was a patzer and my dad had never played a game of chess in his life. When I joined the club and brought some pieces home, I offered to teach him how they moved. "No thanks, Daniel," he said, laughing. "I don't have the mind for it."

I looked back at Eric and Brad and shook my head. "I don't get it. I won't help you much and my dad doesn't play."

Eric dug out a piece of paper. I saw that it was some kind of computer printout. "Your father is Morris W. Pratzer?" he asked, like a prosecuting attorney nailing an evasive witness.

"Yeah."

"We needed one more father-son to join us so we ran the dads of all club members through the Chess Federation ratings database, going back three decades."

He showed me the paper. My father's name and rating were there with an asterisk because his rating hadn't changed in almost thirty years. I stared at it. According to the printout, Morris W. Pratzer had been a grandmaster, rated well over 2500. "This is a mistake," I said. "Don't you think I'd know it if my father was a grandmaster?"

"Apparently not, Patzer-face," Eric said.

"Go home and have a father-son chat," Brad urged, handing me a sheet with info about the tournament. "Find out the source of this little misunderstanding. Tell your dad we humbly invite him to join us this weekend in Manhattan, and if Grandmaster Pratzer doesn't show up we'll wring his son's neck."

2

My mom had cooked a meat loaf that night, with broccoli and rice pilaf. She isn't a very good cook, but there are a dozen or so meals that are family favorites that she's made so many times over the years she's perfected them. Meat loaf is high on the list, and we were all digging in.

My sister, Kate, sat across from me, trying to eat as little broccoli as possible and get away from the table fast so that she could gab with her friends on her new cell phone. She went to the same crummy public school I had gone to for years. My parents were planning to send her to a private high school, too, when she finished middle school.

With the prospect of two kids in private school looming, my mom had gone back to work as an assistant teacher in the local elementary school. She worked in a first-grade class, and even though she was home by three p.m. most days, she now wore a perpetually tired and harried look, as if platoons of six-year-olds had been attacking her nonstop for hours, bel-lowing war cries and firing paper wads at her till she was ready to raise the white flag.

"I don't hear anyone talking so I guess the dinner is okay," she said.

"It's delicious, Ruth," my father told her, carving another slice of meat loaf for himself. He wasn't a big man, and he sat in a chair all day doing people's taxes and figuring out their books, so he probably shouldn't have been eating so much. His paunch was expanding into a sizable potbelly. "Kate, chew with your mouth closed, please."

She rolled her eyes at him, but so slowly that it was hard to tell if they were circling in irritation or just moving around the room in an innocent round-about pattern. "Can I be excused?" she asked.

"After you finish your broccoli."

She picked up a tiny floret, broke it in two, and put half of it in her mouth. "Yum," she said. "Can I be excused now?"

"No," my father told her. "And if you roll your eyes at me again, that new phone is going to disappear for a week."

"Great," she said. "Threaten me. What parenting book have you been reading?"

My father let out a sigh, as if to say "I work hard all day and come home to this." He looked at me. "How's school, Daniel? Tell me something fun."

"We dissected rats in bio lab today."

Kate lowered her fork. "That's it. I'm out of here."

"Not till you finish your broccoli," my father told her. "Daniel, that's not suitable dinner conversation."

"Well, we did," I said.

"Especially when we're eating meat loaf," Kate noted, grinding a piece of broccoli against her plate with her fork, as if attempting to break the limp vegetable up into subatomic particles that would then float away into the ether. "Who knows what goes into meat loaf."

"Ground sirloin," my mother said. "There were no rodent ingredients in the recipe. Could we get off this subject?"

"Try again, Daniel," my father said. "Something fun and interesting must have happened today."

I took a deep breath. "Okay. Something unusual did happen in chess club."

"It's kind of hard to believe that anything fun and exciting could happen in a chess club," Kate muttered.

"Go on, Daniel," my mother encouraged me. "I'm sure we'd all like to hear what happened, including your sister."

"There's going to be a tournament in New York this weekend," I said. "They're only bringing three players from the whole team. They want me to come."

"That's exciting," my mom said. "Do you want to go? Will the school pay for it?"

"It's not a regular school tournament," I told her. I was watching my dad as he chewed his meat loaf. "It's a father-son tournament."

His eyes flicked to me for a moment and then quickly down

at his plate. He swallowed the meat loaf he was chewing and had a long drink of water, then slowly put down his fork.

"I'm afraid I don't understand," my mother said.

"Neither did I," I told her. "And I still don't."

"When are we getting to the fun and interesting part?" Kate wanted to know.

"Your dad doesn't play chess," my mom observed.

Dad looked at her and then back at me.

"That's what I told them," I said. "Why would you want my dad? He can't play at all. But they said they had done a computer search on all the team fathers, and he used to play really well."

"They must have had the wrong Morris Pratzer," my mother said. "It's not a common name, but there are dozens of Pratzers out there."

"They had looked up Morris *W.* Pratzer," I told her, emphasizing the middle initial. "You're Morris William Pratzer, right, Pop?"

"Yes," my father answered softly, putting one hand flat on the table as if preparing to resign a chess game.

"According to their information, Morris W. Pratzer was a grandmaster." I heard a little anger creep into my voice. "But that can't be, because if you were a grandmaster, Dad, your son would know about it and not have to be told by a bunch of chess club bozos. Right? If you were a grandmaster, we would be playing games every night, and you would be teaching me openings and endgame theory and helping me out so I wouldn't be just a patzer."

My father stood up from the table and drew himself up to his full height of five feet four inches. His fist came down on the tabletop so hard that it rattled the silverware. "I'm not playing in any chess tournament in New York next weekend, and neither are you, Daniel. You're going to help me clean the basement. Now, excuse me. I've lost my appetite." He walked quickly away from the table.

My mother and I watched him go, and then looked at each other. She stood up and started after him.

"Well, that *was* kind of interesting," Kate admitted to me. Then she shouted: "Hey, Dad, aren't you going to finish *your* broccoli?"

DON'T MISS MORE THRILLING READS FROM DAVID KLASS!

★"An emotionally taut story."
—*Publishers Weekly*, starred review

"A highly engaging, timely, and thought-provoking read."
—*Booklist*

"A captivating first-person narrative with an original voice."
—*Kirkus Reviews*